PRAISE FOR

PAPERBACKS FROM HELL

Winner of the Bram Stoker Award

"Pure, demented delight."—*New York Times*

"It's a gorgeous, lurid deep-dive into horror's heyday and a must-read for any self-respecting horror fan."—*Tor.com*

"Horror fiction is alive and well, and *Paperbacks from Hell* is a grand, affectionate, and informative celebration of the genre." —*NY Journal of Books*

"Fans of horror fiction will love this funny and insightful history." —*Library Journal*, starred review

PRAISE FOR

MY BEST FRIEND'S EXORCISM

"National treasure Grady Hendrix follows his classic account of a haunted IKEA-like furniture showroom, *Horrorstör* (2014), with a nostalgia-soaked ghost story, *My Best Friend's Exorcism.*"—*Wall Street Journal*

"Take *The Exorcist*, add some hair spray and wine coolers, and enroll it in high school in 1988—that'll give you *My Best Friend's Exorcism*...Campy. Heartfelt. Horrifying." —Minnesota Public Radio

"Readers who thought *Heathers* wasn't quite bleak enough will find this darkly humorous horror tale—filled with spot-on 80s pop-culture references—totally awesome."
—*Booklist*, starred review

PRAISE FOR
HORRORSTÖR

One of NPR's Best Books of 2014

"*Horrorstör* delivers a crisp terror-tale…[and] Hendrix strikes a nice balance between comedy and horror."—*Washington Post*

"...wildly fun and outrageously inventive..."—*Shelf Awareness for Readers*, starred review

ALSO BY GRADY HENDRIX

Horrorstör

My Best Friend's Exorcism

Paperbacks from Hell

This is a work of fiction. All names, places, and characters are products of the author's imagination or are used fictitiously. Any resemblance to real people, places, or events is entirely coincidental.

First paperback edition, Quirk Books, 2019.
Originally published by Quirk Books in 2018.

Library of Congress Cataloging in Publication Number: 2017941584 (hardcover edition)

ISBN: 978-1-68369-340-6

Printed in the United States of America
Typeset in Sabon, American Typewriter, and Moderno

Cover design by Faceout Studio, Tim Green
Interior design by Doogie Horner
Production management by John J. McGurk

Quirk Books
215 Church Street
Philadelphia, PA 19106
quirkbooks.com

10 9 8 7 6 5 4 3

Grady Hendrix

QUIRK BOOKS
PHILADELPHIA

True as Steel

Kris sat in the basement, hunched over her guitar, trying to play the beginning of Black Sabbath's "Iron Man." Her mom had signed her up for guitar lessons with a guy her dad knew from the plant, but after six weeks of playing "Twinkle Twinkle Little Star" on a J.C. Penney acoustic, Kris wanted to scream. So she hid in the park when she was supposed to be at Mr. McNutt's, pocketed the $50 fee for the two lessons she skipped, combined it with all her savings, and bought a scratched-to-hell Fender Musicmaster and a busted-out Radio Shack amp from Goldie Pawn for $160. Then she told her mom that McNutt had tried to watch her pee, so now instead of going to lessons Kris huddled in the freezing cold basement, failing to play power chords.

Her wrists were bony and weak. The E, B, and G strings sliced her fingertips open. The Musicmaster bruised her ribs where she leaned over it. She wrapped a claw around the guitar's neck and pressed her sore index finger on A, her third finger on D, her fourth finger on G, raked her pick down the strings, and suddenly the same sound came out of her amp that had come out of Tony Iommi's amp. The same chord 100,000 people heard in Philly was right there in the basement with her.

She played the chord again. It was the only bright thing in the dingy basement with its single 40-watt bulb and dirty windows. If Kris could play enough of these, in the right order, without stopping, she could block out everything: the dirty snow that never melted, closets full of secondhand clothes, overheated classrooms at Independence High, mind-numbing lectures about the Continental Congress and ladylike behavior and the dangers of running with the wrong crowd and what *x* equals and how to find for *y* and what the third person plural for *cantar* is and what Holden Caulfield's baseball glove symbolizes and what the whale symbolizes and what the green light symbolizes and what everything in the world symbolizes, because apparently nothing is what it seems, and everything is a trick.

This was too hard. Counting frets, learning the order of the strings, trying to remember which fingers went on which strings in which order, looking from her notebook to the fretboard to her hand, every chord taking an hour to play. Joan Jett didn't look at her fingers once when she played "Do You Wanna Touch Me." Tony Iommi watched his hands, but they were moving so fast they were liquid, nothing like Kris's arthritic start-and-stop. It made her skin itch, it made her face cramp, it made her want to bash her guitar to pieces on the floor.

The basement was refrigerator cold. She could see her breath. Her hands were cramped into claws. Cold radiated up from the concrete floor and turned the blood inside her feet to slush. Her lower back was stuffed with sand.

She couldn't do this.

Water gurgled through the pipes as her mom washed dishes upstairs, while her dad's voice sifted down through the floorboards reciting an endless list of complaints. Wild muffled thumps shook dust from the ceiling as her brothers rolled off the couch, punching each other over what to watch on TV. From the kitchen, her dad yelled, "*Don't make me come in there!*" The house was a big black mountain, pressing down on Kris, forcing her head into the dirt.

Kris put her fingers on the second fret, strummed, and while the string was still vibrating, before she could think, Kris slid her hand down to the fifth fret, flicked the strings twice, then instantly slid her hand to the seventh fret and strummed it twice, and she wasn't stopping, her wrist ached but she dragged it down to ten, then twelve, racing to keep up with the riff she heard inside her head, the riff she'd listened to on Sabbath's second album over and over again, the riff she played in her head as she walked to McNutt's, as she sat in algebra class, as she lay in bed at night. The riff that said they all underestimated her, they didn't know what she had inside, they didn't know that she could destroy them all.

And suddenly, for one moment, "Iron Man" was in the basement. She'd played it to an audience of no one, but it had sounded exactly the same as it did on the album. The music vibrated in every atom of her being. You could cut her open and look at her through a microscope and Kris Pulaski would be "Iron Man" all the way down to her DNA.

Her left wrist throbbed, her fingertips were raw, her back hurt, the tips of her hair were frozen, and her mom never smiled, and once a week her dad searched her room, and her older brother said he was dropping out of college to join the army, and her little brother stole her underwear when she didn't lock her bedroom door, and this was too hard, and everyone was going to laugh at her.

But she could do this.

34 YEARS LATER

CALLER: . . . you're not part of the solution, you're part of the problem.

KEITH: You sound like a hippie, Chester.

CALLER: I tell it like I see it. You guys are asleep. Your Texas owners tell you what to play. Why don't you play real music that talks about what's going on in the world?

CARLOS: We love what we play, Chester. You don't like it, get satellite radio.

CALLER: I dare you to play Nervosa, or Sepultura, or Torture Squad. You're too [censored] to play Rage Against the Machine.

CARLOS: How's the weather in your mom's basement, metalhead?

—96.1 ZZO, "Keith & Carlos in the Mornings"
May 10, 2019

Welcome to Hell

Kris stood behind the reception desk at the Best Western off US-22 in navy slacks and a vest, watching a naked man walk through the sliding doors, his penis flopping from side to side. Even though he had a pillowcase over his head, she knew exactly who he was.

"Mr. Morrell," she said, "We're going to have to charge you for cutting eyeholes in that pillowcase."

"Fuck you, skank."

"Okay, I'm calling the police." She picked up the phone.

"I'm not Josh Morrell," Josh Morrell said.

Kris dialed the station house number from memory.

Josh Morrell reached over the desk and slapped down the hook switch, disconnecting her call. That was when Kris realized that it was 3 a.m. and she was the only clerk on duty in the middle of a half-empty hotel in the center of a mostly empty parking lot with a naked man wearing a pillowcase over his head. If she wasn't a woman, it would have been funny.

"We have cameras recording the lobby area, Mr. Morrell," Kris said, her voice getting thinner even as she tried to make it sound firm.

"I'm not Josh Morrell," Josh Morrell repeated.

He was so close Kris could smell Old Spice and light beer. She could see his eyes glittering through the two holes he'd cut in the pillowcase. She could see the fabric going in and out over his mouth way too fast. Kris knew any movement she made was dangerous, so she froze.

Josh Morrell took two steps backwards and cut loose with a massive stream of urine, turning his hips from side to side, making sure he sprayed the entire front of the reception desk. Its ammonia stink crawled up Kris's nose. Its stream drummed hollow on the wood and high-pitched on the tiles.

Once upon a time, Kris Pulaski had beaten entire rooms into submission. Once upon a time she'd walked into strange buildings in faraway states where the only people who knew her name stood next to her onstage. She'd stood, surrounded by crowds who hated her in Eugene, and Bangor, and Marietta, and Buckhannon, and calmly tuned her guitar in front of those jostling drunks who put bullet holes in the band van, who tucked notes under their wipers that read "Metal faggots get AIDS," who once threw a shit-dripping diaper onstage, who started fights because they wanted to beat without mercy anyone who came from more than fifty miles away.

Kris had stood in front of those cross-eyed, thick-skulled, small-brained cow tippers whose veins flowed with Blatz and Keystone instead of blood, who stunk of Schaefer and Natty Boh, and Lone Star, and Iron City, and she waited quietly for the drum intro to begin, then strummed in lazy on the downbeat and started building her first riff, and then the bass slid in easy behind her, and the other guitar followed her lead before suddenly breaking free and starting to crunch over her rhythms with violent arpeggios, and the first blast beat smashed out of the bass drums and they leaned back into the pocket, thrashing that room without mercy, beating those bearded faces with a wall of sound until their heads started nodding, their shoulders began to twitch, their chins went up and down against their will—until the one with either the least impulse control or the most to prove shoved the person in front of him, and the pit began to swirl in front of the stage.

The aggressively casual thrashers in their long-sleeved black tees and long black hair, the old metalheads in their battle vests and beards, the milk-white school shooters, skinny wrists cuffed with underage wristbands—Kris had turned these haters into dancers, fighters into lovers, hecklers into fans. She had been punched in the mouth by a straight-edge vegan, had the toes of her Doc Martens kissed by too many boys to count, and been knocked unconscious after catching a boot beneath the chin from a stage diver who'd managed to do a flip into the crowd off the stage at Wally's. She'd made the mezzanine bounce like a trampoline at Rumblestiltskins, the kids pogoing so hard flakes of paint rained down like hail.

Now she stood watching Josh Morrell piss all over the floor of the Best Western at three in the morning, and she was too scared to do a thing about it. When he finished, he shook the final drops off his boneless dong, turned around, let out an enormous wet fart, and marched back through the automatic doors.

Reflexively, before she could stop herself, Kris called after him, "Have a great stay."

Then she waited for her hands to stop shaking, picked up the phone, and called the police.

Half an hour later her brother showed up. She let him into the lobby and he stopped short before the puddle of urine on the terracotta tiles.

"Aw, c'mon Kris, that's nasty. You didn't even clean it up?"

"He's in room 211," Kris said.

"Probably just drunk," Little Charles said.

"I have to set out breakfast in two hours," Kris said. "Everything has to smell piney fresh before people start eating their little Danishes."

"I'm not filling out an incident report."

"The guy peed at me," Kris said. "The evidence is right there. I can show you the camera log."

Little Charles didn't get angry with Kris anymore. Instead he turned it back on her.

"You sound stressed," he said. "Did you do the candle and flower like Dr. Murchison showed you? Breathe in the flower, blow out the candle. Want to do it with me?"

"I am not stressed," Kris said. "I'm pissed."

"I hear a lot of tension in your jaw and chest."

"I'll do candle and flower," Kris said, "if you please take care of this guy for me. He'll come down and do it again the second you leave."

"It's okay, Kris," said Little Charles, in the same tone of voice he used whenever a woman was upset. "I'll take care of it. You wait here and clean up. It'll all be okay. I'll go talk to the man."

Once, in Wichita, an owner refused to pay the band's cut of the door. He'd told Kris that if she wanted the $200 so bad she could suck his dick. The instant he turned away she leaned over the bar, grabbed his entire cash box, and ran. Scottie already had the van running, and they tore out of the parking lot, spraying gravel like the *Dukes of Hazzard.*

Now, twenty-two years later, she just said, "Thank you, Little Charles."

The sliding glass doors whisked him outside and Kris watched him walk up the sidewalk to the guest rooms, and she inhaled the flower and blew out the candle five times, which didn't work because the flower smelled like Josh Morrell's pee.

For eleven years, Kris had been able to go anywhere in the world by picking up the phone. She'd cold-called clubs and mailed out demos and swapped slots on bills with Corpse Orgy and Mjölnir and mailed letters to kids who organized shows. Then they'd gotten in their van with its secret loft for the mics and its "No band stickers" rule they'd made after it'd been broken into four times, and they drove all over America playing shows.

Kris had survived one thousand three hundred and twenty-six shows, emerging at the end of each one with her ears ringing, forearms sore, hair dripping, blood crusted beneath her nails. She'd played shows to eight hundred people, and she'd played shows where she knew the names of every single person in the bar. She'd played a few times to five thousand people who were there to see Slayer.

She'd played the humiliation shows, the favor shows, the fuck-you shows, the going-through-the-motions shows, the endless shows that kept rolling for one more song and one more after that, the shows that were over in eleven minutes because there were too many bands on the bill, the out-of-control shows, the empty room shows, the shows where no one gave a shit about the band because they were just there for the beer, and the tear-off-the-roof shows whose only possible conclusion was to burn the venue down, Viking funeral style, when it was all over. She'd played shows where there was no difference between the stage and the crowd, kids sitting behind her, beside her, crawling on the stacks, knocking beer bottles off the amps. She'd played shows from a high riser that looked down onto steel barricades holding back a surging crowd that formed multiple pits.

Now she was forty-seven years old and her knees hurt when she climbed stairs, and her right shoulder ached all the time, and she had tinnitus in her left ear, and for the past six years this hotel lobby after midnight had been her safe space. It was where the phone didn't ring with debt consolidation services and no one knew her last name. It was where you wound up when nobody wanted your band, when you never signed that big contract, when your sales never took off, when you missed your big break by inches, when you came close but no cigar. It was the last job she'd been able to get, and even then only with Little Charles's help, and there probably wouldn't be another one after it, so she went, and got the mop, and filled a bucket, and cleaned up Josh Morrell's piss.

The doors slid open and Little Charles walked back into the lobby, one hand hooked on his overloaded belt. Kris heaved the mop into its yellow bucket, forced down the squeeze handle, and made it barf gray water.

"Did you see what he did to his pillow?" Kris asked.

"He says it wasn't him," Little Charles said.

"You left him there?"

"Running him in won't do anybody any good," Little Charles said. "It'd be a he-said she-said situation."

"I'm mopping up his piss right now," Kris said. "It's a she-said she-said situation."

"I told him that if anything happened, and I had to come back here, then he and I were going to have a problem."

"I already have a problem," Kris said. "He's probably watching the parking lot so he can come back down here and take a shit the second you leave."

"I put a scare into him," Little Charles said. "And that's all I'm going to do tonight. The subject is closed."

He walked back to the doors, which hummed open, then picked the dramatic moment right before his exit to turn and say, "I sold Mom's house. You need to be out in six weeks."

Kris watched him get in his car and roll away through the parking lot, headed toward Route 22.

She clenched both fists so hard her tendons groaned. She dug her fingernails into her palms so deep they bled. For eleven years Kris and Dürt Würk had fought the world, and she'd fought the world alone for another ten years after that. They'd survived the death of metal, and made it through the grunge years without ever once covering "Smells Like Teen Spirit," and it felt like they were going somewhere. But now the music was over, the money was gone, and in six weeks she would be losing her house. This was what she had left. So she lifted the dripping mop, and dropped it onto the floor, and continued cleaning up Josh Morrell's piss.

MARK METAL: In a decade, the LVA's lost one rock landmark after another: Croc Rock, American Music Hall, Wally's, and this past Sunday one more casualty was added to that list when Gurner's Sporting House burned down. A bar with the state's smallest stage and warmest beer, it was where local bands like Dürt Würk and Powerhole played their first shows, which earned it semilegendary status. Owner Bobby Dali closed the place in September of this year to upgrade the PA and the bathrooms, both of which were disgusting, but six weeks ago he hung himself, and at 3 a.m. this past Sunday morning, an electrical fire burned the Sporting House to the ground before a single firefighter could respond . . .

—90.3 WXLV, "The Mark Metal Show"
December 11, 2013

Powerslave

Kris fell into the maroon interior of her dad's car, exhausted. No matter how old she got, the nineteen-year-old white Grand Marquis with maroon interior would always be her dad's car. He'd bought it back in 1999 when everyone actually thought his cancer wouldn't be so bad. She'd told him it looked like a pimpmobile, and he acted like he hadn't heard her, but a year later, on their way to the kidney clinic, he'd said out of the blue:

"This car. I deserve a little style."

She squeezed her eyes shut so hard her lids cramped. Sleep tugged at her brain. Eyes still closed, she reached out and turned the key and the engine roared, hyper-accelerated, then calmed back down to a wheezy growl with a *clunk* that meant she would probably owe the mechanic more money soon. Everyone kept telling her she should trade up, but Kris liked her dad's car. It didn't have all that stuff in it that told everyone where you were—no LoJack, no GPS pinging her location out to anyone who was listening. Kris liked to be invisible.

She opened her eyes, ran the wipers to clear the early morning dew, reversed out of her space, and cruised through the Best Western parking lot toward US-22. Her brain was in neutral, stewing in a skull full of sleep juice, and she could smell the sleepy smell rising up from her chest. Her bed was covered in pillows, her room was dim, her blankets were soft: it would feel so good to have a beer and fall in.

Little Charles had sold her mom's house. She had six weeks to find someplace to live. Kris put that thought in a box and stuck it on the shelves in the back of her brain where all her other problems slept in the dark. It was hard to find room, but she managed to slide it in between "Credit Card Debt" and "I Didn't Cry at Mom's Funeral, Something Is Really Wrong with Me."

She turned east on 22, driving between the abandoned Standard Cement factory and its derelict bride, GB&B, the old ball-bearing plant, rising up like twin tombstones that marked the entrance to Gurner. She passed the weedy lot where the Sporting House once stood. It had been a roadhouse where every single Lehigh Valley band played their first show, and the tiny cubbyhole where bands waited to go onstage was lacquered with graffiti from Teeze, Dirty Blond, even Vicious Barreka, all memorializing that Geronimo moment before they jumped off the cliff for the very first time. Kris's inscription read:

Dürt Würk - Sept. 27, 1989 - METAL NEVER DIES

Now it was just another weed-choked lot with a sun-faded "Available" sign out front. Turns out, everything dies.

Kris's leg lashed forward and she stood up on the brake, her chest slamming into the steering wheel. Adrenaline flooded her veins, sleep fled, and her eyeballs vibrated as a car horn blasted and almost plowed into her rear end. More cars screamed around her, laying on their horns, but Kris couldn't move. Frozen in the right-hand lane of US-22, she stared up at what loomed on the horizon and felt her spit turn thin and bitter. Her breath got fast and high in her chest as she witnessed the hideous thing rising over Gurner, sprung up overnight like some dark tower from *The Lord of the Rings*.

The Blind King was back, staring down at her from the massive billboard with his black, pupil-less eyes. In Gothic font, the billboard read:

KOFFIN — BACK FROM THE GRAVE

Beneath it was a photo of the Blind King. A brutal spiked crown was nailed to his head. Black blood streamed down his face. The digital retouchers made sure he hadn't aged a day.

Across the bottom it read:

FINAL FIVE CONCERTS MAY 30–JUNE 8, LA, LV, SF

Kris stared up at the Blind King, and her guts turned to water. He was vivid. He was legion. Made up of lawyers and accountants and session musicians and songwriters, a colossus that could be seen from space. In contrast, she was puny and small, and stood in the empty lobby of the Best Western, seeing herself reflected in the glass doors, a shadow in navy slacks, nametag pinned to her vest, smiling at people as they ground out their hate on the ashtray of her face.

In the dark storeroom at the back of her brain, the overloaded racks tipped forward and the packages slid to the edge of their shelves, and she scrambled to push them back up. Her hands started to shake, and the world lurched and spun around her, and then Kris stood on the gas, and hauled ass, desperate to get to the toilet before she threw up, yanking her dad's Grand Marquis onto Bovino Street, taking a right at Jamal's Sunshine Market, plowing through the Saint Street Swamp.

Back here, abandoned houses vomited green vines all over themselves. Yards gnawed away at the sidewalks. Raccoons slept in collapsed basements and generations of possums bred in unoccupied master bedrooms. Closer to Bovino, Hispanic families were moving into the old two-story row homes and hanging Puerto Rican flags in their windows, but farther in they called it the Saint Street Swamp because if you were in this deep, you were never getting out. The only people living on St. Nestor and St. Kirill were either too old to move, or Kris.

She slammed into park in front of the house where she grew up and ran up the brick porch jammed onto the sagging facade, put her key in the lock, banged the water-warped door open with one hip, and bit her tongue to keep herself from calling out, "I'm home."

Buy your mom a house. That was the rock-star dream. Kris had been so proud the day she'd signed the paperwork. Hadn't even looked at it, just scrawled her signature across the bottom, never thinking one day she'd wind up living back here. She ran down the same front hall where her nineteen-year-old self had once stormed out, soft case in one hand, screaming at her mom and dad that just because they were scared of the world she didn't have to be. Then Kris slammed open the fridge door and let the cool air dry her sweat.

She uncapped a green bottle with a brisk hiss. She needed to slow down for a second. The billboard had her too jacked up. She wanted to go online and get details, but she knew the most important thing already: the Blind King was back.

On the white plastic tablecloth draped over the kitchen table sat the Tupperware box with her nail stuff. Five months ago, she'd still been coming home every Sunday and sitting down across from her mom and painting her nails. It always made Kris conscious of how soft her mom's hands were compared to the big spatulas she had, laced with faded scars and stained yellow with old callouses. Looking at the box felt like falling into a hole, so she stuffed it under the sink. Her skin itched. She needed to *do* something.

Her Rolling Rock was empty and her mouth was still dry. The veins in her temples throbbed, her blood felt molten. The Blind King was back. She opened a second beer.

The thought of the Blind King gave Kris a fluttery feeling behind her breastbone. She'd been able to keep it together as long as he was off the radar, but now he was back. Why couldn't he leave her alone?

The shelves tipped forward, and the boxes slid off and smashed open on the floor, filling her brain with shrieking bats: her puny three-digit paychecks, constant overages from MetroPCS, Christmas presents bought at the 99-cent store, trying to scrape together a deposit for a new place from the empty hole that was her bank account.

Watching the ambulance load her mom inside, pulling away at a pace you used to pick up groceries. Sitting in the front row of the nearly empty Sacred Heart as some unknown priest delivered insert-name-here platitudes about her mother, all pomp and no passion, standing and sitting on command, mumbling sunshine hymns full of false rhymes and bad meter, trying so hard to make herself cry. Sitting across from the kid with the smear of acne on his forehead at Grabowski's Funeral Home and telling him they wouldn't be doing a viewing, or any embalming, and she'd just like them to burn her mother to ashes and use an urn she'd already bought online, and watching this kid's kindness click off when he realized that she was just another poor person wasting his time.

The money it would have cost to give her mom the funeral she deserved was what the Blind King spent on massages each week. The money separating Kris from the edge was a rounding error in the Blind King's bank account. She saw him huge and colorful and loved, looming over US-22, and herself at his feet gazing up, gray and small.

She saw herself too scared to play, too scared to get angry, too scared to fight, too scared to escape Gurner. She saw the UPS van, and his lawyers, and the settlement she signed, and the Paxator and the Wellbutrin and the Klonopin spilling down her throat, all the things they prescribed to make her less angry, that made her feel dead, and she'd thought she was okay, for eight years she thought this was over and she was fine, but she was wrong.

And then she was shoving the basement door with her shoulder, shoving it hard because it hadn't been used in forever, and it groaned open, and the air smelled like sour dust and Kris dove down into it, clattering down the wooden stairs, diving toward the one thing she'd sworn she'd never do again.

REV. CARSON: . . . you've been studying fans of heavy metal music, Satanic music, occult music—whatever you want to call it—for a long time. Who listens to this stuff?

DR. PADMERE: By and large, these are low-functioning individuals who score poorly on most metrics we use to examine human behavior: low IQ, low patience, low confidence, low reliability. Where they score highly are in areas like anger, deceit, narcotic and alcohol abuse, suicide rates . . .

REV. CARSON: In other words, these are not people you want marrying your daughter?

DR. PADMERE: Definitely not.

—WCYI 580 AM, Denver Praise and Christian Leadership Network
December 14, 1993

Reign in Blood

The basement was dim, with gray light filtering through the dirty, half-buried windows. Even in summer it was lake-bottom cold. A dusty plaid sofa sat in the middle of the room, piled high with boxes of old tax returns and bills. Chairs with busted seats stood against the walls, the floor cluttered with everything Kris and her brothers grew up with that their mom had clung to: boxes of old toys, a sagging playpen, a tricycle with bent wheels.

Before she could second-guess herself, Kris plunged across the room and yanked open the closet door to reveal a sagging tower of cardboard Stor-All boxes printed with dark wood grain. They contained the corpse of all her old lawsuits, all her old battles, with the Blind King. Her knees cracked when she squatted down, and her lower back ached when she slid the boxes aside. Behind them leaned a single soft case and a striped beach towel draped over a Laney Supergroup amp. Kris pulled out the soft case by its neck, flicked off the dusty towel, and heaved out the amp. Her lower back gave another twinge.

She pulled a ladder-back dining room chair to the center of the floor, sat down, unzipped the soft case, and pulled out her guitar.

Six years ago, Kris had locked her guitar in this closet like a bad dog. At night, she dreamed she heard it scratching to get out. But she had steeled herself and ignored its whimpers. For two years, she'd felt guilty every day she didn't play, but eventually her guilt had faded into the background hum of self-loathing that formed the backbeat of her life. She hadn't played since. She'd cut off her hands and buried them underground, and now here she was, digging them back up.

Her white Gibson Melody Maker balanced itself on the curve of her thigh. After that first Fender Musicmaster, this was the only guitar she'd ever owned. There were gouges on the back from her belt buckle and a groove worn on its face from her wrist. She found a cable in the soft case's side pouch, wrapped it through the strap and plugged it in, then flipped on her amp. The hum sounded like coming home.

She found a pick and played an open G, surprised by how easy it was to tune. The notes were all right there inside her ears, waiting to be heard again.

She played "Iron Man." She played it badly. She played it slow, stumbling through the chord changes the way she had that very first time. She missed her transitions, her hands were soft spaghetti that didn't go where she told them to, her picking was tentative, her fingertips were fat. After she finished, she started again, really bearing down hard on the E string behind the nut for the intro and making it moan. Then she turned up her amp and did it again. The steel strings tried to slice her fingertips in two. She felt the dust in the air vibrate. Her left ear began to whine a high shrill E.

She played "Iron Man" again, coming down hard on the

downpick. Then she played it again. And again. And again. And her breathing slowed, and the bats stopped screaming, and the Blind King faded away.

How had she ever given this up?

When Little Charles went off to college in 1982, he'd left five records behind: Bruce Springsteen's *Darkness on the Edge of Town*, which Kris had honestly never heard him play, Olivia Newton-John's *Physical*, which he only bought because of the cover, *The Cars*, which he bought because all his friends had it, the bright-orange *Fresh Fruit for Rotting Vegetables* by the Dead Kennedys, and Black Sabbath's *Paranoid*.

She listened to the Dead Kennedys the most because they were loud and funny. *Paranoid*'s cheap cover with its blurry flash photo of a guy with a sword jumping out from behind a tree kept her away, but the older she got, the more it wound up on her Sears turntable. By the time she was fourteen, the hooks from "Electric Funeral" and "Paranoid" were baked into her brain.

She'd started to play because it was the only way to get the songs out of her head, down her arms, through her fingers, and into the air.

On a cold September evening in her sophomore year, she was down in the basement stumbling through "Iron Man" for the nine thousandth time when, *tik-tik*, someone tapped on the window with a penny. Kris stood on her chair and slid the window open and a kid stuck his face against the screen and said, "Is that Sabbath?"

Even as a dark shadow she knew who he was. He was skinny, with almond eyes, high cheekbones, and golden hair. He came equipped with an enormous, mouth-mangling set of braces. He was a year older than Kris and she didn't know if she was more surprised that he was talking to her or that he knew who Sabbath was.

"Yeah," she said. "It's Sabbath."

Without a word, the kid stood up and left.

The next day, after school, he showed up at her front door with his acoustic guitar. Thank God neither of her brothers were home. Her mother let them sit in the basement as long as they kept the door open.

"Play something," he told her.

So she played "Iron Man," because in metal, everything starts with Sabbath, the very first metal band, the original losers from middle-of-nowhere Birmingham, the ones who forced the world to sit up and listen. She was terrible.

Having an audience made her fingers extra clumsy and she kept saying, "Hold on. Wait a minute," and her cheeks were burning hot, but he didn't interrupt, and she'd spent a lot of time woodshedding, and finally there was a flawless, euphoric forty-five seconds of "Iron Man" falling forward from note to note, Kris's fingers racing ahead of her brain, dancing up and down the neck of her guitar. She didn't know how to mute strings, and her Musicmaster's tone was better suited to "Happy Birthday," but for the first time in her life she felt like the world had room for her. Then she blanked on how to move her fingers from G to D and it all fell apart.

His name was Terry Hunt and they became each other's audience. He didn't care that everyone thought he was boning the sophomore. They were the only two people who took each other seriously. By Halloween, they were trading tapes, and then, after Christmas, Kris went to his house for the first time, and sat in his dad's hi-fi room as the shrink wrap came off his brand-new copy of Sabbath's *Seventh Star*.

"The only one left is Tony Iommi," Kris said.

"But if he says it's Sabbath, it's still Sabbath."

"He can say whatever he wants," Kris said, "but if a band has four people in it, and three leave, it's not the same band."

"It is if the person who stayed behind is Tony Iommi. Same as if it were Ozzy."

"What if it's Geezer?" Kris asked.

"Bass players don't count," Terry said.

That was the year when Metallica and Megadeth, not her mom or her teachers, taught Kris everything she needed to know. Her dad could tell her what she couldn't wear to school, and her mom could tell her when to go to bed, but Metallica's *Master of Puppets* told her that anger opened doors, and Megadeth's *Peace Sells . . . but Who's Buying?* taught her that some fights were worth having.

All through the summer of '86 she and Terry hid in their bedrooms, hunched over their turntables and guitars, debating the talmud of heavy metal. She thought David Lee Roth's *Eat 'Em and Smile* was goofy; Terry thought it was "masterful showmanship." Kris thought Iron Maiden made a huge mistake adding synths to *Somewhere in Time*; he thought synths added body and sounded rad.

They argued endlessly over whether the Judas Priest song "You've Got Another Thing Comin'" should actually be "You've Got Another *Think* Coming." Kris defended Mercyful Fate's new album against Terry's charge that they were "Dungeons and Dragons bullshit." They stormed out of each other's houses. They ate dinner with each other's families. They rode their bikes to Wall to Wall Sound and got Terry's mom to drive them to the mall where the big record store was. They didn't agree on anything except the most important thing: heavy metal was their religion. It tore the happy face off the world. It told the truth. It kicked down doors.

Heavy metal saved their souls and they saved each other. When a kid told everyone that Kris had VD, Terry stole his homework notebook and filled it with drawings of pentagrams and the rough draft of a suicide note. The kid's mega-Christian parents pulled him out of Independence High and sent him to boarding school in Delaware. When Kris heard that Metallica's bass player, Cliff Burton, had died in a bus crash, she ran for her bike and pedaled like hell to Terry's house. He opened his door, red-eyed, and without saying a word, they hugged each other for the first time. The two of them spent that entire month hiding in Terry's bedroom, listening to Metallica. Terry even bought some black candles and used what he said was graveyard dirt to make a pentagram so they could speak to Cliff's spirit, but nothing happened except they set off the smoke detector.

They talked about forming a band, but it was all talk until Christmas, when Terry went to visit his cousins in Ottawa. His weird uncle Mark worked as a gravedigger and he loved telling Terry stories about his "dirt work." When Terry came back home he showed Kris what he'd drawn in his notebook in razor-edged lightning bolts: Dürt Würk. He'd borrowed the umlauts from Mötley Crüe.

"Righteous," Kris breathed.

"Metal up your ass," Terry agreed.

He spent three months in art class coming up with their logo while Kris focused on recruitment. She spotted Scottie Rocket at the Lehigh Valley Mall. He was the only person she'd ever seen wearing a Plasmatics T-shirt. She followed him for an hour, lurking outside Toones and the arcade, before she finally got the courage to tap him on the shoulder.

"Cool shirt," she said.

She was wearing the exact same one. After a basement audition they put Scottie on rhythm guitar. What he lacked in skill he made up for in energy. His dad had taken off for Alaska when he was three, and his mom was a nurse, and Scottie's after-school activities mostly consisted of going to shows and getting in fights. His biggest claim to fame was a scar on his hip where a skinhead had stabbed him with a screwdriver at a Dead Kennedys show. His mom was so relieved he was doing something after school besides getting stabbed that she put the deposit down on their first PA system.

Tuck's high school orchestra performed at Independence later that year. He played electric bass on Pachelbel's Canon. Kris caught him just before he got back on the bus and wrote her phone number on the palm of his hand while his buddies shouted out the windows, "Once you go black, you never go back!"

Her parents were nervous that she had yet another boy in the basement, and a black one at that, but she kept the door open while she played him Dio's "Don't Talk to Strangers" on her boom box. Starting with a gentle acoustic intro that erupted into shredded electric chaos, Kris thought it was exactly the kind of structured, challenging metal that a guy who played classical music might like.

Tuck was huge—six foot three and wide as a wall—and there

was no way he wasn't getting pushed onto his school's offensive line, and probably onto its basketball team right after. It didn't matter that he didn't like sports, that he lacked a killer instinct, that he'd rather play Mozart. He was a black guy the size of a house in small-town Pennsylvania. His dad and his coach had already planned his future: high school ball, athletic scholarship to a state school, seventh-round NFL draft pick, five seasons, then dumped back into the world at thirty-one with a blown knee and brain damage. He was looking for anything that would help him say "no." Metal was his answer.

She couldn't remember how JD, their first drummer, wound up in the band. Whatever happened to JD? Nothing good, probably. He was the stupidest, angriest kid they'd ever known. He thought Jewish was a country and claimed his dad invented the question mark. When a kid called him a liar, he tried to throw a hornet's nest at him. He got stung so many times the paramedics had to inject him with adrenaline to restart his heart.

What she did remember was when Bill came up to them after that epic backyard show at PJ White's house and said they needed to get rid of their drummer and play with him instead. Bill was an uptight control freak who constantly panicked about fingerprints on his cymbals. He played by math, counting the beats instead of feeling them, but Kris still remembered the blissful look on his face the first time he lost himself in their noise that night at the Sporting House.

In the basement, she played Europe's "The Final Countdown," the same song they opened with at the Sporting House the night they finally became a band instead of five people onstage playing their instruments at the same time. They'd screamed through the five-minute song in three minutes because they were so nervous to be on a real stage for the first time. But when they closed their set with their first original song, "Get in Your Coffins," it sounded bigger than themselves and they all leaned back into the pocket, suddenly feeling like old pros, knowing that there was finally a place for them in the world, thinking that they could keep doing this forever.

Then Terry went and fucked it all up.

No, Kris fucked it all up.

Actually, it was both of them working together. But sometimes, Kris was scared that it was mostly her.

"Angel of Death" was Scottie's favorite song, and down in the basement Kris ran through it for an hour and a half until she could tear it off, note perfect. By the time she finished, her fingernails were bleeding and sweat dripped onto her strings.

None of what she played would pass onstage. Too many finger scrapes and missed notes, a million lazy chord changes and sloppy progressions. But the longer she played, the angrier she got. She hadn't felt angry in a long time. For years, Dr. Murchison had taught her to breathe in the flower, and blow out the candle. Now she breathed in Slayer and blew out Black Sabbath.

Everyone told Kris that anger was her enemy. They told her to accept things. They told her life wasn't always fair. So she took pills. She took anger management classes. She listened to relaxation tapes. She gave up playing. But now the music kept punching her in the ears and her fast-moving fingers rekindled a fire from dead ashes. Something woke up inside her that had long been declared dead: an old desire so painful that it used to keep her up in the middle of the night, gnawing at her guts. After six years of silence, there was no way she was stopping now. She turned up her amp. She filled that dead house with sound.

Everyone had told her it was a silly daydream, an adolescent fantasy. Back in the day, none of them even dared say it out loud. But it was the only reason anyone ever formed a band. Everyone pretended it was about the three P's (party, pussy, paycheck), but that was a lie. No one ever formed a band to make money. You formed a band because you wanted to be legendary. Kris wanted to press her fist to the planet and leave a mark. She wanted to be remembered. It's why they put up with the cold vans and the sweaty venues and the cheap beer and the shady promoters and the constant grind. Because they wanted to live forever.

She didn't find the right guy, she didn't get married, she didn't go to college, she didn't even graduate from high school, she didn't save money, she didn't have a career, she didn't do any of that because she'd bet everything on Dürt Würk. And she'd lost.

The final chord of "Angel of Death" reverbed off the walls and faded. It was getting bright outside now, the morning sun washing out the dim basement lightbulb. In the sudden silence, her amp humming quietly beside her, Kris knew what she had to do. She had to go to the Blind King and demand what was hers. It was time to stand face-to-face with Terry Hunt and make him pay. Money? An explanation? An apology? Breaking his nose? She didn't know how he'd pay, but all she knew was that she'd paid the price for his success for so many years, and now it was his turn. There was no other way to put this anger back to bed.

Around the base of the wooden staircase clustered Dollarmax bags with their handles tied shut. Some of them contained her mom's magazines—*National Geographic*, *TIME*, *AARP*—

but most were filled with mail that Kris was too tired to sort and her mom had been too nervous to throw away. Now she ripped them open and pawed through the envelopes until she found a Christmas card from Scottie Rocket with his return address on the envelope.

Upstairs, Kris reached into the back of her closet for the heavy plastic hanger and pulled out her Bones. It gleamed back at her, the black leather Brooks motorcycle jacket that everyone had worn back in the day. Kris had worn hers for so long that it still held the shape of her body, the bend of her elbows, the curve of her spine. Terry had painted a spinal column up its back in white paint and a curving ribcage that met in front when she zipped it up, wrapping her in its skeletal embrace. She hadn't worn it in years, but now she slipped it on, grabbed her soft case, and got in her dad's car.

On the way out of town, she drove past the billboard of Terry Hunt, the Blind King. He'd taken everything and left her behind, and he thought it was over because his lawyers said it was over, but she wasn't ready to quit fighting yet. They'd been a band once, they'd been good, they might have even been great.

But then the Blind King betrayed them all. He had broken her, ruined her, and stolen her music. He'd sold out and gotten rich, while she stayed poor. Now she was coming for him and the first thing she needed to do was get the band back together. There was only one problem: Kris was the only person they hated more than they hated Terry.

GRAY MANNING: The owners and management of WDIY want to apologize to our listeners for this morning's broadcast of "Good Morning, Gurner." Although protected by a tape delay, the crudeness of the band known as Dürt Würk was unprecedented in this station's history. We have taken steps to ensure that future guests are screened more carefully, and we are undertaking a review of our practices that led to this morning's incident. Thank you."

—88.1 WDIY, Lehigh Valley Community Public Radio,
announcement from the station manager
September 5, 1995

Under the Blade

It was a sign from heaven, a shaft of light slicing through gray clouds, the lone blast of color in a beige world. Nothing gave Melanie more hope than the billboard of the Blind King towering over Star City, West Virginia. She clung to it so that she wouldn't drown. The final dates had been announced online, and Koffin's comeback was all over drive-time radio, and the landing pages of *Loudwire* and Spotify. But all the dates were on the West Coast, so they felt dreamy and faraway to Melanie, like a story about someplace she'd never go. But this billboard was right here. It was real.

She was working bottomless brunch at Pappy's, smiling at the frat boys in their Wet Vagina University T-shirts, pulling frozen margaritas for these couch-burners bellowing "Country Roads" at the top of their lungs, ignoring the shoulders brushing her breasts and the eyes boring into her cleavage when she bent over tables to drop off another pitcher of Bud. Suddenly, a table erupted into a ragged, drunken chorus of Koffin's "Burn You Down."

I know where you live
Got a can of gas
And I park

Splash a spark
It's dark
Turn my frown
Upside down
When I burn you down
Down to the ground.

She had a platter of wings for their table and when she dropped it off she saw they were passing around an iPhone with the billboard on the screen.

"Y'all Koffin fans?" she asked.

"That get us a free beer?" a lanky ginger with cheeks full of acne shot back.

"You know it," she said.

He handed her his phone, letting his fingers run over hers when she took it, but after two years at Pappy's that didn't even make her blink. The phone showed the massive Koffin billboard, the Blind King staring down on West Virginia with his pupilless black orbs, black blood streaming down his face from the crown nailed to his skull. She handed the phone back with a smile, and asked, "Was that Bud, or Bud Light?"

After work, she drove out and parked her 2008 Subaru in the Sheetz parking lot, facing the Monongahela River and the Blind King's enormous face.

MAY 30–JUNE 8, LA, LV, SF

She'd never wanted anything more than she wanted to see those shows. The need to get away from this place tasted bitter in her throat. In West Virginia, everyone drove the same cars, and they clogged the highways at the same time, and they ate the same food at McDonald's, and Starbucks, and Wendy's. Sometimes there was a Taco Bell. Everyone pumped their gas at Chevron and BP. All their kids were honor students, they all put yellow ribbon decals on their cars to show they supported the troops, or pink ribbons to show they hated breast cancer, and they were insured by AAA, and Liberty Mutual, and State Farm, and Smith & Wesson. They got married, and had kids, and played on the internet, and argued about the latest superhero movie. They filled up their time between childhood and old age trying to be as unremarkable as possible.

Melanie was only twenty-six years old and already felt exhausted. The light looked exhausted. Colors looked exhausted. The whole world was exhausted. She thought, "How can I be so young and feel so dead?"

But she knew the answer. She got out of college with $29,938 in debt and Navient scratching at her door demanding repayment before her diploma was even in its frame. She worked a job that'd only allowed her to pay that down to $27,309 in three years. She discovered that her degree in computer animation wasn't a ticket to a good job in Atlanta or LA, because she was stuck in West Virginia, living in the same three-bedroom shoebox she grew up in because she couldn't find a job that would let her save enough for a deposit on a new place.

She tried. She tried so hard for so long. She went to group interviews where she sat in a circle with fifty-five-year-old men, all of them in their good suits, taking turns telling the HR rep why they'd make the best bank teller at Citizens. She vowed to apply for a job a day, and created six different versions of her résumé that she sent out to compete with the thousands of other résumés from kids with better degrees from better schools, who could afford to take unpaid internships in New York City, who were willing to animate shorts for free because it would look good in their portfolios. She tried to brand herself by starting a YouTube channel, because content creators are king, and she uploaded her best work every other week for an entire year, but by the end of that year not a single one of her videos had over 337 views.

Pappy's started as a part-time gig because two years ago she couldn't imagine working full-time at a place where training consisted of Big Pappy giving a lecture on the difference between being a tease and being a sleaze (key difference: teases stayed on the floor and let guys pull them into their laps, sleazes took too many breaks and got pregnant). But she made between $60 and $80 a night in cash tips, and close to $100 in credit card tips, and after six months she went to swallow her pride and realized she didn't have much of that left, so she went full-time.

Through it all, Koffin was there for her. She drove herself home every night shouting "Stand Strong" or "Burn You Down" at the top of her lungs. She whispered "InFANticide" to herself over and over while she waited in the hospital after her dad's accident. "Get in Your Koffins" was playing when she met her boyfriend Greg. Whenever she heard someone else from her graduating class had died of an OD (twelve and counting) she played "A Grave Is a Hole Your Heart Makes."

But as the years passed and no new albums came out, and no more tours were announced, and Terry Hunt stopped giving interviews, her love got rusty. She forgot everything except her next shift at Pappy's, and losing herself at depressing parties where she pretended to have fun, and reading *TMZ* on her phone during her breaks, gossiping to the other waitresses about famous people who had no idea she even existed. And now here was Terry, staring down at her, back from the grave, and there was nothing Melanie wanted to do more than go out to Vegas and see him play live. They were a band that had given her so much, and she had never even seen them live, and these were their last shows.

It was only a billboard, but it felt like reconnecting with a younger part of herself that was good, and pure, and true. It felt like a door to a world where she wasn't tired all the time. But she didn't have the money. Navient owned all her potential future earnings, and anything she saved had to go to a deposit on a new place. The world was a trap and there was no way out. Melanie started to cry. When she realized she was sitting in her ten-year-old Subaru in a Sheetz parking lot, looking at a Koffin billboard in West Virginia and crying, she cried even harder.

Terry Hunt looked down at her with his all-black eyes, black blood streaming down his face. Melanie knew his story. He came from a crappy little town in Pennsylvania. He came from a poor family of steelworkers. He put himself out there and played in any band that would take him. He wrote his own songs. He developed his own material playing bar after bar after bar. He pulled his way up out of that hole all by himself, and now here he was on a billboard, the most famous rock star in the world, and he did it all by himself.

If he could do this, she could do this. If he could claw his way up out of Nowhere, Pennsylvania, she could claw her way up out of Nowhere, West Virginia. She swiped the tears off her cheeks and came up with a plan. Then she started her Subaru, whose transmission kept making a noise that sounded like metal screaming, and she drove home to tell her boyfriend that they were changing their lives. The Blind King gave her strength. The Blind King gave her hope.

She could do this.

NANCY: Lollapalooza! Monsters of Rock! Ozzfest! Now, get ready for another of rock's landmark events: Koffin's Farewell to the King Tour. Five nights of mayhem.

SID: Oh, brother.

NANCY: In LA, both shows at the Rose Bowl sold out in under thirty minutes. Three shows at the T-Mobile Arena in Las Vegas sold out in under an hour. Every single ticket to their concerts in San Francisco was gone in six minutes.

SID: Koffin isn't a band, they're a corporation. Koffin condoms, Koffin headphones, Koffin black scented candles, Koffin panties with Terry Hunt's face on the crotch, Ibanez's Terry Hunt Signature guitars . . . He doesn't even play guitar. Trust me, this is the first of what's going to be many "farewell tours" from Terry Hunt. The man is everything bad about KISS rolled up into one person.

—100.7 WLEV, "The Sid & Nancy Wake-Up Rumble"
May 11, 2019

Appetite for Destruction

Scottie Rocket lived a half-hour drive from the Saint Street Swamp, but to Kris it was another planet. Gurner had a suicide rate four times the national average and so much lead in the ground that the EPA put up a chain link fence around Bovino Park. Scottie lived in a nice part of Allentown where everyone had yards, the trees were healthy, and big houses lined pothole-free streets.

The drive gave Kris time to calm down. She didn't want to storm out to LA and rip Terry's head off anymore. She just wanted to talk to someone else who knew what it was like to live in Terry's shadow. Worried that Scottie still hated her, she parked a few houses down from his place and watched a bunch of kids play basketball in their driveway while she gathered her courage. She hadn't seen Scottie in six years. He probably didn't want some ghost from his past showing up and invading his home. Then again, he *had* sent her that Christmas card.

She checked her hair in the rearview mirror, checked her teeth, checked her hair again, smelled her breath, then launched herself out of her car, across the sun-dappled front yards, up the front walk, and rang Scottie's doorbell before she had time to stop herself. The electric chimes echoed deep inside the house, someone shouted at someone else, and the door opened to reveal a skinny beanpole in a white hoodie eating a bagel.

Kris ransacked her brain and came up with, "Martin?"

His Adam's apple worked as he swallowed.

"I'm Kris," she explained. "A friend of your dad's? From his old band?"

"Mooooom!" he shouted, turning away into the house and disappearing into the gloom.

A woman in sweats emerged.

"May I help you?" she asked, wiping her hands on a paper towel.

"I'm—" Kris began, but the woman recognized her before she could finish.

"Oh, shit," the woman said. "You're Kris."

"Hey," Kris said, like an idiot. "It's been a while. Angela, right?"

The woman nodded, and they stood there, Angela inside the dark house and Kris outside in the bright morning sun.

"You're here to see Scott," Angela said.

"Is he here?" Kris asked.

"Downstairs," Angela said, and didn't move.

"Should I go around you?" Kris finally asked. "Or . . . how do you want to work this?"

Angela stood aside and Kris walked into a house that smelled like scrambled eggs. In the living room, Martin slumped on the sofa, next to an identical skinny blonde girl, both of them playing on their phones and ignoring the cartoon blasting from the flat-screen TV. Angela led her down the carpeted hall.

"Ursula," Angela called, as they passed the living room, "you have to be at practice in an hour."

"I! Know!" Ursula said, not taking her eyes off her phone.

"What does she play?" Kris asked.

"Soccer," Angela said.

They entered the kitchen and Angela leaned back against the sink, facing Kris, who froze in the doorway. Bright sunlight streamed in the window looking out over the block's unfenced backyards. Angela nodded toward a door on the other side of the room, dim and hazy in the shadows.

"He's in there," she said. "Knock loud so he'll hear you."

Kris walked across the tiles.

"Kris," Angela said, "find me before you go. You've known him longer. I need to know if this is just some midlife crisis or if I should be worried."

Then she disappeared down the hall, and Kris turned to the basement door. She knocked, then knocked louder. Something scuffed behind the door and then a muffled voice called, "I said I don't want any breakfast."

"It's me," Kris said. "Kris. Kris Pulaski."

She heard a padlock pop open, then a deadbolt turn, then a chain slide aside, and finally the door swung open and a short man she'd never seen before stood there, one step down, giving her a perfect view of his bald spot. He had long hair that hung past his collar in greasy wisps. He needed a shave. A woven leather belt barely held up his sagging jeans. His belly pushed a small black fanny pack down over his crotch.

The man rubbed his right hand over his face like he was cleaning off spiderwebs, and Kris recognized the hand she'd stared at for years. A thick white scar ringed his first finger and a matching scar ringed the second. Faint white puckers bunched on the backs of his knuckles, long-faded scars from punching dry wall, from punching unruly stage divers, from punching the sides of vans, from punching the lead singer of Powerhole.

After his hands, the rest of him came into focus. All the years disappeared. The knot that was her heart unpicked itself, her knees loosened, her belly gave an embarrassing flip from way down low, and Kris was twenty-four again and her entire life stretched out ahead of her and she had never made any mistakes. Everything could still be saved. She still had her friends. She still had her music. She still had Dürt Würk. Possibilities filled her like helium and she stepped forward and threw herself into Scottie Rocket's arms.

"Scottie Rocket!" she shouted, and it was the first time in six years she'd felt truly happy.

Kris had never been a big hugger because she had a body like a bag of knives, but this felt right, like picking up her guitar again.

"Hey, Kris," he said, muffled.

"I forgot how much I missed you," Kris grinned, her chin on his shoulder.

"You look," he said, holding her back at arm's length and studying her face, "you look really good."

Kris knew what she looked like. Ever since she'd moved back to Gurner she'd stopped wearing lipstick and eyeliner, stopped dyeing her hair and plucking the gray. Her necklines had gotten higher, mostly to cover up the tattoo on her left breast, and her basic black wardrobe had more beige in it, more white, even some prints. She'd left behind boots and embraced flats. But now, with her Bones on, she knew what he meant. He meant she looked like herself, not like this imposter who'd been living her life for the last six years.

"You look good too," she said. "Like an Earth Sciences teacher."

He didn't reply, just kept watching her, standing so close Kris could count every wild hair growing out of his salt-and-pepper eyebrows.

"I should have come sooner," she said.

"You came at the right time," he said. "I don't like to keep the door open. Come on."

He locked the door behind her while she clomped down the stairs and entered a pharaoh's tomb of brown cardboard boxes, stacked up as high as her head, lining every wall, each one carefully labeled with black magic marker: S, M, L, XL. CD. 3" STICKERS. The boxes, sagging and broken with time, were filled with unsold Dürt Würk merch. Hoodies and bandanas spilled onto the floor. In a collapsing pile of boxes on an air hockey table were posters for *All That Cremains*. A cardboard pyramid beneath the stairs contained unsold cassingles of "Reaper's Harvest."

It was the graveyard of all their hopes and dreams, the dusty rubble left behind after a band implodes, and it pushed Kris's breathing higher in her chest and made her hands itch. Inside all these boxes was the crap they sold at shows to pay for their gas and stay on the road. It had once been more precious than gold. Now it was worthless.

"Over there are the studio tapes for *All That Cremains* and *Digging to China*," Scottie said.

Kris looked at the boxes he pointed to, containing their first two albums that she no longer felt much affection for. But if they were here, maybe Scottie knew about the other one.

"What about *Troglodyte*?" Kris asked.

"No one knows what happened to those," he said. "I thought maybe the masters were in my mom's house, or at the Witch House, but I've been looking for years and can't find even a single copy. Terry buried that one deep."

There was a cot in one corner with a sleeping bag on top. An electric kettle sat on a box of "Chinagirl" 7" singles. Beside it was a plastic shopping bag full of ramen. A faint whiff of sour sweat filled the room. Kris looked at Scottie, and he looked back, and they held each other's eyes.

From their very first show until contract night at the Witch House, Kris and Scottie Rocket had stood shoulder to shoulder for eleven years and delivered twelve strings of heavy metal death to their frontline. They'd played every kind of venue that existed, from all-ages shows in Mexican restaurants outside Baltimore to the cramped basement of Wally's in Allentown. They'd played biker bars in New Jersey where a girl bit off the tip of some guy's pinkie, and Zoot's in Detroit where a kid in the pit had glued razor blades to his watch and no one noticed until Kris saw flecks of blood speckling Terry's face.

They'd slept on the roof of a Chinese restaurant in Florida, and they'd slept in the back of their broken-down Volvo waiting for a new fuel pump after playing the Burnstock Chili Fest in West Virginia. She'd taped up his split lips, he'd guarded bathroom doors while she peed, they'd thrown up in the same toilet, had a terrible twelve-hour acid trip together in Atlanta, and like every guitar duo in metal, they were a little bit in love and a little bit in hate all at the same time. For Kris, Scottie was the brother she'd always wanted and the marriage she'd never had, and she suspected that if she ever did get married it would be a shallow thing compared to what she'd shared for eleven years on the road with Scottie Rocket.

That's why she could say, "Scottie, are you living in your basement?"

Scottie unfolded two bright-blue canvas lawn chairs and set them in the middle of the floor. He wiped at one with his shirt sleeve and offered it to Kris. It creaked when she sat down, and her butt nearly touched the floor.

"Scottie?" Kris asked again.

"Angela and the kids," he said, sitting across from her. "You know, they just don't get the journey I'm on. Ha. Sometimes I don't get the journey I'm on. Check this out."

He leaned over, belly resting on top of his thighs, and scratched at his jeans until he'd raised one leg halfway up his calf. A bright orange and black butterfly rested in the middle of a patch of red skin. It was so vivid Kris could see its wings pulse. A needle pricked her heart. Scottie had only ever had one tattoo, the same one she had. Back in the day, they'd each gotten a corny red rose, its stem wrapped in barbed wire, from a tweaking ink jockey in Perth Amboy, New Jersey, around four in the morning It had been a joke, but not really. Her rose was a faded, rusty smudge at the top of her left breast, an ugly duckling compared to this bright, living thing on Scottie's calf.

"I don't even remember getting it," Scottie said, and grinned, but his eyes looked worried. "I just woke up a couple of days ago and was like, 'Holy shit!'"

"Are you drinking again?" Kris asked, but before she finished her sentence, Scottie started shaking his head.

"I'd never, ever, ever do that," he said. "I went back to rehab this winter, but not because of that. Just to get my head together. Top up, you know. I keep getting these flashes . . . these headaches, like I lost something but I don't know what it is, you know?"

"Oh, Scottie Rocket." Kris leaned forward and touched his knee. "You should have called me. I would have come."

"I know why you came today," Scottie said.

"Yeah?" Kris asked, smiling back at him.

"I invited you," Scottie said. "In your dream."

"You wish I dreamed about you," Kris joked uneasily, her smile fading.

"It's the only secure way to communicate without Terry hearing," Scottie said.

"You saw he was going on tour again this summer?" Kris asked, trying to divert. "I was thinking about going out to LA, talking to him, trying to get paid up. Maybe he's changed and . . . "

She trailed off because Scottie was laughing at her, a hissing, whispering giggle, his eyes crinkled shut, bouncing up and down in his lawn chair like a happy baby.

"What?" she asked, embarrassed.

"Kris," Scottie said. "You think Terry will let you get anywhere near him?"

"I know we had problems, but a lot of time has passed and . . . "

Scottie stood up fast, threw himself to the other side of the room, and came back with a box full of Ziploc bags. He yanked one out and thrust it into her hands. It held a little black metal tube with two wires at one end and a glass lens at the other.

"This was in my wall," Scottie said, then passed her another Ziploc bag with a tiny circuit board inside. "That was in the handset of our land line." Then he handed her an empty Ziploc bag. "That was inside my cell phone."

"There's nothing in here," Kris said.

"It's too small to be seen with the naked eye," Scottie said, sitting back down, pulling his chair so close their knees touched.

"Do you know why I'm down here? The TVs are upstairs. Three of them, all internet accessible. I took a look at their activity and they're bouncing video and audio packets to a secure IP address. But I can't disconnect them because then he'll know that I know. And if Terry knew what I knew, he might take steps."

"What steps?" Kris asked, feeling nervous.

"Like killing me," Scottie said.

"That's—" Kris began, still hoping this was all some elaborate put-on.

"The Blind King has been asleep for years," Scottie plowed on. "Now he's awake. And you're here. That's not a coincidence. He's calling this his 'Farewell Tour,' but come on, we all saw what happened with KISS. He's back and he's going to keep coming back until the whole world is Black Iron Mountain. Or until we stop him."

Kris had come to Scottie for comfort, she didn't want to feel sorry for him, but Black Iron Mountain was just a song, the evil bad guys off their third album, *Troglodyte*, and he was talking about them like they were real. If it was a joke, it wasn't funny. If it wasn't a joke, then he was doing worse than her. She'd talk to Angie. She'd go home. She'd come back when she was prepared for this. She braced her hands on her thighs and pushed herself up, her right knee aching.

"I need to go," she said. "But let's get together again soon, okay?"

Scottie's forehead wrinkled, his cheeks turned red.

"You think I'm crazy."

"No," Kris lied. "You're going through something, though. Let's reconnect later this week."

"I thought if anyone would believe me it would be you," Scottie said. "You're the first one who saw Black Iron Mountain. That's why I went into your dreams last night and told you to come."

"I was working last night," Kris said. "I didn't have any dreams. Let's take a break. I'll come back tomorrow."

Scottie's jowls and chin trembled, and his eyes filled with tears. Kris made herself turn and walk to the steps. This had been a mistake. She never should have come.

From, behind her, Scottie chanted, "You like drugs, you like brew. You won't believe what I can do."

Kris froze. She turned back around, saw him sitting on the floor of his basement, trying not to cry, and something inside her unclenched. She said in rhythm, "Dead-end kids in the danger zone," and dropped her voice an octave. "All of you are drunk or stoned."

Scottie laughed. Kris felt like she might cry. She'd found her best friend again, and he was broken.

Right after Dürt Würk recorded *All That Cremains* they'd done a tour from Portland, down to San Diego, then over to Texas—six grueling weeks in the van. At first they'd listened to their regular tapes, but eventually they'd started digging around in the bottom of the tape crate and gotten religious about some of the weirder nuggets they found. One of them was the Runaways' first album.

The Runaways were a bunch of sneering seventies teenaged punkettes in black leather jackets and spandex tights and Kris had bought their album back in high school when she was trying to figure out what she liked. Outside of "Cherry Bomb" with its snarling bratitude it turned out she hadn't much liked the Runaways. She'd thrown the tape in the tape crate without even thinking. Terry put it on while they drove across New Mexico and the whole band had gotten obsessed with "Dead End Justice," the seven-minute epic that ended the B side. It featured a beat poetry interlude and climaxed with a high-camp rock opera between Joan Jett and Cherie Currie playing two girls sentenced to juvie for the crime of being too cool.

They listened to it so many times the lyrics became Dürt Würk's secret language. When they showed up at a venue full of grim skinheads, someone would growl, "You don't sing and dance in juvie, honey." When one of them jerked awake on the midnight drive to the next show and asked, "Where are we?" the response was inevitably, "You're in a cheap run-down teenage jail, that's where."

Now, Scottie sat in a faded lawn chair in his basement that smelled like armpits, and delivered the line they never quoted because it always sucked the fun out of the room.

"On the planet sorrow," he said, "there is no tomorrow."

Kris couldn't think of anything to say. Water ran in the pipes in the walls. They were twenty years, a lot of lawsuits, and a car crash away from the good old days. It was a long way back home.

"Come on," Kris said, realizing Scottie needed her help more than she needed his. "Let's get out of this place. It's depressing. Let's go to Gino's. When's the last time you had a really filthy Italian?"

"I know I didn't find everything he had in my walls," Scottie said, shaking his head. "Now he knows you're here."

Kris was desperate to get out of there, to be in the sunlight, away from this underground merch crypt.

"Come on, Scottie," she said. "I'll drive."

"Terry did something to us, Kris," Scottie said. "There's a hole in the center of the world. And inside that hole . . . "

Kris knew the rest of those lyrics because she'd written them for *Troglodyte* twenty-one years ago. In the *Troglodyte* mythology, there is a hole in the center of the world, and inside that hole is Black Iron Mountain, an underground empire of caverns and lava seas, ruled over by the Blind King who sees everything with the help of his Hundred Handed Eye. At the root of the mountain is the Wheel. Troglodyte was chained to the Wheel along with millions of others, which they turned pointlessly in a circle, watched eternally by the Hundred Handed Eye.

No one in Dürt Würk ever spoke about this mythology except in lyrics they passed back and forth, expanding it, building on it, adding, subtracting, contradicting. It felt thick and lived, like a fairy tale, like something that existed before they sang about it. Troglodyte was chained to his wheel, and he couldn't even dream of escape because he couldn't visualize anything besides Black Iron Mountain. He lived in a prison as big as the world.

"Terry's a shithead," Kris said. "But you can't get obsessed with him. Look what that did to me. You—"

A tinny version of some song interrupted her. Kris recognized the tune and the walls got closer. It was "Stand Strong" by Koffin.

"Sorry," Scottie said, as he unzipped his fanny pack and pulled out his phone.

That's when Kris knew something was seriously wrong.

Scottie's phone was wrapped in tin foil.

He carefully unwrapped it, placed the sheet of foil on the floor, and answered.

"Hello?" he said. "Uh-huh. Uh-huh."

He flicked his eyes over to Kris. His shoulders slumped and his face went slack.

"Okay," he said, and hung up. He put his phone on the ground next to the foil.

"Please, Scottie," Kris said. "Let's get out of here."

Scottie unzipped his fanny pack again, rooted around inside it like a sad kangaroo, and pulled out a small gadget the color of pencil lead and cradled it in his hands. It was a gun.

"I'm sorry, Kris," he said. "Terry told me I have to kill you now."

CALLER (East of the Rockies): . . . the Monarch Mind Control program operated by the illuminati. They invaded my life and turned me into a Piloted Person using psychic driving techniques. They manipulate their slaves with certain wavelengths. Different songs on the radio make me violent.

PAUL GIBSON: What about school shootings? Could those be MKUltra sleeper assassins being activated?

CALLER (East of the Rockies): Britney Spears is a programmed Beta alter with kitten sex slave programming. You can see an alien intelligence peering out of her eyes on MTV's *For the Record*. She's not a real person anymore.

—KIXW-AM "Resistance America AM"
May 12, 2019

Destroyer

There's no point fighting," Scottie said to the gun in his paw. "Terry always gets what he wants."

Kris's throat was lined with something dry and gummy. "That wasn't Terry on the phone," she croaked.

"It was Black Iron Mountain," Scottie told his lap. "They speak with the same voice. You called it, Kris. Way back on *Troglodyte*. There is a hole in the center of the world, and inside that hole is Black Iron Mountain."

"You're not making any sense," Kris said.

Kris had always assumed that if she encountered a gun in real life, she would be strong. If some punk pulled a piece, she'd smack their wrist to the side and disarm them, point their own weapon back in their face. But right now, her hands and feet were freezing cold and her mouth was numb and all her little strategies stood revealed as wishful thinking.

"I wrote it down for you," Scottie said, and his eyes were the same color as the gun. "Because I have a hard time keeping everything straight."

Scottie squeezed his eyes shut and twisted his face into a silent scream of pain.

"They put a concentration camp inside my brain," he said.

He relaxed his face, pulled the gun off his knuckle, and placed it awkwardly in his lap, kneading his temples with his fingertips. If Kris were a warrior, now was when she'd kick his lawn chair backward, immobilize him, take his weapon. Instead she stood there and tried to reason with him, like a victim.

"You don't need the gun, Scottie," she managed. "We're friends."

"They turn me on like a radio," he moaned, "and the song won't stop until somebody drops. I'm never going to reach the Blue Door, but one of us has to. Do you know what *Troglodyte* is?"

He opened his eyes, picked up his gun, and smiled.

"*Troglodyte* is a bullet fired from the past," Scottie said. "You made the weapon we needed years before you knew we needed it. Why can't I think of things like that?"

Kris couldn't come up with a plan. She couldn't think of anything beyond the next second. Her brain short-circuited. Upstairs, feet stomped across the living room floor, and she wanted to shout for help, but any loud sound might make him pull the trigger. Her mouth had been too dry before, but now it was too wet.

"Please, Scottie," Kris whispered. "Nothing you're saying makes any sense."

Scottie began digging around in his fanny pack. "I wrote it all down," he said. "It's in here somewhere."

This time, Kris moved. She made herself take a step backward, then another step, then another. The farther she got from the gun, the clearer her thinking became, and now she had a plan. She needed to get upstairs and get everyone out of the house.

"He canceled *Troglodyte* and buried it deep," Scottie said, looking up, and Kris froze. "And now it's just the five of us who know what it means. Terry wants it to just be him. You can't fight something if you don't even know its name. Jeez, I swear, it's around here somewhere."

He pushed himself up out of his lawn chair and for a second the gun pointed directly at Kris, its barrel a black hole so big it swallowed the world. Then Scottie had his back to her, rummaging through papers by his bed. Kris took a deep breath and turned her back to Scottie, put her foot on the stairs, and it was the hardest thing she'd ever done in her life. She took one step, then the next, then the next. The stairs didn't creak, Scottie didn't turn around, and in seconds she was at the top, out of sight. Quietly, she turned the deadbolt, slowly she slid the chain, and then her fingers went numb.

The padlock was snapped shut.

She pulled on it, praying it would pop open, but it held. From the other side of the door, she heard the muffled soundtrack from the cartoon in the living room. Sick on adrenaline, veins full of bees, she looked down and saw Scottie standing at the bottom of the stairs, the gun tiny in his enormous paw.

"I found it," Scottie said, holding out a white envelope. Then he cocked his head. "Where are you going?"

"Scottie," Kris said, her voice weak. "Please."

She pressed herself to the door, as far away from him as she could go.

"Come down," Scottie said.

"Please," Kris begged.

"Now!" he shouted, launching himself up the stairs.

Kris begged and flailed her arms, but he grabbed her by the

collar and dragged her back downstairs.

"'My Master's Eye,'" he said, as she tried to cling to the wall. "'Beneath the Wheel.' 'Little Sounds from Underground.'"

He listed *Troglodyte* tracks in a loud, flat voice. Beneath all the chub, he still had the muscles of the guy who used to lug their amps onstage every night. He tossed Kris onto the concrete floor, then lowered himself into his lawn chair, and turned the gun over in his hand, considering it for a minute before resting it in his lap.

"Joan, I'm getting tired," Scottie said.

Kris realized he was still, grotesquely, quoting "Dead End Justice."

"I've run out of fire," he said.

Scottie and Kris locked eyes. The sound trapped inside Kris's throat escaped her mouth as a sob.

"I can't . . . " Scottie began, and took a great, shuddering breath. "I can't go any farther."

His look made it clear that it was Kris's turn. She didn't think she could do it, but she didn't have any free will. Scottie had the gun.

"But Cherie," Kris said, her voice cracking, "you must try harder."

Scottie Rocket smiled at her through the spit and snot sheeting down his face. He looked relieved that a long day was finally done.

"You have to watch out for the UPS trucks," he told her.

"Scottie," she said. "Don't."

"They told me I had to kill someone," he said. "They didn't say who."

In one motion, he raised the gun to his temple and pulled the trigger.

The loudest sound Kris had ever heard exploded every air

molecule at once, slapped the walls of the basement, reactivated her tinnitus. She caught a glimpse of the brightest red she'd ever seen leaping through the air and clawing toward the boxes of merch, then she squeezed her eyes shut and covered her head with her arms because she didn't want to see that. It got quiet again except for the relentless high E whining in her left ear. She could hear something wet trying to breathe. It got the hiccups, then stopped.

Running footsteps overhead, then a tentative knock on the basement door.

"Scott?" Angela called down, voice muffled. "Scott!"

Through the whine in her left ear Kris heard the knocking become pounding, then rattling as Angela twisted the knob and shook the door in its frame. The padlock. She needed keys.

The rattling continued as Kris crawled to the body of her best friend and went through his pockets. She felt his skin already cooling through the denim as she pulled out his keys. When she turned to crawl away, her hand brushed something white on the floor and she picked that up, too. Scottie's envelope.

Crawling step by step, a huge weight pressing her to the floor, she finally made it to the top of the stairs and popped the padlock. The door burst open and Angela shoved her backward, but Kris grabbed both sides of the doorframe and pushed herself up and out, shoving Angela back into the kitchen, slamming the basement door behind her.

"Don't," she said.

They stood in the sunny kitchen, Angela frozen in front of Kris, Martin in the doorway, eyes moving between his mom and this strange woman covered in white dust, red smudges on her hands.

"What did you do?" Angela asked.

"He—" Kris started, but the words were too big for her throat. "Call 911."

"Martin," Angela said, not moving, not taking her eyes off Kris. "Go in the front room and turn off that TV."

"Mom?" he asked, voice quavering.

"Go!" she barked.

He went. Still watching Kris, Angela stepped to the wall phone and pressed three buttons.

"This is Angela Borzek," she said, and gave her address, slow and calm. "We have a gunshot wound here, I'm not sure what happened, but we need the police and an ambulance. Right away."

She hung up.

"Are you sure?" she asked Kris.

"I'm sorry," Kris said. "I'm so sorry."

"You're sorry," Angela said, and looked for somewhere to sit, but she was blind and lost and spun in place.

Kris took her arm, careful to only touch the fabric of Angela's sweatshirt. "Come on," she said.

Angela yanked her arm away. "I have to see," she said.

Kris stepped in front of her. "No. You don't."

The doorbell rang, loud chimes, and they both froze.

"Martin!" Angela called. "Wait for me."

She stepped into the front hall as Martin called back, "It's not the police, Mom. It's UPS."

The front door opened and then air slapped the walls of the house, a dry *snap-pop*, exactly like the sound Kris had heard in the basement.

"Wait," Angela said to someone Kris couldn't see, and then the noise cracked out again and Angela fell backward into the kitchen, the back of her skull hitting the floor tiles with a sound like a coconut. Her right eye oozed a slug of black liquid down the side of her face.

Footsteps started down the hall, and Kris backed up, considered the basement door, then saw the pantry door and slipped inside, sliding it shut behind her. She sank to the floor and hugged her knees tight. Through the louvers she saw two men in brown UPS uniforms standing over Angela. Kris thought about Ursula, somewhere in the house, changing into her soccer shorts, looking for her shin guards. These guys didn't know she was home.

Upstairs, a toilet flushed.

One of the men left the room. Kris heard him on the stairs. The flushing sound got louder as the bathroom door opened, then a sharp *snap-pop* cut through the air, and there was a sound like a sack of laundry falling over.

Kris breathed as quietly as she could. She wanted to live so bad.

The first UPS man walked the perimeter of the kitchen. He paused at the back door, then stopped in front of the pantry. Kris could see the brown laces in his shoes.

The other UPS man returned to the kitchen, the man at the pantry door turned, and together they went downstairs. The kitchen got quiet. Kris smelled the stink of a struck match. There were footsteps coming up the stairs and one of the UPS men walked past carrying Scottie's box of Ziploc bags. Kris heard him go down the hallway and out the front door.

She had to go before the other one came upstairs. Quietly, she rattled the pantry door back on its tracks, stepped out, and closed it behind her. Gun smoke swirled in the sunlight. Angela lay on her back, still staring up at the ceiling with one eye, the other eye weeping onto the tiles beneath her head. Her upper lip was pulled up, showing slightly bucked teeth.

The sound of feet coming up the basement stairs pushed Kris through the back door, and out into the warm air and the far-away sound of kids playing basketball. She sprinted around the side of the house, away from the boxy, brown UPS truck parked in Scottie's driveway. Another UPS truck passed her and the driver parked in front of Scottie's house and got out.

Kris reached her dad's car and pulled away while she was still closing her door, driving straight past Scottie's house where the UPS driver stood on the porch. He looked up from his tablet as she sped by.

Scottie had been right about the UPS trucks. But who would believe her? No one. Where could she go? Nowhere. If she told anyone, they'd say she did it. Or something. She didn't know. What else had Scottie been right about? She couldn't think. What Scottie had done, what had happened in his house, to his family—it was a big black mountain pressing her down. She would never get out from beneath its weight. It was too much. All she knew was that Scottie Rocket was right. Terry was going to kill them all.

DAVE THE METAL GUY: . . . and *Insect Narthex* is a radical departure. You're more in the mold of Marilyn Manson, or Trent Reznor at this point in your career.

TERRY HUNT: I've got more showmanship than Reznor, and I'm more intense than Manson, but really I'm about transcending genres. My fans are some of the most intelligent listeners alive. They listen to Metallica, they listen to Tool, they listen to Wagner. They listen with what I call "honest ears."

DAVE THE METAL GUY: So you don't think Koffin is a heavy metal band?

TERRY HUNT: Koffin sings about real things, about social change, about actual emotions, about 9/11. Metal is an act. Koffin is real.

—90.7 WVUA, "The Combat Zone"
July 8, 2004

Awaken the Guardian

"Hold still, you little bitch, and let me shoot you," Greg said. A shotgun went off and he giggled. "Suck my left one!"

Melanie had come to his place after work, hands sticky with spilled margarita, and found her boyfriend where he normally was, in the center of the couch, headset over his ears, an Xbox controller in his hand. She used to sit next to him while he gamed. The places he took his avatar were sometimes eye-searingly beautiful and there were nights when she wanted to live in those fantasy forests with their golden motes floating in beams of sunlight so bad her heart hurt. But now, more and more, he bounced around the same desert ruins, trapped inside a chain-link fence, murdering other players he referred to as "whores" and "little bitches." It sounded too much like real life to her.

"Hey," she said, putting down her bag. "We need to talk."

Greg muted his headset. "Are you breaking up with me?" he asked.

"No," she said, surprised.

"Okay, hold on," he said, and unmuted.

Twenty minutes later he took the headset off and said, "What's going on, babe?"

She came over and sat down next to him on the couch, trying not to wrinkle her nose when it puffed out a blast of dirty socks, Cheetos, and Axe body spray. He shared this townhouse with three other guys. The stuff she kept here was in a plastic bin so their boy stink didn't seep into her clothes.

"Look," she said. "You know things are really hard right now."

"The fucking Boomers," he said. "I just read today that the debt-to-GDP ratio is 103 percent. You know what it was for the Boomers? Thirty-five percent. They sucked everything dry."

"Okay, yeah," Melanie said. The two of them had met at an Occupy protest, and the longer Greg went without a steady job, the more horrible facts he learned about the Boomers. "But geography is destiny, right? If we want to change our lives, and get out of this rut, we need to move. You know Koffin?"

Greg laughed and spun invisible DJ turntables.

"Wicky-wicky-wicky," he said. "Black latex! White girls! Around your neck! Drip my pearls!"

Then he did the robot while making terrible industrial music noises.

"That was a really bad song," Melanie agreed. It was off 2010's *9 Circles* and was maybe one of the worst songs ever written. She mostly ignored it. "But they mean a lot to me. And they got me inspired with this idea. They're playing Vegas in June, that's six weeks away. I can get tickets. Let's drive out there for the show."

"White lady! Smoke curls," he kept going. "Black, black latex! For my white, white girls!"

Melanie persisted. "Then when we get out there, we don't come back."

That shut Greg up. He blinked at her for a moment.

"We kill ourselves?" he asked.

"We keep driving," she said. "To LA. I can wait tables there just as well as here. We'll live way out in the Valley—"

"The Valley's expensive," Greg said.

"We'll live in Pasadena."

"That's worse."

"We'll live in Covina," she said. "Wherever. But it's not here. We go and start fresh. Are you in?"

He slouched against the back of the couch and picked at his cargo shorts.

"We need money," he said. "Even just for gas. And how're you going to pay off your loans?"

"We have to try *something*," she said. "Remember Sheila Bartell? She was homecoming queen my senior year? She just overdosed. That's the thirteenth person from my graduating class. My dad said a guy OD'd in the Walmart today and knocked over a laptop display. They're going to make him pay for the laptops."

"Fucking Boomers," Greg muttered.

"If we don't get out of here now, we'll never get out of here," Melanie said. "This town is a hole sucking everyone down. We're going to wind up dead inside."

"Yeah," he said. "I'm totally supportive of whatever. You know I'm feminist, and I love it when you go all kickass, but we have to be practical."

"Fuck practical," she said. "We are going to die if we stay here. Either we will OD, or get run over by some fucker who ODs in his truck, or our hearts and brains will fucking die because this is the worst place in America and we'll become zombies. Do you want to turn thirty and never have taken a single chance?"

"All right, all right," he said. "Take a pill. How're you going to pull off this grand plan?"

She told him. She'd work nonstop—with a goal in mind, she could work doubles two or three times a week, maybe more. They'd cancel their Netflix. They'd get cheaper phone plans. They'd sell a bunch of her clothes. If they were smart, and worked hard, and focused on being positive, they could do this.

"Yeah, totally," he said. "I'm down."

He leaned forward, holding her hand, and then grabbed her left breast. She jumped backward. He cupped it again.

"You get all fiery and your eyes flash," he said. "Like Selena Gomez."

She knew she should let him, just to keep the peace, so she kissed his mouth that tasted like Cool Ranch Doritos, and put one hand around his neck. There was a tag on the back of his shirt, and she tried to fold it back down inside his collar.

"Ow!" he said.

It wasn't a tag—it was stuck to his skin. He yanked away, but Melanie grabbed his shoulder and looked. There was a white gauze pad taped to the back of his neck.

"You didn't," she said. "Show me."

He peeled it down. On the red, shaved skin at the back of his neck, shiny with antibacterial ointment, were the letters FML in Gothic script.

"You're never going to get a job with 'fuck my life' tattooed above your collar," she said. "And we're supposed to be saving money."

"No Boomer knows what this means," Greg said, his face mottled red. "And it's my money, too."

The fight was ugly and ended when they both stormed off in opposite directions. She went to his bedroom, which she paid part of the rent for, so it was technically her bedroom, too. He headed out the front door. Probably to Farmer Don's to smoke weed.

Melanie's phone dinged, and she saw a Kik message from Hunter.

HEY BEAUTIFUL ——> BEEN THINKNG ABOUT U

U THINK ABOUT WHAT WE TALKED ABOUT?

Then there was Hunter. She hadn't told Greg about him, because nothing was going on, and he didn't need to know because he'd just freak out over nothing. They weren't having an affair, even though she sent him the occasional sexy picture, but everyone did that. She'd met him on Tinder when she was mad at Greg. His profile pic showed him shirtless and tanned on the prow of a motorboat holding up an enormous fish.

I FEEL SORRY FOR THE FISH, she'd typed.

THREW HIM BACK, Hunter had typed. HE WAS AN EGOMANIAC AND LOVED THE CAMERA TOO MUCH.

She actually laughed through her sniffles, and they talked all night. And the next day. He lived in Las Vegas where he was into CrossFit, was a professional gambler, and had his real estate license.

32, he'd typed. FIRST MILLION BY 35.

26, she'd typed. FIRST THOUSAND BY NEVER.

THAT'S ON YOU, he'd typed.

Then he'd told her that geography was destiny. If she wanted to know the maximum salary she could ever make, she should take the average salary of her five closest friends. Her result was barely even a number. Hunter was smart, and he had ambition, and they weren't cheating because she wasn't leaving Greg. Hunter was more of a friend lifting her up to a higher level, which was why it was okay to keep talking to him on Kik.

He'd offered to sell her tickets to the Koffin show in Vegas. He'd bought two extra ones as an investment, he told her, and she was tempted. Go out there, stay with Hunter, feel like she was going somewhere. Now she typed:

I WANT THOSE TIX

Hunter sent: ☺

FOR ME AND MY BOY, she typed.

Hunter sent: ☹

CHANGING MY LIFE, MOVING OUT THERE, A NEW PAGE, she typed. CLOSER TO YOU.

SEND ME A SEXY PIC, Hunter typed. TO MAKE UP FOR HURTING MY FEELINGS.

She smiled, and lifted her shirt. It was the least she could do. He was going to help her and Greg see Koffin and escape from this trap their life had become.

DEMARCOS: A tragic shooting left four victims dead in Allentown late this afternoon, and authorities with more questions than answers. Local resident Scott Borzek allegedly shot his wife and two children, ages fifteen and seventeen, before turning the weapon on himself. Police say that Borzek, a onetime member of the defunct local band Dürt Würk, had a history of drug and alcohol abuse and had recently been seeking treatment. A UPS driver discovered the scene while attempting to deliver a package. Police are seeking an as-yet-unidentified witness who may be able to fill in key details. In Allentown, I'm Rick Demarcos, Newsradio 790.

—790 AM WAEB, "Top of the Hour News and Weather"
May 11, 2019

Holy Diver

Anger had driven Kris to Scottie's house, but fear sent her driving in circles for hours after. If Scottie was right, Terry could see her phone. He was in her email. He was tracking her car. The second she pulled over, UPS trucks would surround her, and their drivers would gun her down.

Her phone buzzed with incoming calls, then texts, from Little Charles. She turned it off and locked it in the glove compartment—another way for them to find her. She didn't know what to do or where to go until she turned on the radio and heard how they were shaping the story. Terry could turn a murder into a suicide, he could turn an assassination attempt into a domestic dispute, he could steal her music and turn it into millions. She needed to warn the band.

Twenty minutes in a public library outside King of Prussia, a little bit of Google stalking, and Kris was driving up and down suburban streets outside Philly looking for the entrance to Eaglecrest, a planned community that paid to keep itself off Google Maps, because privacy was the new status symbol. It was where Tuck lived, and he seemed like the best place to start.

Eaglecrest was a spotless, micromanaged walking community full of gracious green lawns, public spaces, clearly marked bike paths, and sustainable, eco-friendly McMansions. By the time she pulled up in front of Tuck's impossibly perfect house with its impossibly green yard, beneath cotton-candy-pink sunset skies, Kris felt like an intruder, a leper clad in black, bringing bad news no one wanted to hear. She got out of her car and almost hit one of Eaglecrest's perfect citizens power-walking past in a herd, burning off their calories at the end of the day. She planned to take a few minutes and get her head together before ringing Tuck's doorbell, but when she looked up, he was watching her.

He stood in his open garage, a white cooler in one hand, two yellow life vests in the other. A streak of white slashed his goatee in half. His electric-blue polo shirt was big enough to make ten shirts for Kris. His faded olive cargo shorts hung to just above his ankles, which were thick as tree trunks.

Kris wanted to get back in her car and drive away, but it was too late. She had come here on a mission, and she couldn't back down now. She kept her eyes on Tuck's Chuck Taylors as she closed the distance between them. As she approached, he put down his cooler and the vests. She stopped walking when he loomed over her, inches away. He hadn't done anything yet, and she took that for a good sign. She stepped forward, arms open for a hug.

Tuck jumped backward.

"Whoa, whoa, whoa, whoa," he said. "You can't come in here. After all this time? After what you did? Looking for a hug? Are you out of your mind?"

She tried to say something, but only a small noise came out.

"I don't dwell on the past," Tuck said. "I don't dream about the future. I focus on the present. And in the present, I don't want you in my driveway."

"You're not still—" she began.

"I am," he said, picking up his cooler. "But it's been a lot of years, and I have found the forgiveness in my heart. But Lily is home and she is not as evolved on the subject as me. She hears you out here, and she will slit your throat and stuff you in a ditch, and I can't stop her."

Kris remembered going to visit Tuck in the hospital and his father not allowing her in the room. She remembered taking the elevator back to the first floor and walking toward the parking lot, hearing quick, fast footsteps behind her, and turning as Lily, just his girlfriend back then, all bones and tendons and teeth, threw a cold cup of Dunkin' Donuts coffee in her face.

"We need to talk about Scottie," Kris said.

"I heard on the news," Tuck said, picking his way through his cluttered garage. "I was going to call you after I hosed down the life jackets. Phone is okay. You being here is not. Goodbye."

He hit the door-close button on the wall and the big garage door began to rumble down. Kris stepped into the doorway and it detected her, its gears ground, and it rolled back up. Tuck jabbed the button again but nothing happened.

"It's not going to close on me," Kris said. "I'm standing in the electric eye."

"Goddammit," Tuck said. "Go away."

She followed him into the dim garage.

"Scottie thought we might all be in danger," Kris said. "He thought that Terry might try to hurt us. He thinks Terry is spying on us."

"That sounds exactly like what someone who shot his family would say," Tuck said.

"You need to read this," Kris said, and she held out Scottie's note. "It's the last thing he wrote."

"Where'd you get that?" Tuck asked.

"From Scottie," Kris said.

Realization dawned in Tuck's eyes.

"You're the unidentified witness," he said. "They're all looking for you."

Kris threw all her cards on the table at once. "He shot himself," she said. "Someone called him, someone from Terry, and he was living in his basement, and I was down there with him and he shot himself, but he didn't kill his family."

"Aw, Kris," Tuck said. "You cannot do this to me."

"I was there!" Kris said. "Your family is not safe."

"The man was on drugs."

"Scottie's been sober since rehab."

"Maybe that's what he told you—" Tuck began.

"Fine," Kris said. "You keep hosing out your cooler and I'll read it to you."

For the first time, Tuck's mask slipped, and terror showed in his eyes. He snatched at the note. Kris took a big step back, yanking it out of reach. Tuck came toward her, forcing her to back up.

"Kris," she read, backing into a dog carrier, going fast. "I'm sorry for whatever it is they made me do—"

"Please," Tuck said, and stopped. "Don't. Just . . . just let me get my readers on."

Tuck put on his reading glasses and stood by the open garage door, reading in daylight's last pink wash. Kris had memorized the note by now and it played along in her head as Tuck read it to himself.

Kris,

I'm sorry for whatever it is they made me do. I'm not strong enough to stay myself, but you are and that's why I wrote this. I am tired all the time. I thought I was taking allergy medication and also Paxator for my panic disorder but that is not what they are. I stopped taking them 2.5 months ago but it is too late for me.

Terry put something inside my head in case you ever contacted me again. He watches everything we do through our televisions and our phones. He must make sure we do not wake up.

Something is wrong with me. I look up and I'm in places I do not remember going. I think I have something dark living inside of me. But I do not think it is just me. I think it is all of us.

Do I sound crazy? That is their goal. But ask yourself: why can't we remember contract night? Ask Tuck and Bill. I bet they do not remember it either. Do you? Nothing has been the same since then. What happened to us? What did the Blind King do?

Find the answers in TROGLODYTE. *They are there. I don't want to write what they are because I cannot be sure my thoughts are my own. But Black Iron Mountain is the conspiracy behind the conspiracy. They watch us through Terry's eyes. They run us in circles. They make us hurt each other.*

Trust TROGLODYTE. *We are all targeted individuals. Black Iron Mountain will try to stop you. But metal never dies. Metal does not retreat. It does not surrender.*

Metal tells the truth about the world.

You never let me down, Kris. You never disappointed me. There is no one else left. Carry the fire.

I love you.

Scottie Rocket

Tuck lowered the note and took off his glasses. Still holding them in his hand, he pinched the bridge of his nose, eyes closed.

"I had no idea things were this bad," he finally said, scrubbing his eyes with the heel of his hand. "Did you?"

"I hadn't seen him since he went into rehab," Kris said, "but I was at his house today and I saw what happened, and we need to go warn Bill before it happens again."

"Are you high?" Tuck raised his voice, then got self-conscious and dropped it again. "You are the last person I'd take to see Bill."

"You read the note!" Kris said. "Something is wrong with us!"

Tuck's face closed down and he shut the garage door. As it rattled down, closing off the endless stream of happy people jogging past in their Lululemon tops and black yoga pants, Kris spelled it out.

"It was UPS," she said, knowing how crazy that sounded even as it came out her mouth. "Obviously, not UPS, but it was guys dressed like UPS drivers. After Scottie shot himself, Angela, his wife, called 911. But the fake UPS drivers showed up instead and killed her and his kids."

"Kris," Tuck began.

"I hid in the pantry, and ran," she said. "But they saw me and they're looking for me. We have got to go warn Bill."

"Kris," Tuck said.

"Something is going on, Tuck, and I don't understand it, and you don't understand it, but why don't I remember contract night? Why is one entire night missing from my brain? Why did Scottie think we're all in danger? We need to go find Bill, we need to make sure he's safe, and we need to get you away from your family. What if you're a danger to them? What if they can make you do what Scottie did?"

"KRIS," Tuck barked.

She shut up.

"Let me make a phone call," he said. "But for the record, you sound crazy. Wait here."

He opened the white door in the white garage wall and went into his house. Air-conditioning billowed out and wrapped itself around Kris's ankles. Faraway music drifted out the door, peaceful and lazy on a Sunday evening. Then she recognized the breakdown: "Stand Strong" by Koffin.

First she swayed toward the closed garage door thinking it wasn't too late to get out and drive away, then her feet were on the brick steps leading into the house, then they were on the tile, walking down the dim hallway. This was the song Scottie Rocket heard on his phone before he took out his gun, and it drew Kris in. If Tuck was getting a gun it was better to face it head on.

The hushed sigh of central air swaddled her in cool, sweet clouds. The dark hall ended in a bright, modern kitchen. Kris had just passed the island when she heard a human noise behind her. She turned. Lily stood by the opposite counter, a cutting board and a pile of carrots before her.

Lily's face was tight, her mouth pinched shut. Her eyes were the same hard chips Kris remembered from the hospital. In her right hand was a butcher's knife, held low at her side, her knuckles around it bloodless.

She took a step forward. Kris took a step back, bumping into the counter with her butt.

"What the hell are you doing inside my house?" Lily asked, pointing the butcher's knife at Kris.

"I'm here to keep you safe," Kris said.

"Get out of here, now!" Lily said, stepping closer to Kris.

Then Tuck was in the kitchen, getting between the two of them. "Whoa, whoa, whoa," he said. "Lily, put the knife down. Kris is leaving."

"I'm not leaving," Kris said. "Not without you! You have to get away from your family. That Koffin song is everywhere."

"What the hell is she talking about?" Lily shouted.

Two boys about to turn into teenagers and one six-year-old girl, attracted by the commotion, stood in the living room and watched the adults. Seeing the kids sent Kris into a panic. She saw Martin on the floor with a hole in his chest, mouth lolling open, Ursula upstairs, half in and half out of the bathroom in her soccer uniform. Angela stretched flat on the kitchen floor, one eye staring up at the ceiling.

"We have got to go *now*," she said to Tuck.

"Hold on, Kris," Tuck said, arms outstretched, putting himself between the two women. "Hold up. Look, I talked to Bill, just now, on the phone, and he says come on down. You can sleep in your car, or at a hotel, or I don't care where, and we can ride down in the morning."

"You are *not* getting in any car this woman drives," Lily said.

"I'll drive," Tuck said. "Okay, Kris? So go on now."

"We are going now," Kris said. "This is happening now. Any minute there's going to be a knock at the door and UPS will be there. Or you'll get a call and you won't be able to help yourself. You look around and see your family? I look around and see a bunch of potential murder victims!"

The kids in the living room had been following this, and now the six-year-old started to wail.

"Dad," one of the little boys said, "what's wrong with UPS?"

"Everybody stop!" Tuck tried.

"She has a knife, Tuck!" Kris said. "Koffin was on the radio. The song is the trigger. No one is safe."

"Calm down," Tuck said. "No one wants to hurt you—"

"I do!" Lily said.

"Quiet!" Tuck shouted. "Fine, we'll go tonight. That's fine. I'll feed my family and we'll drive down after. Lily, we'll be gone in an hour. Kris, you will sit in your car and wait for me to get ready. This is not a debate."

Kris sat outside in her car and watched Tuck's family eating through the front window. She tried to convince herself that this was what families were like, loud and rambunctious, and fighting over who got too many mashed potatoes, and which one got extra chicken fingers. That they didn't look like Angela, and Martin, and Ursula.

It took Tuck forever to get ready, and Lily watched them from her bedroom window the entire time. Kris watched the street. Even in the dark, the power walkers kept going past on their merry-go-round to nowhere, identical faces staring back at Kris, giving identical good-evening waves, as Tuck loaded up his road snacks, water bottles, phone chargers, and two suitcases.

Kris only had her Bones and her guitar.

When they finally got in the car, Kris crawled out of her skin as Tuck arranged himself: his phone, his seat, the satellite radio, the rearview mirrors.

To distract herself, Kris asked, "Where is Bill, anyways?"

"Bill?" Tuck said. "Bill's still living in the Witch House."

"How do you know that?" Kris asked, shocked.

"We exchange Christmas cards," Tuck said.

"I never got one," Kris said.

"Why would Bill write you?" Tuck said. "I've forgiven you, but Bill . . . he's with Lily on this one. No one likes you, Kris."

Then they hit the road. And Kris remembered the night she broke up the band.

DÜRT WÜRK

All That Cremains

Steeltown road warriors Dürt Würk—as in "grave diggers"—seem to live in their mangy secondhand van, which means that they've given up on stuff like washing and cleaning their teeth, and the cover of their new, self-penned album, *All That Cremains*, is as ugly as an orthopedic shoe. But what was it mum said? Don't judge a book by its cover, and that proves to be the case with these razor-sharp riff-slingers who have made an underground name for themselves by delivering tight power metal to rough crowds in the former colonies (what about coming over here, boys?). You could be forgiven for almost giving up after wading through trite trash like "Keep on Digging," the misguided showcase for drummer Bill Cameron, and the forgettable '80s throwback "Reaper's Harvest." But the final three cuts are near genius—"Chained to the Wheel," "Troglodyte Rising," and "Blinded by Darkness" veer perilously close to Gothic bombast, but wrest themselves away at the last minute and showcase Terry Hunt's soaring vocals and Tuck Merryweather's organic bass, while easy-on-the-eyes Kris Pulaski's rock-solid lead guitar and Scottie Rocket's electrifying solos clash in all the best ways. With better production, they could score some serious airplay.

—Nick Sharman, *Kerrang!* magazine
February 15, 1996

From Enslavement to Obliteration

It was always raining at the Witch House. They'd found it one summer when they were touring and needed someplace near the Midwest where they could store their gear and hole up for a couple of nights between shows. It was a two-story wreck of rotten brown planks sagging against a cinderblock chimney, hidden deep in a forest that grew between two Kentucky hills, and it rented for $140 a month. Trees grew too close to its walls, so it was always damp. Even in the dead of winter, it smelled like mold, and the dirt track that led to the road was mostly mud.

After that, they came there every summer to write, to practice, to drink beer, to kick holes in the walls, to stash their gear in the padlocked, ice-cold basement where they practiced. That summer they'd gone there to record *Troglodyte*, and it had been the best two months of Kris's life. Then, after the Slayer tour blew up, they went there to fire Terry.

Their new manager, Rob Anthony, had gotten them the spot opening for Slayer on the northeastern leg of their tour. At that point, Dürt Würk had a following, but they were either a big bar band or a small club act. Opening for Slayer got them closer to the big time, and with *Troglodyte* in the can, they were ready. The plan was that Rob would bring A&R reps to hear them. Reps would come for the free Slayer tickets, and hear Dürt Würk in the process. If they were interested, the band already had an album ready to go.

No one had counted on Terry. It had taken them so many years to get there, but it took him less than a week to blow it all up.

The Slayer tour had them sleeping in Holiday Inns, not the van. There was actual food backstage, and something to drink besides Rolling Rock. But Terry had taken nonstop potshots at Tom Araya and Kerry King, accusing them of selling out, telling interviewers that Slayer was going to rap on their next album. He acted like such an obnoxious prick that Slayer's road manager finally demanded he apologize. Instead of smoothing things over, Terry trashed his hotel room and disappeared. The road manager was waiting for them when they showed up at the venue that night, ready to play with Tuck filling in on the vocals. He told them they were off the tour. Powerhole would fill in for them. After they paid for the damage Terry did to his room, they only had $700 of their fee left over.

No one understood why Terry had destroyed everything. No one knew where he was. At loose ends, they headed for the Witch House to regroup. Bill drove in a daze, Tuck and Scottie dozed in the back, and Kris rode shotgun, hypnotized by the falling rain and the whoosh of the wipers. It was four in the afternoon, but everyone on the road already had their headlights on. Bill came to a full stop before rolling the van off the two-lane blacktop onto the muddy track to the Witch House. Their headlights barely lit the black air as they took the spookhouse ride through the tunnel of dripping trees and emerged in the Witch House's clearing. Rob Anthony's midnight-blue Porsche 911 was parked out front. No one said a word.

They ran through the pouring rain to the kitchen door, and shoved their way inside. The smell of wet, rotten carpet was so thick Kris gagged. The interior of the Witch House was a seventies dungeon, all water stains and rotten wood. The doors were gone, replaced by tacked-up tie-dyes and beaded curtains. The carpet was a blood flood, wall-to-wall eye-searing crimson that sloshed through the halls and poured down the stairs and covered the entire first floor. Every inch of it was cigarette-burned or water-stained.

But this afternoon, the dark kitchen was full of warm and friendly candlelight. The coffin-sized cooler they used as a fridge was sitting wide open, piled with ice and Champagne. In the living room, black candles burned on every surface, like someone was about to shoot a bad music video. Terry and Rob Anthony were sitting on the busted green velvet sofa, grinning like best friends. Rob was, as always, sculpted out of raw honey and sunshine. In front of him, lined up on the three-legged coffee table they'd rescued from a dumpster, were five contracts. They gleamed in the dim air, the cleanest things in the room.

"What the fuck are those?" Kris asked.

"Those," Terry grinned, "are our future."

"Dürt Würk is dead," Rob Anthony said, standing, hoisting

a bottle of champagne. "All hail Koffin." He popped the cork.

"You ditched us," Tuck said. "You screwed up our gig and took off. And what the hell is a Koffin?"

"It's all in the contracts, Tuck," Rob explained, flashing his blinding smile.

"What's all in the contracts?" Bill asked. Then he pointed at Terry. "You're fired. We're firing you."

Terry found that funny. "Welcome to the big time," he said. "You get inside the headliner's head and mess with them so they play a weaker show and we look better to the reps."

"That doesn't make any sense," Tuck said. "How high are you right this minute?"

"Fellas, fellas, fellas," Rob said, taking up a position between Terry on the sofa and the rest of the band. "Let's not relitigate the past. Let's pop a little bubbly, hoover a few rails, and welcome your future."

"He got us thrown off the biggest tour of our lives," Bill said. "This is a crisis."

"Did you know," Rob said, "that the character in Chinese for 'crisis' is the same as the one for 'opportunity'? An Oriental girl I lived with told me that. I almost got it tattooed on my wrist because that idea is so powerful. She killed herself, and I was sincerely bummed for a while, but then I wound up dating Neve Campbell, right when she was doing *Party of Five*, so see? Nothing is ever really good or bad, it's all about your perspective.

"Slayer fired you because their manager felt threatened by the potential he sensed inside Dürt Würk. It's what I sensed in this band. It's why I'm doubling my investment. But Dürt Würk isn't popping. It's a dead end, so you're going to become Koffin. I've got designers coming up with a whole new look, I'm bringing in makeup and costume people to put a serious show together. Interscope has already made an offer."

Kris didn't want to touch Rob's champagne, but she needed something, so she snatched the bottle off the table and slugged back half. The band drifted to windowsills and folding chairs.

"I thought you'd like that," Rob smiled. "It's a five-year, three-album deal."

"*Troglodyte* and two others," Bill said. "That's not bad."

"*Troglodyte* goes back underground," Rob said. "Don't get me wrong, it was a great calling card, but calling cards open doors, they don't move units. But you should be proud, okay, no frowns. It earned you the advance you need to write your first real album."

Anger built inside Kris's brain. *Troglodyte* wasn't a calling card, it was everything in her life poured into nine songs (ten, actually, but Terry had cut "The Door with Cerulean Hue" from the final mix for reasons that still pissed her off). Pried from her journal, taken from her life, forged from ideas and melodies and fragments that had floated in the dark ocean of her brain for years. She couldn't imagine writing another album after *Troglodyte*. It was her masterpiece.

"I know what you're thinking," Rob said to Kris. "But *Troglodyte* is no masterpiece. You should have seen the reaction the engineers had when we mixed it in LA. It fell flat on its face. But the next album? As Koffin? We have Das Jacks writing some killer hooks, Terry has some next-generation lyrical ideas, Koffin is going to get major airplay."

Bill looked up. He was already halfway through his contract.

"I'll want my lawyer to look this over," he said.

"Pussy," Terry said from the couch.

"Any questions you have, I'm happy to answer." Rob's smile gleamed in the dim light.

"I'm still going to want to run it past my lawyer," Bill said.

Terry erupted up off the couch. "Rob had lawyers going over them for a month," he shouted. "I'm sick of this shit. Sign tonight or get the fuck out."

"I can't do that!" Bill said.

"Do you know how long I've been putting up with your shit?" Terry said. "All of you! Where're my carrots? For ten years it's all been the stick. I'm tired of waiting!"

"This says you can fire us anytime," Bill said. "You own the name, we're hired guns."

"I'm offering you seats at the table," Terry said. "Don't you dare fucking hate me for being smart."

"You keep the publishing rights," Bill said, pointing to another clause, his voice cold. "You keep the name rights. We all get a salary instead of royalties. Why the fuck would I sign this?"

"Because I own the name," Terry said. "Because I registered the publishing rights. Don't spaz, I gave you guys a fair share based on how Rob and I assessed your contribution."

"Assessed our contribution?" Scottie screamed, getting up in Terry's face. "When the fuck did that happen?"

"Let's de-escalate—" Rob began.

Scottie Rocket grabbed his folding chair and flung it at Rob, who dodged just in time. Two of its legs spiked the cheap pine-paneled wall and it hung there, suspended.

"Hey," Kris said.

She hadn't spoken yet, so at first no one listened. Then she stood up, and said louder, "Hey, Terry!"

He turned to her. Scottie shut up.

"What do you mean Koffin's going to get major airplay? What are you changing? How's it different from Dürt Würk?"

"We missed out on grunge because we weren't ready," Terry said. "We thought we were better than our audience. That's not going to happen this time. Koffin's nu metal."

The loudest sound in the room was a candle flickering in the cold draft that whined beneath a window.

Nu metal was metal lite, the flavor of moment that was ushering hardcore acts to mainstream success at the cost of their dignity. Bands that had been growling were suddenly rapping. Bass lines that had previously blasted now bounced with "get on the dance floor" funk. It was all about branding, fan outreach, accessibility, spray-on attitude, moving crowds of white kids smoothly from the pit to your merch booth where they'd buy $20 Limp Bizkit beer cozies and $30 Korn bandanas.

"Nu metal isn't about anything," Kris said. "Nu metal kids are cul-de-sac crybabies with their baseball hats on backward. Every song is a little boy crying in his bedroom about how his girlfriend won't make him a sandwich like his mommy used to do."

"Can anyone really say what's good or what's bad?" Rob asked. "A band is a business, and you have to think like businessmen. Nu metal moves units."

"If I wanted to go into business I would have gotten a job," Kris said.

"For once in your life, stop being so goddamn stubborn," Terry said. "You're fucking it up for everyone else."

"Fuck nu metal," Scottie enunciated. "If I'm going to play metal I don't want that whiny baby crap. I want fucking dragons and shit."

"You know where Slipknot is right now?" Rob asked. "They're in Malibu, recording their first major label release."

Scottie ran at his chair and tried to tear it out of the wall to throw at Rob again. Tuck wrestled him back.

"I can't believe that asshole's talking to us about Slipknot!" Scottie shouted, struggling in Tuck's arms.

"That 'asshole' is going to make us rich," Terry said. "And don't knock fucking Slipknot. They got a half-million-dollar advance from Warners."

"And they wear Halloween masks," Kris said.

"Because it's their look," Terry said.

"Because they're ashamed of their playing," Kris said.

"They're the future of metal," Terry said. "They have a point of view."

"*Troglodyte* is a point of view," Kris said. "You want to turn us into Korn."

"Don't be a snob," Terry snapped. "*Follow the Leader* debuted at number one. Korn flies around the country in a chartered fucking jet. I don't want to be eating fries and sleeping in the fucking band van for the rest of my life."

"Fuck nu metal," Scottie said, and stormed into the kitchen. They heard him kick the cooler, then grunt, pick it up, and a mountain of ice crashed to the floor. They heard the bottles roll across the linoleum.

Tuck sat down heavily on the sofa, a sad, silent Buddha, rolling a cigarette.

"We need a new approach," Terry said. "In case you haven't noticed, we're going nowhere fast. It's been ten years. Ten years! Just saying that pisses me off. We're lucky someone the caliber of Rob is even giving us the time of day."

"I'm just grateful for the opportunity to channel your talent," Rob said.

"Someone shut him the fuck up!" Scottie shouted from the kitchen.

"Man, I'll sign this shit just to get some peace and quiet," Tuck said.

Rob held out his hands. "What do you say, everyone? Terry's worked hard on this. I mean, you should have seen him with those lawyers. He fought like a lion to make sure each and every one of you was taken care of. He reminded me that you can have a Porsche, or a Lamborghini, or even one of those luxury Hummers, but friendship comes first. Why not support your friend?"

"Because he's ripping us off!" Kris shouted.

She shoved past Rob, stalked into the kitchen and almost busted her ass on the ice. She grabbed two bottles of champagne and stormed out of the house. She'd be fucked if she was going to sit there and take this. She walked into the dark, dripping woods, knocking back champagne even though she knew it was going to give her a headache in the morning. Where were their lawyers? This wasn't right. When did Terry become the owner of everything?

She wandered for hours, getting drunker and angrier. After that, things were patchy, but she remembered throwing the empty bottles against a tree and being disappointed they didn't break. She remembered how cold she was, even with her Bones on. She remembered going back to the Witch House. No way were they signing tonight. If the deal was legit, showing it to a lawyer wouldn't hurt. Her little brother was an entertainment lawyer, he'd know somebody. Or she'd find someone to look at it in Allentown. Or Philly.

The house was quiet. No one was in the living room. All the contracts were lined up on the coffee table, all of them signed, except hers. She went into the front hall and saw that the blue door leading to the basement was open. She went down the stairs.

Everyone was in the basement except Rob and Terry. There was a gap in her memory here, maybe caused by the champagne, but she remembered panic suddenly buzzing in her veins, knowing she had to get them out of there right that minute. Tuck was passed out on a damp sofa, Bill lay sprawled across a half-filled beanbag, and Scottie lay on a deflating plaid air mattress by the wall. For reasons she couldn't understand, Kris thought they were dead. She ran around the room, slapping them awake. She had to get them out.

She remembered slapping Tuck's fat cheeks, rocking Scottie's shoulder with her Doc Martens, yelling "Hey, Bill!" Panic fizzed in her blood. She had to get them away from the Witch House. She improvised as she yelled at them, frustrated they weren't waking up fast enough.

"Terry's taken the contracts!" she lied, grasping at anything. "We have to get to the airport before he takes off with Rob."

They were groggy, they were drunk, they were stoned, but she infected them with her panic. They did what she said because she was loud, and she yanked, and she pushed, and she pulled them upstairs and out of the Witch House.

"Hey," Scottie said. "Rob's Porsche is still here."

Kris ignored him, grabbed his wrist, and pulled him into the band van. It was raining hard when she slammed the back doors. As she grabbed the handle of the driver's side door, rain pattering loud on the leaves overhead, she realized how drunk she was, and a smart part of her thought, "This is not a good idea."

Then she yanked the door open, almost clipping herself in the nose. The rest came in flashes and slashes, like seeing a show through flickering strobe lights. Twisting the ignition, flooding the engine, the band complaining in the cold darkness around her. The van lurching up the track, rear end fishtailing in the mud, bouncing through the woods, Kris terrified she was going to veer into a tree before remembering to turn her headlights on, clinging to the steering wheel, knuckles cold and aching. How good it felt to finally hit the hardtop, press the accelerator down, and Tuck next to her, all stoned, saying, "Whoa," and looking over to see him brace himself against the dashboard. Looking back through the windshield, into the headlights of that UPS truck.

CALLER: . . . oceans are past the point of no return, there is no water in thirty percent of the populated countries, DNA-mapping services have fifty-one percent of our population's genetic sequences coded, FEMA just purchased 30,000 body bags, the CIA just got seven billion dollars added to their black-ops budget, we've had false flag active shooter situations every week for months. This is the tipping point. Something's coming.

RUTH MOORE: What's coming, caller? Caller? Are you still on the line?

—1030 AM "Braintronics Newswire"
May 13, 2019

Countdown to Extinction

Kris jerked awake, her head leaning against the passenger window of Tuck's white Chevy Equinox. It was dark outside.

"Nightmare?" Tuck asked from the driver's seat.

Kris nodded.

"Good," Tuck said.

Kris watched the Koffin billboards go by. There was a new one after every exit because no driver escaped the Blind King's commercial solicitations. It was exhausting seeing Terry's face again and again proclaiming that shows were sold out, that there would be pay-per-view packages available, that Atlantis would be streaming it live to select theaters. Around them flowed an endless stream of cars and trucks with Gothic *K* decals on their back windows.

A drone flashed by, 200 feet above the highway. Kris stared at it until its lights turned into a speck and it disappeared in the blackness.

"Traffic drone," Tuck commented.

There were so many ways for Terry to follow them. GPS,

Waze, Google Maps, traffic helicopters, tollbooths, dashboard cams. It didn't matter anymore. Terry might know where they were going, but it was too late to stop them. As anxious as she was about seeing Bill, by seven o'clock in the morning the surviving members of Dürt Würk would be together again.

West Virginia was a haunted house. Grocery stores sat dark, empty diners stared out from blank windows, farmhouses collapsed beside the highway like rotten teeth. Billboards featured opioid addiction hotlines, debt consolidation services, and car loans for anyone with a guaranteed monthly income from the government. The cars got rustier, the men wore more camo, and the road began to dip and wind as it threaded through the hills.

Finally, Kris couldn't keep it inside any longer. "What do you think Bill will say when he sees me?" she asked.

Tuck eased back in his seat and spoke diplomatically. "I'm sure Bill has come to terms with what happened on contract night," he said. "Same as the rest of us."

"If it even really happened," Kris said. "Scottie said we can't trust our memories."

"Scottie also went crazy and killed his family," Tuck said, and Kris had to bite the inside of her cheek to keep from starting an argument. "If you have any doubts that contract night really happened, I'll show you my scars."

Kris looked out the window while she talked because the SUV suddenly felt closed up and tight. "I used to do jigsaw puzzles sometimes with my mom," she said. "I never thought that's what I'd wind up doing on my Friday nights, but she liked them. You ever do those?"

"I'm familiar with the concept," Tuck said.

"There's always that moment when you know that this piece has to go into that hole," Kris said. "It's the only one that'll fit, but it won't go. So you turn it, and you twist it, and you force it, and you think, well, maybe it got cut wrong in the factory, maybe it's defective. So you work on other parts of the puzzle, but you can't stop obsessing about that one piece that won't fit. That's contract night. I can't make it fit."

"We were in a band, Kris, not the Super Friends," Tuck said. "We smoked some grass, drank some wine, played some shows. Then it ended, and not in a good way. But we all moved on. Everyone except you."

"If Terry moved on, then why is Scottie dead?" Kris asked.

"Terry is done with Dürt Würk," Tuck said, pulling himself forward on the wheel, shifting his weight. "And now he's richer than Jesus. What does he care what we're up to? We all cashed out and went our separate ways. It ended."

"*Troglodyte* would have put us over," Kris said. "All we had to do was hold on. We were so close. Why'd he stop us?"

"You have a timetable I didn't have access to?" Tuck asked. "When were we scheduled to break big? Wait one more day, one more day, one more day, suddenly you're pushing fifty, and what do you have to show for it? Nothing."

Kris changed the subject.

"What happened after I left the house?" she asked. "On contract night?"

"I'm not sure this is a productive conversation," Tuck said.

"Do you honestly not care?" Kris asked. "Can you honestly say nothing about that night feels like unfinished business? Nothing about it bothers you?"

They drove silently for a while. Kris sensed Tuck was thinking, so she didn't say anything. She didn't even move. After two miles, Tuck shifted his weight, and said:

"We did what any band would do that just signed a major deal. We partied." He licked his lips. "You missed some fine champagne. The next thing I know, we're in the basement and you're slapping me in the face, saying we got to go."

Kris watched another Koffin billboard roll by outside Star City and remembered the most vivid ninety seconds of her life. The blinding UPS headlights. The hollow metal boom. A violence done to her body she'd never felt before or since. She remembered every revolution as the van rolled off the road, two full turns and one half turn before they hit the tree, her stomach flipping into her feet, vomit spraying out her nostrils. The top of her head smashing into the roof of the van again and again. The wet meat sounds of everyone in the back bouncing off the walls. The van landing on its roof and the windshield shattering into her eyes, and then that moment of perfect silence before Bill started screaming in the dark, high-pitched and unvarying, like a dying animal.

"I still don't know why you all came with me," she said.

Their voices were lower now, more honest and straightforward. Neither one trying to impress the other.

"We all felt a little guilty for signing without you," Tuck said. "Everyone respected your talent back then, even Terry. I mean, every single song on *Troglodyte* was your idea. So you're yelling at us and saying 'Pack up, pack up,' and I guess none of us had the heart to argue. I wish we had."

Unconsciously, he pulled the seatbelt strap away from his chest, fiddling with it. In the silence, Kris gave voice to what had been circling around inside her head ever since she'd woken up.

"What time do you think that was?" she asked.

Tuck rolled his bottom lip between thumb and forefinger. "Beats me," he said. "You took off into the woods around seven? Eight? We partied until midnight, passed out early. You came back, woke us up, we got in the car."

"I found a copy of the accident report," Kris said. "In all the insurance stuff. It says the ambulance was dispatched at 4:14 a.m."

"Sounds about right," Tuck said.

Kris took a deep breath, careful not to look at him. "Let's say I really did walk around in the woods with two bottles of champagne for four hours," she said. "Let's say I woke you guys up at midnight, even 1 a.m. It took us three hours to drive a quarter of a mile?"

"That's what time the ambulance was dispatched," Tuck said. "We might have sat there for a while."

"The UPS driver radioed it in," Kris said. "Right after it happened."

"Your point being?" Tuck said.

"The pieces don't fit," Kris said. "I walk in the woods for five hours? Then we drive four hours but only make it just up the road? I leave the house at seven and come back at midnight, why is the truck we hit calling the EMS at four?"

"We were drunk and stoned," Tuck said. "You forgotten that part?"

"Not that drunk," she said. "Not that stoned. There's missing time in there, Tuck. Didn't you read Scottie's note?"

"I wish I hadn't," Tuck said.

"What happened to us that night?" Kris asked, talking faster.

"What happened in those four or five hours? Terry did something to us. He did something to our memories."

It was getting light outside. More cars appeared, passing in the other direction.

"You planning on talking this kind of conspiracy craziness to Bill?" Tuck asked. "After what you did to him? I beg you, Kris, hold off on the UFO abduction theories until he has some time to process this thing about Scott."

"Scottie didn't kill his family." Kris leaned forward, the shoulder strap of her seat belt cutting across her chest. "And we're missing hours of our lives. Don't you want to know what happened?"

"We were stoned, stupid kids who shouldn't have been operating a motor vehicle," Tuck snapped. "That's what happened." He leaned away from her, his shoulder resting against his window, shaking his head. "I knew you were crazy, but this is really crazy."

They traded around Huntington so Tuck could sleep while Kris drove, and then they were in Kentucky, the morning sun coming up over the hills. They were lost. So many lanes closed, so many trees cut down, so many of their old landmarks erased. They made U-turns, took the wrong exits, pulled over twice to consult Tuck's phone.

Finally, they came around the curve of the road and saw a familiar stand of pine trees on the crest of a hill. Kris rolled off the two-lane highway onto a dirt road. They bounced down it, taking the same old familiar turns, then she eased the brakes and they rolled to a stop before a massive, white wooden gate flanked by a pair of stone pillars.

"What happens now?" she asked, her stomach starting to crawl all over itself again.

The gate performed a smooth, professional swing inward to reveal a gleaming white gravel road winding through the trees.

"I don't know if I'm ready for this," Kris said, a panic monkey gibbering in her chest.

Tuck's SUV crunched down the drive. The dark, dripping forest Kris remembered had gotten plastic surgery. What had been wild and dank was now manicured and rustic. Meditation gardens set back in the trees flashed by, carved wooden "Horse Crossing" signs appeared alongside the road. Finally, the white gravel lane terminated in a perfect circle that flowed around an abstract V-shaped sculpture made out of two jagged, lightning-struck tree trunks. Kris pulled around the circle and stopped, shoved the transmission into park, and there, in front of them, stood the Witch House.

It was bright and glossy, its wood gleaming and oiled. No longer sagging, it stood up straight, its cracked cinder-block chimney replaced by a rustic British fairy-tale chimney made of hand-baked bricks. Where it had previously raised blank walls of slimy wood, now it was bisected with glass cubes and rectangles at dramatic angles, forming sunporches, skylights, and solariums. A wooden ramp flowed from its front door, spread across the grass, and terminated in a raised dock next them.

Sitting at the end of the dock in his wheelchair, waiting for them to arrive, was Bill.

RUSS STARLIN: . . . and I say, Jeremiah, 13:17, "the Lord's flock is carried away captive." They destroy your individuality, they destroy your free will, they destroy your personality and replace it with one of their own. I've got JD here on the line.

CALLER: Russ, I want you to think about this. They say you have to be "healthy," they say you have to be "sober," then they put you in programs that are secret brainwashing camps. Alcoholics Anonymous. Narcotics Anonymous. The only Anonymous are the globalist elites using these camps to manufacture MKUltra mind-controlled assassins.

—WWCR Shortwave Radio, "Unchained with Russ Starlin"
May 13, 2019

High 'n' Dry

Kris got out of the car and met Bill's gaze for the first time in over twenty years. Hard lines hacked their way from his nostrils to the corners of his mouth. His blue eyes had faded to a watercolor wash. His blond hair was coarser and mostly gray. His expression was blank.

With two economical arm movements, Bill sent his chair rolling to the lip of the dock. The two of them stood face-to-face.

"Bill—" Kris said.

Bill leaned forward, eyes locked onto hers, and she remembered that long, unbroken scream in the dark that felt like it would never end.

"I'm sorry, Bill," she said, in one great outrushing breath. "I should have come sooner, I shouldn't have driven. I should have—"

He reached up and cradled her face in his hand.

"Blondie," he said, "you're gonna be here until you're eighteen, so get used to it."

Hearing him quote "Dead End Justice" melted something inside Kris she didn't know was frozen. In a flurry of black wings, something enormous escaped the cage inside her chest and flew away. Scottie Rocket was dead, but at least they were all back together again, the three survivors. For the first time in six years, Kris felt like everything might turn out all right. She threw herself forward and wrapped her arms around Bill's shoulders and the two of them held each other while Kris cried.

After a minute, Bill pulled back from the hug, and Kris used the opportunity to turn aside and wipe her eyes and nose on her sleeve. Bill brushed aside Tuck's beefy hand and hugged him, too.

"How was your drive?" he asked, then laughed at himself. "Who cares? What do you think of this dump? I made a few changes."

Bill made a hand signal and a young white woman with fine bones in her face and thick dreads appeared, followed by two aggressively healthy-looking attendants in white linen shirts and pants. One of them approached Kris and one went to Tuck. They offered warm hand towels. Kris caught a whiff of lemongrass as she wiped her hands.

"When did you get so rich?" she asked.

"This," Bill said, "is Well in the Woods, a holistic wellness community where we break chains and rebuild lives." At Kris's blank look, he added, "We're a luxury rehab center for rich junkies."

"There's a lot of them?" Kris asked.

"The supply is endless," Bill said. "And they are really rich."

Another attendant appeared with two beaten silver cups on a slate tray.

"Try this," Bill said.

The cup radiated waves of cold, numbing Kris's fingers. The water trembled like mercury and smelled dark, with a mineral edge. It cascaded down her throat, the purest water she'd ever tasted, sharp and cold, like diving into a bottomless mountain pool. Her whole body came alive.

"What is it?" she asked, her voice hushed with awe.

"I have seen thirty-year alcoholics who haven't said a sober, loving word to another human being in their entire adult lives drink that water, fall to their knees, and burst into tears," Bill said, as the water bearer took her cup away.

"Oh, shit," Kris said. "The well?"

"We're famous for it," Bill beamed. "Not the one in the basement. That's been dry a long time. But we found its source out back and tapped that. The government insisted on testing it, and they didn't find a single bacterium, no sodium, zero iron, no nitrates, no sulfates. It's the purest drinking water in the state."

Kris remembered the well in the basement. She'd dragged the plywood cap off one night when she was looking for a place to write, and left it off after that. It was so deep you couldn't see the bottom with a flashlight, but you could always hear it, a roaring, dark ocean buried deep underground. When she was writing *Troglodyte*, Kris sat by that old well for hours, listening to the secret sea rumbling underground as the story of Troglodyte, and the Blind King, and Black Iron Mountain materialized on the pages of her journal. She sometimes still heard that water in her dreams.

"I was just headed to the sweat lodge," Bill said. "I'll show you where you can get changed, then meet me out back and we can sweat out some toxins while you tell me what the fuck is going on."

"What do you mean?" Tuck asked.

"Come on," Bill said. "Terry's tour? Scott dying? Kris showing up at your house? After twenty years, this all happens at once?

I don't believe in coincidence. The universe always has a plan. It's our job to perceive it."

Then he spun his chair and rolled to the glass doors leading into the Witch House. The young woman with dreads swung the door wide and stepped aside.

"Thank you, Miranda," Bill said, and they followed him in.

The old kitchen was now a welcome center that felt like the inside of a Swedish sauna. The stink of old carpet had been replaced by sandalwood and incense. Light poured through a huge skylight and New Age music tinkled from hidden speakers.

"How'd you know to be waiting for us?" Kris asked, as they followed his chair.

"I saw you guys turn off the highway," Bill said. "Then I got a better look at you when you stopped at the gate. Don't let the enchanted kingdom thing fool you—I've got cameras everywhere. The third time an addict has his personal assistant drone a package of cocaine onto the grounds, you learn that you need to know everything that happens on every inch of your property."

As they passed through the back hall, Kris stopped, and so did Tuck. Something was wrong, and Kris realized they were in the hall where the blue door used to be, the one door they could lock, the one that led to the basement where they stored their gear, practiced their set, recorded Troglodyte. But the wall was blank.

Kris ran her hands over its surface, but there was no dip or ripple to show where the blue door had been. Bill rolled back to her.

"I know," he said. "It feels weird, right? But the basement kept flooding, so we had it filled in years ago. And then we walled it up for good."

"It's like a metaphor," Tuck said.

"What?" Bill asked. "Oh yeah, I get it. What once was a door is now a wall. Like you can't go home again. I think we all know that by now."

"I don't think Kris does," Tuck said, and they kept moving.

Miranda led Kris to a small room lined with lockless lockers and three sinks carved out of a single piece of granite. She changed into an untreated linen wrap, grabbed a towel, and walked up a slight ramp, out a plain wooden door, and into a fairy-tale kingdom.

The deck looked over the grounds. Wooden paths curved and swooped out into the forest, circling trees, wrapping around their trunks. Glowing like a handful of scattered jewels, outbuildings dotted the woods, ranging in size from a large phone booth to a massive, glass cabin half buried underground. Everything was lit like a stage set, buried lights and hidden lanterns guiding her eye from one beautifully balanced architectural detail to another. Kris didn't feel like bulldozers and hard hats had been at work here—more like elves and magic spells.

"Big change, right?" Bill said, rolling up next to her.

"I can't believe it's the same place," Kris said.

The back deck vibrated and buckled as Tuck came out, wrapped in a long piece of white cloth.

"Don't say a word," he said.

The sun turned the treetops emerald green as the morning air lightened to gold. Any minute, Kris expected *Lord of the Rings* music to play and elves to come wandering out of the woods and start dancing on the grass.

"Let's get hot," Bill said, as an attendant opened the door of an adobe dome.

Bill levered himself up out of his chair and an attendant helped him inside. Kris and Tuck ducked their heads and followed. Recessed lighting cast a golden glow over a room that was cozy, not claustrophobic. They sat on tiers of beautifully carved wooden benches joined by dovetails and wooden pegs—not a metal nail anywhere.

Another attendant ducked inside, carrying a bucket of hot stones, and piled them in a beaten bronze brazier in the center of the room. Tuck sat near the door, so enormous he had a hard time getting comfortable. Bill sat across the stone pit from Kris. The hairs inside her nose crinkled from the heat. She knew if she inhaled deeply she'd scorch her lungs.

The flurry of activity died out and the attendants withdrew, closing the door behind them, leaving the three of them alone in the gloom. Sound was soft and muffled inside the sweat lodge. Kris's pores opened their mouths and vomited sweat down her ribcage, her collarbone, the backs of her knees. Even her elbows got sweaty.

"Hey, guys?" Bill said. "Don't keep me in suspense. What's up?"

The stones clicked and settled; the room got hotter.

"Kris needs to handle this one," Tuck said.

"I was at Scottie's house when he died," Kris said.

She explained about Scottie Rocket, the gun, his suicide, and then hesitated before telling Bill about the note, the UPS drivers, the listening devices, and Terry. Bill listened, then let out a big lungful of air, spread a towel behind him, and lay down.

"I'm going to meditate on this," he said. "I'd recommend you two do the same. Afterwards, let's clean up and then we'll break bread and talk over our options."

He closed his eyes and the room got silent. Kris tried to make eye contact with Tuck, but his eyes were closed, his glistening chest moving up and down in a slow rhythm. She rested her eyes on the pile of rocks in the bowl in the center of the room.

Her long nightmare had started after the accident. The next morning, Terry didn't show up at the hospital. Instead he sent Rob Anthony, along with two young lawyers, and one thick contract. They found Kris in the family room where she was waiting to hear if her friends would live or die. She told them no, she didn't want to do this now, but they insisted on reviewing the terms of the deal.

The contract turned over ownership of Dürt Würk to Terry and forbade her from playing Dürt Würk material, or even from playing music in the style of Dürt Würk. In exchange, she got a payout of $500,000.

For the first time in her life, Kris got so angry she didn't remember what happened. All she remembered was tearing the contract up, shouting at the lawyers, watching them scuttle into the elevator, pressing the "Door Close" button. She remembered how good it felt to have people afraid of her for once.

That feeling lasted until she got home and called Bill's mom. His brother answered the phone and told her that Bill would never walk again. He told Kris they were going to sue. He hung up before she could say anything.

Two days later, she was in court facing a felony DUI. When she came home there was a message on her answering machine from Scottie's dad. She knew Scottie hadn't talked to him in five years, but now he wanted to sue Kris, too. She found Rob's card in her pocket and called. When he showed up at her door he had a fruit basket in his arms and he didn't mention the scene at the hospital. He didn't have to. He'd won. She signed the contract on her coffee table, then spent the rest of her life living in its shadow.

Every cent of the payout went to Scottie's dad, to Tuck's mom, to Bill's brother. By the time she found out she owed $130,000 in taxes on the money, it was almost all gone. She worked out a payment plan with the IRS and got back to work.

She started a new band. They would play bars, weddings, whatever it took to get cash coming in. But after five shows she got dragged into court by Terry and found out that not being allowed to play music in the style of Dürt Würk meant she wasn't allowed to play music at all. She found a lawyer to sue Terry. Then another lawyer. Then another. The richer Terry got, the more lawyers were willing to give her a consultation. The first few didn't even charge.

Whoever she talked to, they all said the same thing: why fight? Terry would win. The terms of the contract were open-ended and nebulous, every clause studded with legal land mines that would blow up in her face. Why hadn't she had a lawyer review the contract before she signed? They warned her that they wouldn't take her case on contingency. Legal fees would eat up her savings, her house, her life. She started to feel like every lawyer in the world actually worked for Terry.

So Kris didn't fight, she folded. She went home, and locked up her guitar, and got a job at Best Western, and did her best to fit in, living the rest of her life in silence.

In the quiet of the sweat lodge, Bill said, "What do you guys remember about contract night?"

At first, Kris, head light and full of heat, wasn't sure he'd said anything at all. "What?" she asked.

Tuck had his eyes open, watching to see how she'd react.

"I built this place to help people become whole," Bill said, still flat on his back. "But let's admit it, this slice of Kentucky is hardly a vacation destination. I think I founded Well in the Woods here because it's where I lost a piece of myself."

Kris kept her eyes on Tuck as she spoke. "How so, Bill?" she asked, voice calm and level.

"Well," Bill said, "I remember most of that night very clearly, for obvious reasons, but the timing doesn't add up. Let's say you ditched us around six o'clock. We all imbibed various substances, passed out, and then you came back and woke us up around midnight. When I was in the ambulance, one of the paramedics asked for the time, because he thought he had to call a code. I'll always remember the other one saying, '4:56 a.m.' Where did those five hours go?"

Tuck shimmered in the heat and the walls suddenly felt very far away. Kris kept her eyes on him until he solidified, then turned to Bill. Sweat trickled through her eyebrows.

"Yes," she said, louder than she intended. "Exactly. What the fuck happened to the time?"

Bill raised his head and looked at her through half-lidded eyes. "Sounds like you have a theory," he said.

"No," Kris said, and she wanted to get her thoughts organized, but it was so hot in the sweat lodge. "But I do know—"

The door opened and Miranda entered. Kris clammed up. Miranda carried a woven bamboo basket of cool, rolled towels. She closed the door behind her and her skin instantly dewed with sweat.

"You can talk in front of Miranda," Bill said. "I trust her completely."

He draped a cool towel over his forehead. Miranda handed one to Tuck, who wiped his face, then his chest.

"Terry did something to us," Kris said. "He pulled something and I don't know what it was, but it was him."

"Here comes the conspiracy theory," Tuck rumbled.

Miranda handed Kris a towel. Her arms and legs felt weak from the heat.

"But it doesn't make any sense," Bill said.

"Because it's always been Terry," Kris said. "Scottie said to me before he died, 'There's a hole in the center of the world, and inside that hole is Black Iron Mountain.' What if it's real? Or a metaphor for some kind of conspiracy? Something's been wrong with our lives ever since we signed those contracts. Like something's missing. And now this? With Scottie? He didn't kill his family. It was Terry. I know it."

Bill used his hands to swing his legs off the bench and sit up. Kris tried to stand, but the sweat lodge did a lazy half-turn and she plonked back down hard enough to bruise her tailbone. She swiped sweat from her face with the towel. She looked down at it and saw something stitched along the edge. A logo.

"You're right, Kris," Bill said. "Something has been missing from you. We've all been very worried."

Kris unfolded the towel with thick, clumsy fingers and saw a flash of orange and black. The Well in the Woods logo. A butterfly, exactly like the one on Scottie Rocket's leg.

"Tuck . . . " Kris said, and her lips were already numb.

"I'm sorry, Kris," Tuck said from far away. "But you have to let go of the past."

"You'll thank us later," Bill said.

Miranda eased Kris down onto the bench, and Kris felt ashamed that she was too weak to resist. She tried to push Miranda away, but her arms didn't work right. Miranda leaned over Kris and filled her field of vision with her empty, plastic eyes, and Kris knew Scottie Rocket was right, but it was too late. The room was rushing away so fast, and her body felt so heavy, like she was being crushed beneath a mountain, and then it all went black.

FEMALE VOICE: I was lost and drifting through life. Everything was a struggle. I was fighting with my parents and with my boyfriend. I lost my job. Every day, I thought about suicide.

MALE VOICE: But when Rachel Small came to Well in the Woods, we were ready.

FEMALE VOICE: The caring staff helped me confront the issues that held me back. They taught me to stop fighting and to accept the world the way it was.

MALE VOICE: By the time Rachel finished her ninety-day program, the calm, happy young woman looked nothing like the frantic, angry individual who arrived.

FEMALE VOICE: Now, when things get overwhelming, I stop, and listen, and remember what they taught me at Well in the Woods.

—Well in the Woods Radio Promo Spot
May 17, 2019

Theatre of Pain

Kris woke up in a white room. The walls were white. The ceiling was white. A wide rubber sheet kept her body and arms pressed flat to the mattress so she couldn't sit up. She squirmed to make the sheet looser.

"What do you think happened on contract night?" Bill asked.

His voice came from behind her, like a James Bond villain, and no matter which way she twisted, she couldn't see him.

"Did I pass out?" she asked. Her veins felt full of mud.

"The heat made you lightheaded," Bill said, wheeling into view on her right. He smiled down at her, his face open and honest. "How are you feeling?"

"I want to sit up," Kris said.

Bill kept smiling, so she tried to sit up on her own. She thrashed beneath the rubber sheet for a minute, whipping her legs from side to side, but couldn't get any leverage. She started to panic.

"It's okay, Kris," Bill said. "This is standard when someone passes out in the sauna. It keeps you still while your circulation balances."

"I'm claustrophobic," Kris said, voice tight.

"Just breathe deep," Bill said. "In through your nose, out

through your mouth. We were talking about contract night."

To distract herself from her rising panic, Kris focused on her memories. She remembered pushing open the blue door to the basement on contract night. She remembered going down the stairs and seeing everyone sprawled out on the sofa, the half-filled green beanbag, the deflating plaid air mattress, their equipment leaning against walls, cables drooling out of blue milk crates. And then she was in the van, driving, not thinking straight, scared.

"There's a hole in my memory," Kris said.

"Good," Bill said. "The best thing you can do about the past is forget it."

"Where's Tuck?"

"He left," Bill said. "He has a family, responsibilities, a comfortable life. He's moved on. Scott had a comfortable life, too, before you showed up."

"That wasn't my fault," Kris said.

Bill raised his eyebrows in surprise. "Whose fault was it?" he asked.

"Terry's," Kris said. "The UPS drivers'."

"There you go again," Bill said, clucking his tongue. "Refusing to take responsibility for your actions."

Beneath the sheets, Kris felt a tube against her right calf. She got it between her toes and pulled. Immediately, something sharp pinched inside her bladder.

"Ah!" she gasped.

"Don't pull on that," Bill said. "It's the catheter. We put it in to make urinating easier."

Kris's spine turned to ice. "How long have I been here?" she asked.

"There are three phases to your time at Well in the Woods," Bill said. "Orientation, integration into the community and, finally, graduation. Today, you're a caterpillar, but we're going to turn you into a beautiful butterfly. Flying free. Not tied down to the past. Living in the moment. That's what we did for Scott."

Kris saw the tattoo of the butterfly on Scottie's calf. She saw the butterfly logo on the hand towel. She heard Scottie getting the phone call with the "Stand Strong" ringtone.

"Scottie came here for rehab," she said.

"He's one of our biggest success stories," Bill said, then his eyes got sad. "Was."

"How. Long. Have. I. Been. Here," Kris said.

"Three days," Bill said, and Kris felt her stomach go into freefall. "A court-appointed evaluator saw you, and, with your brother's help, you've been admitted to recover from your traumatic experience at Scott's house. We all think you experienced a break with reality. Terry has generously agreed to foot the bill. This place ain't cheap."

Bill laughed at his little joke, but Kris started to panic. There wasn't enough oxygen in the air.

"I need to get out," she said. "I can't breathe."

She struggled against the sheets again, but only succeeded in a little boogying motion that made her catheter pinch. The pain made her angry.

"Why's Terry so scared of me?" Kris asked, fixing her eyes on Bill. "You don't have to do what he tells you."

"There you go again about Terry," Bill said. "Terry is paying for your treatment because he cares about his old friends. He likes to keep up with how you're doing. He enjoys keeping tabs on all of you."

"He's spying on us," Kris said.

"I'd hate to be married to you," Bill said. "You really don't let go of things."

Kris pushed all her air out from down in her stomach, projecting her voice so it bounced off the walls. "Let me up!" she shouted.

"And there's anger," Bill said, pretending to check his watch. "Right on cue. I hope we get to acceptance soon."

"Bill," Kris said, controlling her voice, managing to pull her cheeks into what she prayed looked like a smile. "Come on, we're friends. Just loosen this a little bit, okay?"

Bill considered her a moment, his face blank, not trying to look like he was in charge, just being Bill. Kris saw the kid she remembered in the tightness of his mouth, the way his eyes always looked worried, the unruly bits of hair that always stuck up.

"Okay," he said, and his voice sounded real for the first time since she woke up. "Just a bit."

Kris's heart broke into a trot as Bill leaned forward in his chair, reaching under her bed, grunting with the strain. Then he leaned back.

"On second thought," Bill said, "that's probably not a good idea."

"No," Kris said, struggling to keep her face and voice friendly. "No, Bill, it's fine. I'm fine. I won't do anything. It's not a big deal."

"How stupid do you think I am, Christine?" he asked. "How

stupid did you always think everyone was? You acted like you were better than us, the real musician, with your tortured artist bullshit that made you superior to us."

Kris had been alive long enough to know it was dangerous when men accused you of being better than them.

"No, Bill, that's not true," she said, trying to keep smiling. "I never thought I was better than you, I never thought I was better than anyone. I was shy. Maybe that came across as standoffish."

"You were never happy with anything unless it was your way," Bill said. "Play this song, release this album, don't sign the contracts. We all signed the contracts, Kris, and we're all happy. But that's not good enough for you, and now you've put everyone in a difficult position. I don't want to hurt you, and neither does Terry. We made our peace a long time ago. He helped me start Well in the Woods and today he's our biggest investor. He's the reason we've been able to open centers across the country."

Bill wasn't aware of the small smile he gave whenever he said Terry's name, the way he savored it in his mouth, but Kris saw.

"Bill, I don't have a problem with anything you're saying," Kris said. "I think it's great."

"No," Bill said. "You *are* the problem. You can't let go of the past, and now you're running around, hurting Terry's brand when he's got these concerts coming up. You never made anything of your life, so you want to tear down someone who has. These are the most important concerts Terry's ever given, Kris. The message he is bringing to the world will change everything. He has a dream for humanity, and this is its greatest expression. And because it's not all about you, you want to ruin it."

Everything clicked into place inside Kris's head. The "Stand

Strong" ringtone, the way it changed Scottie's personality, Terry coming out of retirement, all of them being watched. Why now? The concerts.

"What's he doing at these concerts, Bill?" she asked, not just scared for herself anymore.

"You thought you were better than everyone else, but Terry is better than you," Bill said. "He's richer, he's an international celebrity, a rock-and-roll icon, and you're a Best Western receptionist. You're not even on the same level. Don't try to compete."

The door opened, and Kris felt a surge of hope as Miranda entered the room, pushing a rolling steel tray.

"Help me," Kris said to her. "I'm being held here against my will. This is illegal. Please."

Miranda bent over the bed, her crunchy dreads falling into Kris's face. Kris pressed her head back into the foam rubber pillow, trying to get away, but there was nowhere to go.

"We love you," Miranda said, kissing Kris on the forehead, caressing her cheeks with soft hands that smelled like antiseptic. "That's why we're going to make you better."

Miranda smiled and stood up.

"Before Miranda helps you with your orientation," Bill said, calm again, "I want to share something with you. That hole in your memory—it's okay, Kris. Stop worrying about it. Everyone has a hole inside of them, and it's not a problem. The whole world has a hole in it, and eventually you learn to love it."

"And inside that hole," Kris said, "is Black Iron Mountain."

Bill thought for a moment, then his face fell, and looked sad.

"Scottie's note," he said, nodding to himself. "You shouldn't have read that, Christine. Honestly, if we'd had any idea he'd written something like that, we would have gotten there sooner. It's never good to say their name."

"It's a song," Kris said. "I wrote it. I invented it."

Bill looked excited now, practically wriggling in his chair.

"No, Kris. You only named something that existed long before any of us were even born," he said. "Terry took me into his confidence and showed me. It's so beautiful once you see the pattern. The whole philosophy that Black Iron Mountain brings is about embracing your place, not struggling against things you can't change. We all have a place, and standing over all of us is Black Iron Mountain. The sooner you accept your place, the sooner it all stops hurting."

He rolled slightly back from the bed. Miranda stripped the paper from a disposable hypodermic needle.

"Wait," Kris said. "What if I don't tell anyone? What if I promise to stop fighting? I'll talk to Terry. Let me talk to him."

"Terry doesn't have time to talk to you, Kris," Bill said. "He's way up there, and you're way down here. You're just an item on a checklist that needs to be crossed out before the first show in San Francisco. The longer we talk, the more I realize you're not going to be someone useful we can return to the world like Scott. You're probably going to have to stay here for a long time."

"Why is Terry so scared of me?" Kris asked, stalling, one eye on Miranda filling the syringe.

"You're a sparrow, Kris," Bill said. "You think you're so tough, you posture and pose, but you're just a tiny little bird flapping around a mountain. You'll be gone in the blink of an eye, and nothing you've done will be remembered. But the rest of us have chosen to be a part of something larger than ourselves. Something important, that will be here long after we're gone."

Miranda rubbed a cold alcohol swab on the side of Kris's neck.

"Don't do this, Bill," Kris said. "We used to be friends. He's scared of me, don't you want to find out why?"

A bee stung the side of her neck. Ice spread through her throat, something black and oily oozed through her veins. Cement filled her chest, her breathing got tight, her heart slowed.

"You're a hysteric, Kris. Running around, upsetting everyone," Bill said, rolling closer. "But we'll teach you to accept things the way they are. If you ever return to your job at Best Western, you won't feel like it's such a bad fit. You'll finally be happy."

The air dimmed around the edges of her vision.

"What does Black Iron Mountain want, Kris?" Bill smiled. "It wants you. It wants me. It wants everything."

As the air turned black, Kris saw Bill and Miranda smiling at each other, nodding, so pleased with themselves. She saw Little Charles, Tuck, Bill, Terry. Men who could hurt her, men who controlled her. She was one girl, alone, strapped to a bed.

They were bigger than her, they were more powerful, and she had been abandoned by her family, abandoned by her friends. She had nothing. Except her music.

Inside her head, she heard Scottie's voice say, "Trust *Troglodyte*."

Metal never dies. Metal never retreats. Metal never surrenders.

The world went black.

She was ready.

DANIELLE OTOMIES: Security is tight and anticipation is high for the first night of Koffin's Farewell to the King Tour, debuting at the Rose Bowl in just one hour. With only five sold-out shows before bringing his career to a close, Terry Hunt has sparked a media frenzy, especially after the tragic murder-suicide involving his former associate Scott Borzek. The Rose Bowl is locked down, and police are asking concert-goers to arrive two hours before showtime to be screened. No water or laptops will be allowed inside the Rose Bowl for fear of a liquid bomb.

—790 AM KABC, "Today in LA"
May 30, 2019

Fighting the World

Melanie pulled back-to-back doubles. She sold her old textbooks on Amazon. She sold Greg's old textbooks on Amazon. She removed backgrounds from photographs on Fiverr for $5 per job.

R U COMING 2 SHOW? Hunter texted her, three weeks out. NEED TO KNOW.

She converted some foreclosure specialist's logo to vector graphics and made it spin for a $25 iTunes gift card she sold for $20 cash. She mowed the yard at the townhouse where Greg lived for $40. She made big pots of stew and froze them for lunch.

DO I WAIT 4 U OR GO WITH MY BOYS? Hunter texted her two weeks out.

After trying to convince Greg to apply for jobs, Melanie counted it as a victory when she got him to cancel Netflix. She searched her sofas and carpets and rolled the loose change she found. She watched their bank account pile up, penny by penny, building toward the cost of moving out West. But ten days out, she had to admit: it wasn't enough.

SHOW WAS FUCKING DOPE, Hunter texted. SAW BOTH.

She missed the May Rose Bowl shows in LA. She missed the show in San Francisco. Now, the final two Koffin shows at the

T-Mobile Arena in Las Vegas would happen without her, too.

SAW ALL 3, GOING AGAIN IN LAS V, Hunter texted. SO WORTH IT.

"Just watch it on pay-per-view," Greg said the night of the second-to-last Las Vegas show. "You can watch it on the big TV. I'll play in my room."

Melanie tried to explain that it wasn't about the tickets anymore (she couldn't tell him that her online, male friend with a shirtless Tinder profile would have bought the tickets for them), it was about moving out West and doing something with their lives. She tried to explain that the $49.95 pay-per-view package would put them $50 further away from getting out of West Virginia. She tried to explain that they still needed to go, even without the deadline of the Koffin shows, but without the excitement of the deadline, all the gas leaked out of her plans.

That night she dreamed of cold hands reaching up out of the West Virginia dirt to hold her down. She didn't need a shrink to analyze that. On the night of the last Las Vegas show, she went into Pappy's and took herself off the schedule for upcoming doubles. Why work herself into the ground for nothing? She should learn to be more like Greg. At least he was happy. On her way home that night, she caved and bought a pack of cigarettes. She hadn't smoked in years because it was too expensive, but what was she saving her money for? She wasn't going anywhere.

Her phone pinged as she sat in her car, unwrapping the pack.

DID U SEE? Hunter asked. U DOWN?

She looked online. In the final minutes of the final show of his final farewell tour, Terry stood on the edge of the stage and announced that he'd had so much fun, that the tickets had sold so fast, that so many more people needed to hear the message of Koffin, that in September, in the desert outside Las Vegas, he was holding Hellstock '19.

"Fuck Burning Man," he shouted. "This is Burning in Hell, Man!"

Melanie sold the cigarettes as loosies in the Pappy's parking lot to drunk frat boys for a dollar each. She made $20 off her $5 investment, and started piling up her pennies again. She would not miss this.

Even Greg got into it this time. The night he told her he'd gotten a part-time job at the GameStop in Morgantown, she did everything he wanted in bed. It felt like a honeymoon, she felt like his partner, she felt reborn. She had to tell Hunter.

CANT TAKE UR TICKETS, she messaged him, explaining that she and Greg were getting their money together, that they were moving out West together, that they were staying together. She expected Hunter to shut her down, but instead he texted:

GOOD 4 U. COMMITMENT. INTEGRITY. RESPECT.

Melanie almost cried. Hunter insisted that he buy her and Greg two tickets while they were still available, since they were selling out fast.

THANK U, she messaged. PAY U BACK —> PROMISE

The lineup for Hellstock '19 looked insane. With two stages to fill, any band that had an edge, any act that was at all heavy, got booked. The original Woodstock was all about hippies humping in the mud. Woodstock '99 was a disaster where everything got set on fire. Hellstock '19 promised to combine both those events together into an apocalyptic end-times party.

All the bad press from Koffin's Farewell Tour only got everyone even more hyped. In Vegas, a truck full of rednecks had thrown a beer can out their window at some Koffin Kids in corpse paint heading to the show. One of the kids had a .22 and he shot at the truck as it drove away, leaving the driver blind in one eye and with a plate in his skull.

In LA, a woman was attacked in the Rose Bowl parking lot, but rescued by a group of passing Koffin Kids who beat the perpetrator nearly to death. The guy was still in a coma one week later. But then the Koffin Kids dragged the sobbing woman out from under the car where she was hiding. One of them had a pair of scissors. They sliced her tongue in two, right down the middle. Three of them were arrested. One of them hung himself in the holding cell while waiting for bail. He was fourteen and shouldn't have been in there in the first place, but the cops had thought he was older. His parents were suing the LAPD. The other kids were going to trial the weekend after Hellstock '19.

All that just made ticket sales fly faster. Within a week of Terry's announcement in Las Vegas, Hellstock '19 tickets were taken offline. By then 440,000 tickets had sold, 10,000 more than planned. Out of all those tickets, two of them were earmarked for Melanie and Greg.

Hunter became Melanie's life coach. He messaged her at 5 a.m. to make sure she was out of bed and doing her Fiverr jobs before work. She signed back up for all the doubles she could pull and sent Hunter her Pappy's schedule so he could message her inspirational quotes during her shift.

THE PATH OF MOST RESISTANCE IS THE ONE LEADING UPHILL

She bussed massive trays. She pulled pitchers faster than anyone. She turned tables like a motherfucker.

PAIN IS A FOUR LETTER WORD THE WEAK USE TO GET OUT OF DOING WHAT MUST BE DONE

She popped aspirin. She drank coffee. She rubbed Tiger Balm into her aching wrists.

THROW ME TO THE WOLVES AND I WILL WIND UP LEADING THE PACK

She ignored the guys who pressed their boners against her when the crowd got packed in butt to gut. She smiled at the ones who said, "Smile, beautiful." She did fake shots with the ones who said, "Dat butt." She piled up the tips in her bank account. Especially the cash. It was too easy to spend if she kept it at home. She could do this. She was doing this. She had never been more tired. She had never been happier.

Sitting on the couch one Monday, the one day she let herself have off at Pappy's, she almost didn't notice how good the graphics were on Greg's TV. Her head was on his thigh as he played what looked like *Call of Duty*, but from the future.

"What game is this?" she asked.

"*Shockwave: Infinity*," he said.

"Is that new?" she asked.

"Looks rad, right?"

"I thought we weren't buying anything new," she said, sitting up.

"I borrowed it from a friend," Greg said, too quickly. "Stop moving. You're fucking up my score."

"Which friend?" she demanded.

He couldn't even be bothered to lie. He confessed he'd only worked at GameStop long enough to get his employee discount and buy the new Xbox when it came out. That was three weeks ago. When she thought he was going to his shifts, he was getting stoned with his friends. He'd dipped into his account and used the money to make it look like he was still depositing his paycheck into their joint account. He'd opened up a new credit card with a 26 percent APR to buy games. He wasn't just broke, he was $1,100 in debt.

She screamed. She broke his housemate's bong. She Frisbee-d the Shockwave disc so hard it left a divot in the kitchen wall. She raged out of the house as his housemates came back from brunch.

"Dude," they said to Greg as he jogged by them, "she is so on the rag."

"Are we breaking up?" Greg asked, clueless, through her car window.

It took all her self-control not to back over him as she drove off.

At home, she went into her bedroom and turned off the lights. She blocked Greg's number on her phone and crawled into bed and felt her life fall apart while her skull filled up with black static. After a while, she could think again. She could take everything out of the joint account. Even paying Greg back his share, she still had almost enough for one person to get on the road. She needed a new transmission if she was driving the Subaru to Las Vegas, but that was only $1,300 if her cousin did it. Greg wouldn't get out of here, but she would.

She opened Kik. She messaged Hunter:

U STILL HAVE TICKET FOR ME?

After a second her phone pinged back,

2 TICKETS

NO, she messaged. JUST ME.

IF UR DREAMS DON'T SCARE U, he messaged, THEYR NOT BIG ENOUGH

GRETA ULABY: Why stage Hellstock 2019?

TERRY HUNT: I don't "stage" concerts. Conjuring Koffin requires a magikal working. To perform this ritual, hundreds of hours of labor are sacrificed, structures are built, millions of volts of electricity are routed into sacred spaces. To enter those spaces, worshippers sacrifice the most valuable thing they own: their money. At the appointed hour, on the appointed day, they are led to the correct position. They've memorized the chants and they summon their god, losing themselves in a communion where their personalities are subsumed into mine.

GRETA ULABY: There were several incidents of violence by fans on your latest tour. Does that bother you?

TERRY HUNT: Do what thou wilt shall be the whole of the law.

—90.9 WHYY, "From the Culture Desk"
June 11, 2019

Destroy Erase Improve

Every day at Well in the Woods was like a pharmaceutical commercial: sunny, beautiful, and stress free. Everyone woke up with the sun and journaled for twenty minutes before joining Miranda for sunrise salutations. On the back deck, she led them in breath work and a gentle asana sequence followed by silent mindfulness, and their first Paxator of the day.

That was followed by a healthful breakfast, then the Silent Sunrise Session, then crafting in the Activity Barn, followed by midday's Learning to Listen. They had picnics in the late afternoon on a sunny meadow deep within the property, throwing a Frisbee, eating tomato sandwiches, drinking iced tea, laughing and talking about their lives. The day ended with Sunset Review, then they got another Paxator and watched the sky darken to lavender, then purple, then black, and walked home while fireflies sparked in the trees.

Everywhere was safe at Well in the Woods because of the cameras nested in the trees, and built into the walls, and concealed inside artificial rocks, roosting on roofs, in showers, under bushes. If a butterfly went somewhere they shouldn't, an attendant would instantly appear to guide them back. At Well in the Woods, you were never alone.

They had Kris on so many sedatives, mood enhancers, stabilizers, and anxiety reducers she didn't walk across the grass, she floated. Nothing had sharp edges. Well in the Woods was suspended in a bubble of Now. There was no need to worry, because you always knew what was coming next. They were butterflies, and butterflies lived in the present.

Kris stopped speaking. She never wrote a word in her journal. But otherwise, she went where they told her to go, did what they told her to do. Miranda subjected her to numerous one-on-one encounter sessions, but Kris never said a word. They wondered if she'd had a break. They wondered if everything had been too much and she'd simply shut down. They wondered if she even heard them when they talked to her. Bill wanted to schedule an EEG to see if she showed any brain activity at all.

There was plenty. Inside Kris's head, all day, every day, she played the album that Terry had never wanted released, the one that scared him so bad he'd buried it down deep. Song by song, chord by chord, note by note, Kris silently reconstructed *Troglodyte* inside her mind.

The first track on *Troglodyte* was not actually a song, because no self-respecting metal album ever begins with a song. They all begin with an intro. Sometimes it's spooky samples over an ambient soundscape, sometimes it's keyboard swells and distant bells. Some people think intros set the mood. Others think they're pretentious bullshit.

Dürt Würk fought over the intro like they fought over everything. Scottie said they were fucking bullshit. Kris agreed with him because the frontline sticks together. Bill, though, he was nuts about that intro track. He wouldn't shut up about it until they gave in and let him make one, as long as it was less than two minutes long. Every night, while the rest of them drank warm beer from the kitchen cooler, Bill headed out into the woods around the Witch House with their portable DAT recorder, and in the morning they'd wake up to find the kitchen sink stuffed with mangled celery stalks, smashed tomatoes, and broken tree branches. Bits of black gaff tape littered the counter where he'd stuck his mic.

He finally unveiled it to them, a densely layered audio collage called "Little Sounds from Underground." It started with birds in a daylight field and the breeze in the trees before the mic descended into a well, the daylight sounds becoming muffled and fading away, then the sound of digging worms, maggots gnawing corpses, the dead pounding on the lids of their coffins and, far away, the massive creaking of the ever-grinding Wheel. The sound of screaming voices rose up, and then the audio panned across two channels, going from mono to stereo as the mic entered the massive underground cavern that housed the Wheel. Even Scottie had to admit it was an impressive effect. You could hear millions of slaves chained to its spokes, moaning as they pushed its great weight in a never-ending circle. The sound of their torment got louder and louder, and then came the crashing first notes of "Beneath the Wheel."

Just to be a jerk, Bill made the intro three minutes long.

"The world is not a complicated place," Miranda told the group at midday's Learning to Listen. "It's actually very simple."

The nine residents sat in a circle around Miranda. The sun was strong, the grass smelled sweet, and the wind shushed the treetops while Miranda told them the truth about the world.

"Who is right, and who is wrong?" Miranda asked. "What is the value of this thing? What is the value of that thing? What should I be doing with my life? These are the big questions, right?"

The circle nodded.

"Who is right? You are," Miranda said. "What is the value of something? Most actual things come with a price tag. The more it costs, the more valuable it is. What should you be doing with your life? Whatever feels good."

People nodded at her wisdom.

"Worry about yourself, don't worry about people you don't know," Miranda said, and everyone smiled because they'd never thought about it like that before. "We like to create crises where we can be the hero. But life is very simple, my butterflies. We don't need heroes. Take care of yourself. Ignore everything else. Rinse, repeat."

Kris sat, the way she always did, the same neutral smile on her face, but she didn't hear Miranda. Inside her skull, she heard Terry singing the opening lines of "Beneath the Wheel."

History
Is a boot
Smashing your face
Forever

The chords were all magisterial doom-metal tritones, each one a big black slab of sound crashing into the next. She wrote it as a showcase for Terry's voice, letting his high tenor contrast against the draggy, doomcore opening. He hit a high, clear C note on "crushed" before dropping down the octaves to a Cookie

Monster growl for "beneath the wheel." Tuck's bass picked up right off the end of his low note, dragging the song forward like a corpse. And so it went, a grinding, repetitive song designed to replicate the eternal grinding of the Wheel.

Eternity
In the mud
Crushed like a bug
Whatever

Born with a squeal
Die where you kneel
All that is real

Crushed
Beneath the wheel

"Accept each day for what it is," Miranda said, and everyone agreed.

Identity
Scrubbed away
Chemically
Forever

My leprosy
Is all that
Remains of me
Oppressor

"No one is spying on you or controlling your life," Miranda said. "You are responsible for what happens to you. Only you."

Imprison me
Underground
Slaves chained
Together

"Focus on the here, focus on the now," Miranda said. "Forget about the past."

Born with a squeal
Die where you kneel
How does it feel?

Crushed
Beneath the wheel

After "Beneath the Wheel" came "My Master's Eye," the obligatory ballad. No one in Dürt Würk wanted a ballad on *Troglodyte* because they figured a ballad meant a power ballad with the whole band singing on the chorus, a steel guitar making sad cowboy noises on the bridges, and an acoustic intro full of fake finger scrapes. They were thinking KISS's "Forever" or Mötley Crüe's "Without You." But Kris had taken a glam-metal riff she'd been playing with and fit it to an idea from her notebook to turn "My Master's Eye" into the darkest and most cynical love song ever recorded.

Everything I do he studies
Everything I do he knows
He watches me wherever I am
He follows me wherever I go

In her head, she heard the band come in on the chorus, all sickly-sweet cynicism.

He has one hundred hands
He has all-seeing eyes
He is all I am
Without him I die and die and die and die and die

Then it went to a solo with Kris fingerpicking an acoustic guitar that sounded like rose petals falling in slow motion, candles burning in a circle around the band, a sincere guitar player sitting on a broken chair inside an abandoned house, filmed in black and white. Terry sang the next verse with his voice trembling on the verge of tears.

My master won't abandon me
For me there's no escape
His loving hands leadeth me
He owns my mind, he made its shape

Then the band came in again on the chorus, all soaring swoony vocals, the kind of sound that says "Girl, I'll always love you forever," twisted into a message about their total humiliation before the Hundred Handed Eye.

I am deaf and I am dumb
My master calls, I will come
Don't ask for anything

And one . . . two . . . three . . . four . . .

I am numb

One evening at sunset, they had a bonfire behind the Witch House and while everyone watched, Miranda presented Kris with her guitar and her Bones, placing them on the ground in front of her.

"How do you feel when you see those things?" Miranda asked.

Kris didn't say anything. She simply continued her silent smiling. Miranda was starting to get frustrated.

"I know they make you nervous," Miranda said. "That's because they tie you to an unhealthy past. They are your chains."

A white butterfly pulsed on the sleeve of Kris's Bones. Next to it, her guitar lay on top of its soft case, glowing in the twilight. The guitar that Kris had recorded the original Dürt Würk demo on, the one she'd played on *Troglodyte*. It made her think of Scottie Rocket and the next song on *Troglodyte*, the one she gave him as a showcase for all his hyperactive tremolo picking and ascending runs, a song where he could run wild and blow off steam so he'd settle down enough for them to record the other nine tracks.

It was called "Eating Myself to Live."

"It's time to move on," Miranda said. She held out a white plastic bottle of lighter fluid with a red cap. Kris looked at it blankly.

Miranda bent down and picked up Kris's Bones. "Don't think," she said to the group. "Just do."

The fire feature was an enormous rusty bowl anchored to a concrete pad. Miranda dropped the Bones on the fire and it smothered the flames. The air went dark. The white butterfly floated around Kris's shoulders, bouncing up and down on an invisible string.

"Be free," Miranda said.

Then she sprayed the lighter fluid and a blue sheet of flame crawled across Kris's Bones, the white paint bubbled and split, and the leather dimpled and caught. The flames suddenly surged up to her chest. The heat baked Kris's face, stretched her skin tight over her skull. Everyone clapped and hugged her. She didn't resist.

"Next week," Miranda said, "we'll burn your guitar."

Kris thought about Scottie Rocket in this place, chained to the wheel, Miranda and Bill breaking his mind. Sweet, trusting Scottie, twisted into something dark, having that butterfly tattooed onto his calf. She thought about him in the basement, performing one final act of resistance, refusing to hurt anyone but himself, pressing the gun barrel to his own head. Thinking like that almost made her scream, so she thought about what made Scottie happiest, instead: the breakdown on "Eating Myself to Live." He loved that breakdown the way Slash loved Jack Daniels. He played it all the time, and when they hung around the blood-carpeted living room of the Witch House he kept fingering it on his unplugged guitar while they shot the shit and talked about tomorrow's session.

The breakdown was where the song dropped tempo until it practically stopped, Kris chugging her guitar with Tuck following on the bass, as Scottie ran all over the place with his chromatic progressions. After giving Scottie almost a minute to deliver fireworks, Terry cut in like a razor as the tempo slowly picked back up.

And everything's a game
And everyone's been tamed
And everything's the same
And everyone's to blame
And no one wants the pain
The Blind! King! Reigns!

"Poincaré's Butterfly" was the next song on *Troglodyte*. Terry didn't want it because the first half was all soft, trilling runs over the fretboard with echoing, pensive pauses, a rippling fingerstyle opening played by Kris with no pick, just her calloused fingertips, a sudden introspective calm that Terry thought was the equivalent of putting a gun in their mouth on a metal album. But Tuck stuck up for it, which surprised Kris, and that was that.

Bill had come up with the title, taking it from a book called *Chaos* he was reading about how the world was interconnected and a butterfly flapping its wings in Bombay could cause hurricanes in Boston. Kris studied Mark Knopfler's fingerstyle for a long time to be able to play what was inside her head, and it had impressed the hell out of Terry. In the basement studio, he'd watched her lay down her track in one take, then quietly stepped up to the mic and gave it everything he had on the vocals, singing in a high sweet falsetto:

Down
Through the floor
Through the dirt
Through the door

Tunnels
Of darkness
And whispers
And screams
Like a choir

Kris kept smiling. She would not let them into her mind. Twenty-seven-year-old Kris was the only person adult Kris could trust. A girl whose back never ached, whose head never bowed, whose knee never bent, bravely firing a flare into the future called

Troglodyte that warned her tired, slow, failed adult self that this world was really a prison, and its name was Black Iron Mountain.

On wings
Made of red
Made of yellow
Made of fire

It lands
On my hand
This strange thing
With its wings

As Troglodyte turned the Wheel, a butterfly somehow got into Black Iron Mountain and landed on the back of his hand. He'd never seen one before, and it made him realize that there was more to this world than Black Iron Mountain. There was an escape somewhere, a way out, a Blue Door.

Makes me know
This shadow show
My master's voice
They are liars

In one smooth movement at this point in the song, Kris would grab the pick from her mouth, and come down hard:

There is a fire.

She ripped into a G power chord on "fire," then tore into the heavy, shredded ending of "Poincaré's Butterfly," chewing up the air, waking everyone up the way Scottie gave his life to wake her up. At the end of "Poincaré's Butterfly," after Troglodyte realizes he can break his chains and leave, after he realizes that there is a way to the surface, Kris came in with Scottie Rocket on a hard riff that repeated again and again, getting stronger with each repetition, as Terry sang:

There is more
Beyond the pain
And the shame
And the blood
And the screams
Past the flood
And the fire
And the King
And his choir
Through the torture
And the wire
And the murder
And the gore
Above these dark tunnels . . .

It was the sound of rage and triumph as Troglodyte shattered his chains and began his long trek to the surface, because metal woke you up. Metal set you free.

There's a door.

They'd been a band once, they'd been good, they might have even been great. Then the Blind King betrayed them all. No matter how many drugs they gave her, Kris would not forget. Not again.

"When you came to us, you had a strange delusion," Miranda said at their one-on-one session. "Do you remember what it was?"

Kris smiled softly, looking straight ahead.

"You're probably embarrassed," Miranda said. "You thought that people spied on you. You thought Terry Hunt controlled your life. That he kept you down. Do you remember that?"

Kris didn't change her expression.

"But you know why your life was a mess, don't you?" Miranda asked.

Kris gave her nothing.

"Because of you," Miranda said, looking into her eyes. "You're the only one responsible for your problems. It was never anyone else's fault. It was only ever you."

She held Kris's gaze for a long time, trying to get her to flinch, trying to make her blink. But Kris held steady because now she knew why *Troglodyte* was a weapon that could shatter chains, she knew why that album scared Terry, she knew why Black Iron Mountain tried to get it erased.

It told the future. She lived in Gurner, chained to the wheel, and Terry's Hundred Handed Eye watched her. She ate herself to live, but then Scottie showed up with Poincaré's butterfly on his leg, and he woke her up. Well in the Woods was the Wheel, too. Every day the same, everything in chains.

"Kris," Miranda said. "I know you can hear me."

Miranda leaned over and pinched the skin on the back of Kris's hand between her thumb and forefinger. She twisted it around like a corkscrew, squeezing all the blood out, turning it white, looking for a reaction.

Kris didn't give Miranda anything. Partly because in her one thousand three hundred and twenty-six shows, in her thousands of rehearsals, in her tens of thousands of hours woodshedding,

Kris had done way worse to her hands.

But mostly because she knew the truth: *Troglodyte* told the future. Scottie asked her to carry the fire. She would not let him down.

And she knew what track came next.

Miranda let go of Kris's skin, and it throbbed as blood surged back into her torn blood vessels.

"Well," Miranda said. "We'll try again tomorrow."

The next track on *Troglodyte* was "Down Where the Worms Squirm." It was the one about the rain.

Heavy rain and flash flooding is possible in the Clay County area starting as early as tomorrow night as Tropical Storm Stephen arrives off the Atlantic coast. Several inches of rain could fall across Eastern Kentucky in just a few hours, accompanied by severe thunderstorms with damaging winds gusting up to forty-five miles per hour. Hail is expected, lasting into the early hours of Monday morning. Residents are advised to remain indoors.

—162.4 KEC58, National Weather Service Alert
August 10, 2019

Let's Rumble

All day the temperature plummeted. Gray clouds scudded over Silent Sunrise Session. At Learning to Listen, Kris's ears popped as the air pressure dropped. Attendants ran all over the property putting plywood over glass walls and securing doors. At lunch, Miranda announced that a tropical depression was going to make landfall in Virginia, sending high winds and rain into Kentucky, even as far west as Well in the Woods. Sunset Review would be indoors in the Group Awakening room. Afternoon activities were canceled. Everyone got extra Paxator and was sent to bed early.

Now, in the darkness, a bucket of water slammed into her window and Kris woke up. She reached out, found the sconce over her bed, and twisted the switch. It clicked and clicked but the room stayed dark. The window rattled in its frame. Kris stood and the dark room did a merry-go-round. Two fast steps got her to the window without falling down. Outside, flashlights bounced across the grounds. All the landscaping lights were dark. The power was out.

Kris smiled, and this was a real smile. She had trusted *Troglodyte* and *Troglodyte* came true. The storm from "Down Where the Worms Squirm" was here.

With shaking hands, Kris dressed fast. All she had were the linen pants and shirt they provided for her, and the soft shoes with their thin rubber soles, but they were better than nothing. She padded to the door, pushed it open, and crept into the hall. Her heart hit thrash metal beats per minute, rabbiting in her chest so hard she thought she'd throw up. Each corner produced bowel-churning terror, but she forced herself around every one until she reached the stairs that disappeared down into the deep darkness of the first floor. She put one foot on the top step.

A flashlight beam landed on the bottom step and started to rise, and Kris backed up and ducked into an open doorway. It was someone's office, so modern and forward-thinking it didn't even have a door. Instead of a chair, a yoga ball sat behind the desk. A cell phone sat on the windowsill, plugged into a charger. Leaning in the corner was Kris's soft case, and she knew that inside it was her guitar, ready to be burned soon. This must be Miranda's office. As Kris hid behind the desk, she saw the flashlight dust the room, continue down the hall, and disappear.

Kris unplugged the cell phone and shoved it into her pocket, then stepped back into the hall. She started for the steps but froze when, from around the corner, she saw the flashlight beam bobbing back toward her.

" . . . didn't even . . . in the office," the voice said, torn to shreds by the rain. "Windows open . . . or . . . "

Next to Kris was a resident's room belonging to a middle-aged recovering food addict named Gray. Kris turned the knob and stepped inside, closing the door behind her as quietly as she could.

Cold air pinched her nostrils and scraped her throat. It was pitch black. A wet sound filled the room. Kris turned on the phone's flashlight to see what was leaking, raised it over her head, and the harsh light bounced off a thing on the bed and the final piece of the jigsaw puzzle snapped into place, and Kris remembered what really happened on contract night.

Kris stood in the woods behind the Witch House, double-fisting her champagne. It had started to rain and she was cold and wet and pissed off when she came back inside. The first thing she saw were the contracts, four of them lined up on the coffee table, signed by Bill, Tuck, and Scottie Rocket, the last one waiting for her. Stomach acid burned the back of her throat. Her brain gave a deep throb.

Even as she entered the blue door, even as she stormed down the basement steps, she knew something was wrong. It was too quiet. It was too dark. Usually they had the Christmas tree lights on, or the Coleman lantern, and there was always the sound of Scottie talking endlessly, or Tuck noodling on his bass, or Terry indulging in some elaborate fame fantasy, but tonight it was completely silent.

In the dark, she had heard the same soft, rotten, sucking sounds she heard now as she picked up the flashlight hanging halfway down the stairs and clicked it on. At first, she didn't know what she was looking at. She recognized Bill's black jeans from the two identical tears he'd made over his knees, the cotton forming pouty lips, but she didn't understand what he had over the upper half of his body. A pile of towels? A bag of laundry? She swung the flashlight to the beanbag chair and saw a white bag covering Tuck's upper body and face.

The last place the flashlight stopped was the plaid air mattress against the wall. Scottie was passed out on his back, completely boneless, and in that instant she knew what he would look like dead. The air mattress had deflated, pressed to the floor by the thing that crouched on his chest. The light nailed it to the wall, erasing all shadows, and Kris thought it was a woman because of its long hair and two deflated dugs swinging back and forth.

It was a corpse, emaciated past the point of survival, white as house paint, all its ribs standing out, every knob of its spine pressing painfully through its skin. Its fingernails were black and it bent over Scottie, slobbering up the black foam that came boiling out of his mouth. Kris flipped the light back to the couch, and she saw that the same thing was crouched over Bill, a starved mummy, maggot-white, its skin hanging in loose folds. A skin tag between its legs jutted from a gray pubic bush, bouncing obscenely like an engorged tick.

At first, they were so intent on their feeding they didn't notice her. But then the one crouched on Tuck's enormous stomach sensed her. It turned its head, blind eyes targeting Kris, and she could not look away. Its gaze was old and cold and hungry and its chin dripped black foam like a beard. It sniffed the air and hissed, its bright yellow tongue vibrating, its gums a vivid red. Kris's hands went numb and the flashlight slipped through her fingers and spun crazily down the stairs and across the floor, rolling to a rest with its beam shining on an empty patch of basement floor. In the dark, she heard the other two stop feeding. From the darkness came a hungry, chittering hiss.

A white hand planted itself in the middle of the flashlight beam and Kris could not move, because the one that had been on

Tuck was crawling toward her, walking on all fours like a spider, and she tried to run but then she saw that its elbows and knees bent backward, and her joints locked. The thing took careful, slow steps on all fours, and then, in a rush, it scurried up the bannister. The railing creaked under its weight and Kris could feel the painful cold radiating from it in waves, and its blind face turned toward her, and then . . . nothing.

Kris was in the wet woods, time spliced out of her memory, looking up at rain falling into her face. She slid over the cold, wet ground. Sticks and leaves went up the back of her shirt. She raised her head and saw the white creature, on all fours, moving like a spider, dragging her back to the Witch House by one ankle. Her brain short-circuited and she rolled to her right, twisting, and the thing was on her fast, pinning her to the dirt, colder than the rain.

Its mouth was wide and hungry, its fingernails jagged and torn. There was nothing in its eyes except hunger. It pinned her by the shoulders with one hand, then dipped its fingers into her mouth and Kris gagged reflexively, her teeth pressing into its cold knuckles. It scrabbled down her throat, its fingernails grasping the root of her tongue, and panic erupted inside Kris and she moved the only part of her body she could.

Kris bit down. A bitter liquid sprayed the inside of her mouth and trickled down her throat. The thing reared back, yanking its hand free, hunching over its wounded fingers. Kris rolled onto her hands and knees and saw a pile of old lumber from some forgotten renovation project glistening nearby in the rain. She grabbed a two-by-four and she smashed it down on the thing's skull with all the revulsion and disgust of crushing a roach—once, twice, then the thing was squirming in the mud on its back.

Everyone was still inside, and Kris was running before she even stopped throwing up. She slammed through the kitchen door, crashing down the stairs before her fear could catch up to her. The things were gone, and the beam of the flashlight she'd dropped on the floor was watery and weak, and Kris was slapping their faces and kicking their shoulders and shouting, "Come on, come on, come on, we have to get the fuck out of here!"

She remembered getting them into the van, hitting the highway, lurching in the rain, and seeing not headlights in front of her, not a UPS truck, but a flash of white in the rearview mirror. She turned just as the thing from the woods, its head split open and oozing black blood, scrambled up the back of the moving van, impossibly fast.

"What's that?" Tuck said, as the thing pounded across the roof. Then its face exploded into the windshield.

Tuck screamed as it banged one bony fist against the glass, eyes ragged holes, mouth a gaping black maw, and Kris slammed on the brakes and pulled the wheel to the right as far as it would go. The thing went flying as she felt two tires leave the road, and the last thing Kris saw before the van rolled was its face, yanked out of her field of vision. Then gravity stopped, and then the violence, and the stillness, and the long, lonely sound of Bill's unvarying monotone scream. But before she passed out, she heard it coming, picking its way through the wreckage, back to finish its job . . .

The thing squatting on Gray's chest turned its black dripping chin into the cell phone light, and the twenty years between points A and B disappeared. Wind squeezed the sides of the building as the thing sniffed the air, then dismissed her, turning back to Gray's mouth, where it continued to lap up the black foam like porridge from a dog's bowl.

This was what lived in Black Iron Mountain, and Kris knew in a flash that there was us, and there was them. There were human beings, and there was Black Iron Mountain. And it had ignored her, dismissed her like she didn't matter. Like she wasn't dangerous.

Kris fell back against the door, shoved it open, stumbled into the hall. She raced into Miranda's office, crawled behind the desk, unzipped the soft case. She'd forgotten the heft and weight of her guitar. She grabbed it by the neck, its steel strings slicing into her soft hands, and felt strength coursing from it, up her arms like an electric current, as she ran back to Gray's room.

People call guitars axes because that's how they're shaped. A long neck made of mahogany, and the body like a blade. The Gibson Les Paul Melody Maker's body was a ten-pound slab of maple, about an inch thick, a foot wide at the bell. It was unbalanced in Kris's hand, wanting to flip from her thin wrist as she gripped its neck and raised it over her right shoulder. She swung it down and across, throwing her body weight into it, going for a home run. The body of her guitar hit the thing with a *TONK*, and it toppled back against the wall and was on its feet in an instant, hissing at Kris, but she already had her guitar over her head and she brought it down again. It dodged left, but she turned and smacked it again with the full face of her Les Paul. Three metal strings gave comical *TWING*s as they snapped and sliced backward in metal curls.

It gathered its limbs to leap at her, and Kris didn't give a shit.

She let her momentum carry her to the right, and at the peak of her arc reversed and brought her guitar slamming back down to the left, smashing into the knobs of the thing's spine. Something snapped, and the thing collapsed on top of Gray's abdomen, forcing black foam to fountain from his mouth, spattering the wall over his head. The thing's limbs twitched in double time as Kris brought her guitar down on it again and again, the remaining D, A, and E strings vibrating as this piece of shit crunched beneath her blows.

She finally stopped, arms aching, tendons shaking, palms burning, out of breath. Then the thing shoved its torso up, one clawed hand reaching for Kris, and she leaned back from the waist and brought her guitar up in a high arc, behind her back, over her head, and crashed it down onto the base of its skull.

This time, it didn't move.

Kris heard men shouting over the wind outside, voices filtering through the rain. She ran into the hall, damaged guitar in her right hand. She went around the corner, clattered down the stairs, and then she was out the back door in the howling rain, pounding across the deck, and before she knew where she was going, she was running for the Witch House.

Behind her, flashlights danced in windows as they searched for her, while cold rain lashed her chest and face and washed black foam from the body of her battered Les Paul. She ran up the slippery wooden steps and across the back deck of the Witch House and pushed open the door. There was one way out of here that wasn't protected by a fence or a gate. All Kris had to do was count on the fact that Miranda and Bill were liars. She threw her whole body against the back door and pushed it shut in the face of the roaring wind, and then everything was silent.

A flashlight beam nailed her in the face. Kris flinched away.

"You little faker," Miranda purred in the darkness behind the blinding light. "You're going to regret—"

That was all it took for Kris to take aim. Her guitar gave her three extra feet of reach. She jabbed it forward and glass shattered and the flashlight went out. There wasn't room in the hall to swing her guitar to the side, so Kris brought it straight up, then down, onto something soft.

In the dark, she saw a doubled-over shadow, blacker than the air around it, and Kris brought her guitar down on it again. The shadow dropped to the floor and didn't move. Kris gave it a kick, just to be sure.

She felt along the wall until she found the spot where she remembered there had once been the blue door. She braced her legs and gripped her guitar by the neck, one hand near its body, the other close to its head. The wall was smooth and perfect and solid. For a moment she hesitated—Bill had said that they filled the basement in. Then she remembered that they were all liars, and she brought the edge of her axe down.

She swung her guitar twice, three times, four. Its body punched ovals in the dry wall, and then the wall began to break, and fold, and cave in. Kris's wasted muscles screamed as she bashed away at it. The cold leeched the strength from her arms and thighs, her calves cramped. Her palms blistered and tore, her shoulders vibrated down to the marrow with every blow.

But finally, the edge of a door emerged. Kris turned on the light from Miranda's cell phone, and through the clotted dust and rubble, she saw the edge of the old '70s doorframe. She turned off the phone and kept swinging.

She grabbed the drywall with cramped hands, and tore it out in sheets, dropping it to pile up in the hall. Kris stood on the pile and kicked the wall, she slashed at it with her guitar, she punched through it, and finally, she saw it: the Blue Door.

Kris didn't feel foggy. She felt hungry and sharp like she'd finally remembered the name of that song, finally dislodged that piece of food between her teeth, finally completed the puzzle.

In the light of the phone, the paint was so faded the door was barely blue anymore. They'd taken off the key plate and the knob and walled it up, but it was still here, buried behind the Witch House walls, waiting. She braced herself and jammed her guitar forward. The body bashed into the blue door and its hinges gave way, and with a massive, tearing crash it sheared off and crashed down the dark stairs.

Her guitar's center of gravity suddenly shifted and the neck split with a tearing crack, separating from the body. It was twisted and ruined, barely held together by three strings. But it had done its job. It had helped Kris escape, first Gurner, then her long sleep, and now Well in the Woods. She kissed it, getting plaster dust in her mouth, and laid it in the rubble. Then Kris went through the door and down the stairs. They were dark and stained, and they led underground, into the basement, back where it all began.

HOWARD PEARS: Rights issues keep Suzy and I from playing you a recording of Dürt Würk's *Troglodyte*, but because of its place in heavy metal history, we need to describe it to our listeners.

SUZY BAUM: It's this very mystery that has made it such a legendary recording. But those who've heard it reveal the truth behind the legend—it's not very good. The production quality is lacking, the musical technique is somewhat lackluster, and the lyrics can best be described as juvenile.

HOWARD PEARS: And yet this recording exerts a unique fascination, holding your attention despite the very problems that Suzy describes. Its internal mythology indicates more than it states, implies more than it explains, and obscures more than it reveals.

SUZY BAUM: There's a constant sense that there is always some bigger picture just out of sight, hidden behind yet another curtain, that what we are hearing is only the tip of the iceberg.

—BBC Radio 3, "The Story of Music in One Hundred Pieces"
June 14, 2019

Sleep's Holy Mountain

Lit by Miranda's cell phone, the basement was smaller and dirtier than Kris remembered—a bare, concrete cube. Rust streaked the low white wall around the mouth of the well where the plywood cap still rested. She only had a minute before someone showed up and saw the smashed hole in the wall, the torn drywall filling the hall, her shattered guitar. They would be here soon.

Kris limped to the well. The cap was a big sheet of blue plywood braced by two-by-fours, and someone had drilled eyebolts into each of its four sides. Chains hung down to four rings embedded in the concrete. Four open padlocks lay in the filth on the floor. With effort, Kris shoved the lid aside, just a crack, and exposed the dark shaft. The cold smell of graveyard dirt blasted up out of the well and hit her square in the face as she leaned over the mouth, the phone's harsh light showing the grubby cylinder of the well's interior. Rusty rebar rungs ran down into the gloom. Kris flipped one leg over the lip of the well, found the rebar with her foot, and brought her other leg over. She scraped her stomach on the concrete edge of the well, her back on the plywood, and then she pulled the cover back in place over her head and descended into the well.

Her arms shook with exhaustion. She had to force her torn palms to grab each rebar rung, but she kept going. The rungs bruised the bottoms of her feet through the flimsy soles of her soaking-wet shoes. By the time her feet touched the concrete bottom, she was so deep in the earth that all sound had been sucked away except for the quiet, hollow rumble of air rising through the well. Kris lit Miranda's phone and saw there was only sixteen percent left on its battery. By the base of the well, a glossy clay pipe about three feet wide jutted from the wall, facing another just like it on the opposite wall. These must have been what carried the water from the underground river and drained it away again.

Above her, shouts echoed down the well. They were already in the basement. Kris's heart sped up, her breath tightened. She had to hide, but there was nowhere to go. The pipes were too small. There was no way she could fit. The plywood above her scraped a bit, then dropped back into place, punching her in both eardrums. There was rattling noise, and scraps of flashlight flickered on the underside of the plywood cap. They were going to look down the well.

She had no choice. Kris squatted, and stuck her head into one of the pipes. It was clear, except for a line of soil along the bottom. Above her, the plywood cover gave a longer scrape. Kris turned off Miranda's phone and slid it into her pants, raised her arms over her head, and forced herself to slide into the pipe, just as the plywood cap was dragged to one side and crashed to the floor.

Kris rocked her hips from side to side, hands extended in front of her like a diver, dragging herself by her raw palms. The balls of her feet pushed her forward, then left the well floor, and she slithered ahead until she was completely inside the pipe. She stopped—just out of sight, she hoped. She wanted to look back, but when she tried to turn her head it hit the solid side of the pipe.

All she had to do was stay put, and stay calm. Against her will, she started to pant. She would have to get that under control. Suddenly, there was a hollow crash, then metal rattled, twice, three times, four. They'd put the cap back on and locked the chains. Kris thrashed for a minute, but couldn't get any leverage to move backward, and her heart beat so hard it thumped against the pipe. Another boom, then another. They were stacking something heavy on top of the cap. Then silence. They'd sealed her in.

Kris tried to reverse out of the pipe, but her butt couldn't rise up high enough to inchworm back. She was stuck.

"No, no, no, no, no, no, no," she moaned.

She wanted to scream and stretch and thrash but the pipe clamped tight around her. This was going to be her coffin. Down where the worms squirmed. It was the next song on *Troglodyte*, and she tried to focus on its lyrics, tried to replay them in her head to distract herself from her rising panic.

Black Iron Mountain is cold, cold, cold

It started like a sea shanty.

Black Iron Mountain is cold, cold, cold
The language they speak is old, old, old
And their lies are made out of gold

Kris repeated it to herself. She couldn't look up because there was no room to raise her head before it hit the ceiling of the pipe. Her shoulders rested against either side of the pipe. She wiggled her hips, and dragged herself by her palms, and pushed with her toes, and slid forward an inch. She did it again.

Black Iron Mountain is cold, cold, cold

And again.

The language they speak is old, old, old

And again.

And their lies are made out of gold

And again.

Kris shivered in the freezing dark. She imagined rain falling far above her, and then heard Bill's dry drum solo that kicked off the first verse of "Down Where the Worms Squirm."

Welcome to my dark places
Coffins pickling in the dark
Surrounded by blind faces
Their minds bear his evil mark

Inch forward. Inch forward. Inch forward.

All I know is what they tell me
A cat screams inside my brain
And miles above my coffin
Iron skies spit iron rain

Troglodyte was still right. It was raining and she was trapped inside a coffin. But she couldn't die yet because there were four songs left to go. Then Kris's fingers struck a solid wall. She couldn't lift her head to see, so she pushed, she scraped, she pressed, and discovered that the pipe ended.

Instinctively, Kris tried to back up and her shoulders wedged solidly in the pipe. There was no give. In the darkness, something brushed against the sole of her right shoe, and Kris tried to jerk her leg away but only succeeded in jamming her knee under herself, shoving her butt tight against the top of the pipe. She was a cork in a bottle.

The chorus came blasting into her brain.

Down where the worms squirm
Down where the blood churns
Down where the pain burns
In my dark places
Buried with the worms

She was buried with the worms. That's all. It was only a song. She was only an actor in a video. She took three breaths, not too deep, then imagined her right leg muscles relaxing, and slowly stretched that leg out behind her, cautiously, ready to yank it back if something touched it again. She spread her arms apart, laying the side of her face on the dirt at the bottom of the pipe, and felt the walls. Her right arm ran up the smooth, hard curve of the pipe, but her left found air: the pipe didn't end, it took a forty-five-degree turn.

Kris got stuck making the turn, crumpling her lungs into a position where they couldn't expand, and her body stopped bending. She made herself focus on the words:

Black Iron Mountain is cold, cold, cold
The language they speak is old, old, old
And their lies are made of gold

She could go two minutes without air; this was going to be okay. She forced herself to relax. Her shoulders and the base of her neck came unstuck and she slid forward again. She stretched to full length and began the next verse of "Down Where the Worms Squirm" as she rocked forward, inching down the pipe.

Iron rain is falling
On the bodies of the slain
The Blind King keeps calling
Trapped inside a coffin made of pain

A hollow moan echoed down the pipe from up ahead and Kris froze. It sustained, unchanging, and she made herself inch forward again. The moan turned into a howl and Kris felt cold air blowing on her hands, and suddenly, her hands couldn't feel floor anymore. The pipe opened into space. Kris pulled herself out, walking her hands forward on rough ground, gasping with relief. Her feet fell out of the pipe and she squatted, pulled out Miranda's phone, and turned on the flashlight. She was in a rocky wasteland, a small cave, where water once flowed. The river must have been sealed further up. Across the cave, a jagged tunnel of rocks headed downhill beneath a low ceiling, but she could just make it if she hunched over at her waist.

Kris pulled herself over the loose rocks, inching downhill.

The phone was at nine percent battery but she had to keep it on to watch where she put her feet so she wouldn't twist an ankle.

Everything you said you wanted
Rots and falls apart
In the kingdom of the Blind King
He eats your aching heart

At first it was hard to tell that the roof was getting lower, but now the rocks she climbed over were only two feet from the dirt ceiling. Lacy roots hung down like dead hair. Now the ceiling was one foot away, and she crawled over the rocks on her belly like a lizard, phone in one hand.

The battery was at seven percent. She wondered if she'd made the wrong decision, if she should have chosen the other tunnel, or taken her chances with Bill. Maybe by the time she discovered it was a dead end, it would be too late. The walls were getting tighter, slowly bending toward each another like a funnel.

Down where the worms squirm
Down where the blood churns
Down where the pain burns
In my dark places
Buried with the worms

The phone was at six percent when she came to the point where she had to decide: headfirst or feetfirst. After this, she'd be crawling through a rock tube too narrow to turn around in. She went with headfirst, diving into the heart of the mountain, arms outstretched in front of her. Dirt rained down where her back brushed the ceiling, rough rocks tore her hands, her elbows and knees bled. The mountain closed its fist, squeezing her tight.

Finally, she stopped crawling. Before her, the ceiling and floor sandwiched together until they were barely two fists high. She couldn't turn around. The phone was at four percent. She took a look at the lay of the land and realized this flat gap went on for a while. She shut off the phone and stuck it in her pants. In the cold darkness, she felt the weight of the entire mountain pressing down on her. Kris turned her skull sideways and it barely fit. She lay flat on her stomach and starfished, spreading her arms and legs out as much as possible, and slid forward, walking her whole body on her chest, fingers, toes, and the side of her face. She inched forward, inched forward again, her left ear filling with dirt, and then the rock slammed shut and snapped her between its jaws. Stuck.

The top of the cave pressed down on her back. The floor pressed up on her chest. Her lungs couldn't fully inflate. She couldn't even open her mouth to wet her chapped lips.

She couldn't breathe.

Through the darkness his worms swarm
Black water flooding their black caves
This rage I'm feeling is a cold storm
Drowning all his slaves

Kris couldn't tell if her eyes were open or closed. She thought they were closed. She pulled a small breath low into her belly, feeling her stomach press against the rock floor and her shoulder blades press against the ceiling. She took another breath. Then another. She waited, she felt her blood flow slower, her muscles relax.

Let the sky come down
Wash everything away
Worms scream underground
I no longer feel afraid

She could bend her right arm some, but her left arm was stuck, wedged tight by her body weight. She swung her right arm slowly back and forth from her shoulder, like a windshield wiper. Her fingertips walked the rock in front of her. There was a gap there, a crack in the rock through which warm air blew. If it was wide enough, and not a fatal inch too low, she might make it.

Constricting her muscles, Kris slithered forward and the ceiling bent her left ear backward. She wrapped her right palm over the lip of the gap. She tried to get her left arm into it and her elbow felt like it was going to pop out of its socket and then, with a lurch, it was in. Both hands on the lip, she pulled. The rock took skin off her back, stomach, and the tops of her thighs, but she slid into the hole up to her waist, and then toppled forward into space, bruising both knees, landing hands first in mud. The stench of animal musk made her eyes water. She stood in mud up to her knees. She'd lost one of her shoes and her right foot was bare in the hot muck. Instantly she felt her pants leg moving. Shoving her hand into her pants, Kris pulled out the phone and turned it on, and wished she hadn't.

She stood in another small cave, and the floor was covered in bat shit up to her knees, giving off eye-searing waves of ammonia. Its surface seethed with a glistening black carpet of bugs. Rocks raised their sharp heads above the guano like icebergs. Kris forced herself to look up. Four inches above her head, the ceiling rustled with a swaying carpet of soft-bodied bats. One woke and turned its blind eyes toward her, mouth open in a silent scream, showing tiny white teeth like needles. Kris brushed bugs from her legs. Their chitinous hooks nipped at her palms. She made herself turn off the phone and put it in her pants again. With a shock, Kris found that even with the phone off, she could still make out the dim outline of the cave. There was light up ahead.

She sloshed forward and prayed the light wasn't coming from a hole too high to reach. Beneath her, beetles crunched, pinched their way up the backs of her knees, her thighs, clung to her waistband, her belly. Her feet were warm in the guano and rocks shredded their skin. She bounced her kneecap off a rock and fell forward, putting her arms out, and went up to her shoulders in bat shit. A centipede clung to her chin. She pushed herself up, and felt the top of her head brush several bats and send them swaying. One of their soft, hot bodies dropped onto her shoulder, and she slapped it away. It squished under her hand, and its sharp teeth tore into the ball of her thumb like a razor blade, and hung there for a moment as she shook her arm frantically. Then it was gone. Warm velvet and leather slapped past her face. Kris fought the urge to scream. She slogged forward faster.

The beetles had reached her neck. She felt their sharp pincers and feelers searching inside the collar of her shirt, pushing under her hair. She slapped them away, crushed them, got her hands slick with their ichor. Ahead of her, there was a bend in the cave, and when she rounded it, the light was full in her face. There was a jagged cleft, about three feet high, only a foot wide, obscured by roots and grass, but after the jaws of the mountain, it felt as wide as a Walmart aisle.

The ceiling rippled, set off by her frantic movement, and bats dropped, forming a crazy cloud around her. Kris blundered forward, her toenails bending backward on the rocks. Then she leapt for the slash of light, forcing herself out through the crack, hauling herself out into the long grass, desperate to get outside before the cloud of biting, shrieking bats overwhelmed her. She thought she would go insane if they touched her face again.

A root grabbed her waist, kept her suspended in air, then ripped free and Kris slid down the wet hill on her stomach. Her tumble slowed, then stopped, and she lay on her back, panting. The mountain rose up above her. Kris had never been more grateful to be in the open air. Her feet were bleeding, she was covered in bat shit, but she was alive, gulping cold, fresh, sweet oxygen.

Below her, a truck went blasting past in the gray early morning light, headed up the highway. She was on the shoulder of a two-lane blacktop, a scenic overlook on the other side of the road, a huge hill of long grass rising up behind her.

And now what?

She had to keep moving. She had to get away. If they found her and brought her back to the Well, her mind wouldn't survive. Kris slid down the rest of the hill, and after looking both ways, she hobbled across the two lanes to the scenic turnoff. She limped into a clump of bushes, pushed her way out, and kept heading downhill.

Just like that, America reached up and swallowed her whole.

JACK BLAST: For those of you just joining us this is Jack Blast Freedom Radio broadcasting live from the Compound in the great state of Arizona where the men have guns, the women have racks, and every day is hunting season. You're on the air.

CALLER: This is JD.

JACK BLAST: Our old friend. How goes it, compadre?

CALLER: Forces are on the move, Jack. Past sins will be paid for in blood. You hearing this big increase in chatter? They're laying the groundwork to cover their asses. This is the big one.

JACK BLAST: And what's the "big one," JD? Caller? Are you still on the line? [dead air] Okay, I'm sure that caller will return just as soon as he gets back on his meds.

—WJET, "Radio Free America"
August 13, 2019

Stay Hungry

On stiff legs, Kris stumbled downhill, trying to put as much distance between herself and Well in the Woods as possible.

Behind a band of dying trees, she found a little house with no cars in the driveway. She drank from their garden hose until her stomach sloshed, and washed away the worst of the bat shit. There wasn't an inch of her skin that wasn't bruised, cut, scraped, or torn. Her head felt so light it almost floated off her shoulders, but she forced herself down the road in her soggy white linens, squatting behind parked cars or trudging into the woods whenever a truck came along.

At a beat-down shopping center she found a Salvation Army. Two old guys were unloading boxes of children's toys into the back.

"You got any clothes?" Kris asked, her throat rusty.

"Sure," one of the men said. "Inside. For sale."

Kris held her arms out. The white linen outfit she wore was so wet and stained it was transparent. She only had the one shoe.

"Please," she said.

One guy went inside. Kris stood on the asphalt, enjoying the heat from the rising sun. The guy came out and threw a black bundle at her.

"Here," he said, turning his back. "Couldn't sell those anyway."

Behind a dumpster, Kris put on pink sweatpants with a big brown stain down one leg. She hoped it was chocolate. There were a pair of Tevas and a black hoodie featuring a full color, ultrarealistic picture of spilling guts on the front. On the back it read "Slipknot World Domination Tour."

"Wonderful," Kris said.

She turned it inside out. It would be hell to get out West in these clothes, but they were better than nothing. *Troglodyte*'s next track was "Sailing the Seas of Blood," which told her she needed to keep moving. She had to get out West and stop Terry's Farewell to the King concerts. Whatever he had planned, she knew it wasn't good. She was a believer now, both in the pure evil of Terry and the predictive powers of *Troglodyte*. Kris came back around the dumpster.

"What day is today?" she asked one of the men.

She hoped it was still May. Even if it was Memorial Day weekend, that gave her some time. She needed at least a week to get to LA.

"August twelfth," the guy said.

Kris's brain shut off and she walked away blindly. She remembered the sun being in a different position when she ate half a hotdog out a garbage can in a 7-Eleven parking lot. It was directly overhead when she found some congealed fries sitting on the sidewalk outside a Hardees. She ate them. She didn't know what time it was. It didn't matter. She'd missed the concerts. She'd failed.

She kept stumbling away from Well in the Woods, hiding from traffic, forcing herself to keep moving. As it got dark, her legs got heavier, and she started to nod off on her feet. Across the street was a huge, green, tree-studded cemetery, and she figured it made sense to sleep there. Terry had gotten his way again. She might as well be dead.

The cemetery was neat as an architect's model: all straight edges, swept sidewalks, orderly rows of identical headstones. Kris collapsed in the bushes behind a stone gazebo on the side furthest from the road. She woke up at 2 a.m., freezing cold, shivering inside her sweats, wondering what to do next.

She couldn't go home. Little Charles would send her back to Well in the Woods and by now her house already had new people living in it. Tuck had betrayed her. Scottie was dead. Terry had won. Whatever he was doing was finished. There was no place left for her anymore.

Kris spent the rest of the night awake, desperate for dawn to come, hands buried between her thighs to keep them warm. Every time she started to fall asleep, she heard the *snap-pop* in Scottie's basement, saw the tears sheeting down his face, saw Angela on the floor staring up at the ceiling, saw Bill questioning her at Well in the Woods, saw the cold white face hissing at her in Gray's room. How did she ever think she could fight Black Iron Mountain? They weren't even human. She was just a musician. Now she wasn't even that. Twenty years ago, Black Iron Mountain had come for Dürt Würk and their touch had poisoned the rest of her life. All she could do now was hide, and hope they forgot about her.

When the sky finally lightened, Kris walked toward the road, her knees so stiff they felt broken. As she passed the small chapel, she saw a woman sitting with her back against the wall, partially hidden by a shrub.

"Morning," Kris said, taking her hands out of her armpits to let the woman know she wasn't a threat.

There were shopping bags stacked on either side of the woman. Her eyes were open, so Kris knew she was awake. She didn't want to get too close, so she tried again.

"You okay?" Kris asked, and as she said it, she knew the woman was dead.

Kris squatted about five feet from the body. The woman was a hard-living forty, or maybe a young-looking sixty, and her chin rested on her chest. She wore a green windbreaker with a Boca Raton Golf Club emblem over the breast and a stonewashed denim miniskirt. She stared down at something between her feet. Dew collected on her face.

Kris went through the dead woman's bags. In the bottom of one she found a $10 bill inside an empty pack of cigarettes and an Oklahoma driver's license identifying her as Deidre McDeere. Kris stole her sneakers. Feeling queasy wasn't an option anymore.

The sneakers cushioned her feet as she walked through the cemetery gate and down the road. The morning traffic thickened. Her stomach growled with every step. A young black woman with short braids shared half of a doughnut with Kris outside a BP gas station. The glazed sugar made Kris's mouth erupt in a waterfall of drool. "I'm trying to lose some pounds," the girl said. "You're doing *me* a favor."

Kris begged for rides at Sunoco gas stations and Wendy's parking lots. She fell asleep under an overpass across from a silent old man with a dozen pairs of dirty socks pulled over his swollen, seeping feet. When she woke up, a gentle rain was falling, the old man was gone, and there was a can of green beans placed by her side. He'd forgotten to leave her a can opener. She walked down the litter-choked shoulders of highways as cars blasted past and picked her way through the long grass at the exits.

She bought $10 of gas for some Guatemalan guys in exchange for a ride to Louisville. They were headed there to do yards, and only one of them spoke English. Kris sat in the back with him and his teenaged cousins as they smoked cigarettes and played on their phones. When she left, they gave her three striped beach towels she could use as blankets.

In Louisville, she found an access ladder on the back of a Shell station and slept on the roof, staring up at the stars. She woke up with *Troglodyte* playing in her brain, mocking her.

"Stop it," she moaned, wrapped in her beach towels, clutching the sides of her skull. "They took three months of my life. Isn't that enough?"

Terry and Black Iron Mountain had won, she had lost. She wasn't going to fight anymore. Terry had finished his five concerts and whatever he was doing was already done, and the world still looked like the same shitty place it always was, full of empty storefronts and full emergency rooms. Street corners held down by fast food restaurants and pawn shops and check-cashing joints, and strip-mall churches preaching prosperity, and little girls clutching dollar-store dolls, and little boys with WIC grape juice staining their tongues.

The billboards and bus stop ads said Dollarwise and Cash Advance, Loan Star, Fastcash, Money Mart, and People Pawn. The margins Kris slipped through were full of people who spent their lives standing in lines and shuffling forward, sitting in hot rooms, waiting to hear their names called by someone holding their file. This was where she belonged. Terry had been one step ahead of her for her entire life.

Security cameras hung from every building. Dome cameras squatted over every door, bullet cameras roosted on building corners, PTZ cameras scanned parking lots with their unblinking plastic eyes. HD cameras, hardened for outdoor use, clung to long metal poles protruding above cell phone arrays, beaming back street images on the cellular network. Kris drifted between them, trying to stay out of sight.

In downtown Louisville a bald evangelist, his beard dyed black, gave out bus tickets to the homeless he said the city was murdering. Each one came with a flier about his ministry being shut down and his shelter being busted. Kris listened to his sermon and took the ticket to St. Louis.

On the way, head leaning against the greasy window, she saw a billboard flashing past, almost too fast to process:

HELLSTOCK '19
KOFFIN RETURNS!
SEPT 6, 7, 8
RIP LAS VEGAS

She turned to the one-legged guy in the seat behind her.

"Did you see that?" she asked.

"That Satanist is doing another Woodstock," One-Leg said. "I was at the original Woodstock, and it wasn't in Las Vegas, that's for sure."

For the rest of the trip he kept tapping Kris on the shoulder to tell her about how much pussy he scored at the original Woodstock. St. Louis couldn't come fast enough.

Kris limped through downtown, getting to-go food bags at a masjid soup kitchen and eating at a nearby park. She slept, wrapped inside her towels, buried deep down in the bushes, trying to disappear. But the Las Vegas dates were a sharp tack in the soft folds of her brain.

"What do you want me to do?" she muttered to herself, limping through downtown St. Louis.

At night, she fell asleep apologizing to Scottie, telling him she was sorry. She couldn't carry the fire. She was just a girl with a guitar, and she didn't even have the guitar anymore. The best thing she could do was disappear. Make sure Terry never found her. Live quietly inside Black Iron Mountain.

The weekend before Labor Day, she wound up outside the big baseball stadium during a Cardinals game. There was a strip of beer halls and outdoor tables across from the stadium where buskers plucked their guitars under a backbeat of coins rattling into paper cups. She eased herself down to sit on the sidewalk, listening to a girl across the street play a battered acoustic guitar. The girl was trying to play "Brown Eyed Girl." She had scabs all over her face, and a long-suffering pit bull puppy tied to a thick piece of rope. After the girl butchered "Hey Jude," Kris couldn't take it anymore and walked over.

"You're out of tune," she said.

The girl ignored her and started playing "Jane Says." Kris squatted and waited for her to finish.

"You're scaring people away," the girl said, not looking at Kris.

"Let me tune it," Kris said. "Please."

The girl looked at her with eyes that were a spooky washed-out blue.

"Play E," Kris said.

The girl plucked E and Kris tightened the lug. Immediately, it sounded like an actual guitar. The girl ran through all the strings as Kris brought them roughly into tune.

Uninvited, she sat on the side of the girl away from the pit bull while she played "The Wind Cries Mary." The girl still sucked, but at least now she sucked in tune.

"Want me to show you a trick?" Kris asked. "It'll help you make more money."

The largest bill in the girl's ragged Starbucks cup was a quarter.

"Bring your pick down, you're dragging it. Look," Kris said, and reached over and guided her hand. The girl stopped missing her E string and sounded better on her sluggish version of "Wish You Were Here." The pit bull got up, moved over to Kris and lay down again, resting his muzzle on her knee. Kris rubbed him between the eyes and he closed them in sleepy bliss.

"Can I play something?" Kris asked after the girl trailed off uncertainly. "I'm Deidre."

The girl didn't answer.

"Just one song?" Kris asked.

The girl handed Kris her guitar and pulled the pit bull onto her lap. Kris balanced the guitar on her right thigh and started to play, just running through scales and chords, warming up her knuckles, making her joints flex. She didn't think about her fingers as they rippled up and down the fretboard. Finally her strumming started to coalesce into music, and what came out of that cheap, chipped piece-of-shit guitar was the blues.

That didn't surprise Kris. Relax any metal song enough and you went right back to the blues. Led Zeppelin covered Memphis Minnie's "When the Levee Breaks." Black Sabbath blew a harp on their first album. Hell, the first band Ozzy and Tony Iommi were in together was called the Polka Tulk Blues Band. Hard rock, heavy metal, stoner rock, doom metal—it all dragged itself up out of the swamp called the blues. Kris started to strum "Red Cross Store" by Mississippi Fred McDowell. Tuck had taught her that one, but that was okay right now. It wasn't Tuck's music, he was just passing it along, from hand to hand, the songs reaching up through time, ready when you needed them.

It took Kris a few bars to get it tight, and then she was loud and confident, its single-chord vamping primal and hypnotic, the tone from the battered crapbox clear as a glass bell ringing down the street. She rolled into "This Land Is Your Land" and change started to rattle into the cup. It felt good to play, and when she slid into an acoustic version of Sabbath's "War Pigs," the girl surprised her by picking up the verse and singing in a slightly cracked voice that stayed roughly on pitch and at least held the rhythm. That was their pattern. The girl sang, Kris played, and they ran through Black Sabbath, Zeppelin, Lead Belly, Phil Ochs, Woody Guthrie, even the Scorpions.

Every song was the same song. These were songs for people who were scared to open their mailboxes, whose phone calls never brought good news. These were songs for people standing at the crossroads waiting for the bus. People who bounced between debt collectors and dollar stores, collection agencies and housing offices, family court and emergency rooms, waiting for a check that never came, waiting for a court date, waiting for a call back, waiting for a break, crushed beneath the wheel.

Kris's hands could barely keep up with the music, but she rode it forward and it carried her, and all the songs were in the language of the cardboard signs she saw everywhere she went. Please Help. Need Help. Help me. Trying to get home. Lost everything. Signs written in want, need, must, hungry, sick, lonely, scared. Songs for people who couldn't escape the weight that pressed down on their backs like a mountain, crushed them to the ground, who couldn't walk because they were too tired, who couldn't run away because their feet were in chains, who couldn't think of a solution because they were too hungry to think past their next meal.

Everyone plays for someone, and Kris didn't play for the big dogs like Sabbath and Zep, she didn't play for the ones who made it, for the wizards who figured out how to turn their music into cars and cash and mansions and an endless party where no one ever gets old. She played for the losers. She played for the bands who never met their rainmaker, the musicians who drank too much and made all the wrong decisions. The singers who got shipped off to state hospitals because they couldn't handle living in the shadow of Black Iron Mountain. She played for the ones who recorded the wrong songs at the right times, and the right songs when it was wrong. The ones who blew it all recording an album that didn't fit the market, the ones who got dropped by their own labels, the singers who moved back home to live in their mom's basements.

She played for the fallen, the forgotten, the footnotes. The people with an eternal gnawing in their bellies, the ones who died hungry, the ones who wanted it so bad but never got a place at the table. She played for the people who worried about the change in their pockets, who had no crumbs on their counters or cans in their cupboards. She played for the people who believed in themselves long after everyone else wised up and moved on. The ones who died still living in hope. She played for the people who made themselves too hard to love, the ones who never read the fine print, who never listened to good advice, the ones who just wanted to play. She played for Scottie.

She played metal. She played country. She played the blues.

The girl kept up where she could, and listened where she couldn't, silently mouthing half-remembered lyrics to the chords. Her pit bull dozed. Eventually the people thinned out and a cop rode up on his bike and told them they didn't have to go home, but they couldn't stay there. He thought he was funny.

At the end of the day, there was $80 in the cup. Kris knew there should be $120. She knew that the girl had slipped $40 into her own pocket, but thinking about money exhausted her. The girl insisted Kris keep the $80 and take the guitar.

"You're better," she said. "You deserve it more."

Kris took the cash but gave back the guitar.

"Keep playing," she said. "A girl with a guitar never has to apologize for anything."

She walked off down Clarke Avenue, her left ear shrilling its high tinnitus E, money in her pocket, knowing now what needed to be done. Just now, she'd conjured up $80 out of thin air, turning sound into money like magic. She had one weapon left. One they couldn't take away.

Back at the Witch House, she remembered Terry showing them what would become the first nu metal Koffin songs. *Troglo-*

dyte was dead and these songs were scrubbed free of mythology, purged of dark hints of powerful forces shaping the world from the shadows. There was a song about trying to get his dad's attention with a catchy funk hook ("Look, look, look at me / What, what, what do you see?). There was a metal-by-way-of-Springsteen power ballad about growing up in the shadow of the steel mills, a screamer about rejection, a thrash-pop number about being alone. She remembered thinking how small metal had gotten. If this was all they could sing about, why bother singing at all? Suddenly, in a violent rush, Scottie Rocket had snatched the pages out of Terry's hands and ripped them in half, threw the pieces up in the air, gotten in Terry's face.

"Wah! Wah! Wah!" he shouted. "No one loves me! Boo hoo! Guess what? We play fucking metal! I don't want to sing about your sad feelings! I want dragons."

All these years later, she finally understood what Scottie meant. She needed to sing songs about something bigger than this world. She needed to play about something more than the soulless country she saw around her. The blues were about the pain and struggle of living inside Black Iron Mountain. Metal showed you a door.

She wasn't famous, she wasn't rich, she didn't even have her own photo ID. She was just a musician. But you fought with the weapons you had, not with the ones you wished for.

Kris couldn't put it off any longer. She bought a ticket to Wichita, Kansas, with everything she had, and got on the bus with empty pockets and an empty stomach, riding through the Midwest to find the one person who hated Terry more than she did, the one person she could maybe still trust.

DJ GORDON G: We've got Tuck Merryweather here, original bass player for Dürt Würk and close personal friend of Terry Hunt. You know, I didn't actually listen to you guys back in the day—what did I miss?

TUCK MERRYWEATHER: Not a lot. I was the rhythm section. Our original drummer was a guy named Jefferson Davis—

DJ GORDON G: Aw, hell no!

TUCK MERRYWEATHER: That was his name.

DJ GORDON G: Did his mama not love him even a little bit?

TUCK MERRYWEATHER: That boy was his own worst enemy. He bungee-jumped out of a tree once with bungee cords tied around his feet and broke both ankles.

(Laughter)

—WXKC Classy 100, "The Lo Down"
October 29, 2010

Don't Break the Oath

When the door of the little house in Valley Center opened, Kris said, "Mrs. Davis, I'm Kris Pulaski from back in Gurner. Is JD home?"

The old woman sighed. She had short, curly hair dyed a shade of red that does not occur in nature and wore enormous round sunglasses. The front pockets of her cardigan bulged with Kleenex and a remote control. There was an oxygen tube running from her nose to a tank at her feet.

"Who?" she asked.

"Kris Pulaski," Kris repeated. "I went to Independence High with JD. I'd love to see him."

The woman's expression didn't change. "No you wouldn't," she said. "No one loves to see my boy. No one's nice to him. He's having a bad day. Come back later."

She started to close the door, but Kris put her foot against it.

"I need his help," she said.

Mrs. Davis stopped pushing. "That's a new one," she said.

She let Kris into a living room containing every home-decor idea Kris had ever seen on TV, all executed at once: ceramic figurines on the mantle, sofas overflowing with decorative pillows, paintings of unicorns and seascapes in massive frames, doilies, and animal-print throw blankets draped over everything.

"Did my son get you pregnant? Steal your car? Did he once take a poke at your little brother?" Mrs. Davis asked.

"I haven't seen JD in over twenty years," Kris said.

"You'd be surprised at how long people hold onto grudges," Mrs. Davis said. "Come on."

She led Kris down the hall and into the kitchen. The floor was shaking. It sounded like a truck was in the basement, blasting its engine, smashing into everything. It took Kris a second to realize it was someone playing super-fast double-stroke drum fills. They sacrificed expression for volume, blasting away with a machine gun made of drums.

Mrs. Davis stood outside a flimsy wooden door, waiting for a break. The drums stopped, silence snapped into place, and she turned to Kris, one hand on the knob.

"It is easy to be unkind to my son," she said. "He's never gotten much from other people except mean. I hope you're not more of the same."

Before Kris could answer, Mrs. Davis pushed open the door, just as the drums started up again, and a battering ram of noise smashed into Kris. She braced herself, descended the stairs, and stepped into Metalhead Valhalla. The walls of the basement were a shrine to Viking metal: photos of Quorthon blown up to the size of religious icons, Amon Amarth posters, framed limited-edition Bathory LPs, and a series of amateur oil paintings depicting Vikings chopping priests in half with their battle axes.

The room was dominated by an enormous drum kit in a dark corner. Behind it was the shadowy outline of a man wearing a horned helmet, pounding away on his skins. He thrashed on his toms, tickled out a final cymbal swell, then silence. He sat, motionless, watching Kris from the dark.

"Hey, JD," Kris said. "It's me. Kris Pulaski. From Dürt Würk."

He didn't say anything.

"Look, it's been a long time," Kris said. "Things have been pretty crazy. But I came out here to see if you . . . you don't ever hear from Terry, do you?"

Kris's eyes started getting used to the darkness. Beneath JD's Viking helmet, he was made of hair. It sprouted from his cheekbones, knitted his eyebrows together, fell from his scalp in waves that splashed off his shoulders and flowed down his back. It formed a bib that hung from his face and covered his chest.

"I came out to say I'm sorry," Kris said. "Turns out Bill was a fucking asshole. We should have stuck with you. It was just, Bill kind of offered himself up after that show at PJ's house and he seemed, you know, like a good guy at the time. We had to do a lot of rehearsing and you didn't like coming to rehearsals. And we didn't know that Bill would grow up to run some kind of mind-control brainwashing prison camp disguised as a rehab clinic. So we made a mistake. I'm sorry. Sincerely. I offer you my full and complete apologies, and while I can't speak for Tuck, I'm pretty sure Scottie would offer his apologies, too."

JD stayed silent, fixing her with a blank stare. Kris had thought through this conversation on the multiple bus trips it took to get here, but unless he started participating, she was running out of material.

"I need your help," she said. "Something happened, a long time ago when we all signed our contracts and it's a little hard to talk about, so I sort of need you to tell me what page you're on.

Terry did something to us, and I think he's doing it again but on a bigger scale at this Hellstock thing. I don't know what your views are on that, but maybe you should tell me before we continue here."

"Terry didn't 'do something.'" This time his response was immediate. "Terry Hunt sold your souls."

That took the wind out of Kris's sails.

"You sell your soul to Black Iron Mountain," JD said, "and the Special Ones come and suck it from your mouth."

The blood stood still inside Kris's body as she remembered the crawling white thing, cold and greedy, looming over her, holding her down.

"I don't even believe in souls," Kris said. "Never been to church once."

"Souls are the best part of us," JD said from the shadows. "Our passions, our dreams. We sell them and lose our creativity, our songs, our spark. We can no longer imagine anything bigger than what's in front of our faces, we can no longer dream of a better world than Black Iron Mountain. Tell me, Kris, you written any new songs lately? Has Terry?"

Kris thought she could write a song if she wasn't so tired, if she wasn't so hungry, if she wasn't so worried about everything all the time, but the truth was that until recently she hadn't even played in six years.

"It's been going on for centuries," JD said. "But it's getting faster now. Terry is speeding everything up. They targeted the musicians first. The bards traveled between tribes, transforming our hopes and fears into epic sagas: Paganini, Robert Johnson, Tartini, Jimmy Page. Once they were perverted, Black Iron Mountain used them to spread their message of emptiness around the world. They couldn't tempt us with anything important, but they could offer us things of minor value, like money and fame. We fell all over ourselves selling the one priceless thing we possessed for trinkets and glass beads.

"Now, people sell their souls for nothing. They do it for a new iPhone or to have one night with their hot next-door neighbor. There is no fanfare, no parchment signed at midnight. Sometimes it's just the language you click in an end-user license agreement. Most people don't even notice, and even if they did, they wouldn't care. They only want *things*. So they sell their souls, and they go to sleep, and the Special Ones crawl out of the dirty corners and lap them up.

"They control everything, they keep us hungry, they keep us in pain, they keep us distracted. Have you noticed how soulless this world has become? How empty and prefabricated? Soulless lives are hollow. We fill the earth with soulless cities, pollute ourselves with soulless albums.

"When the soul is removed it leaves a hole, and we try to fill that hole with so many things—the internet, and conspiracy theories, and CNN, and drugs, and food, but there is only one thing inside that hole, Kris, and that is Black Iron Mountain. It is our jailer, and this is our jail: an eternal, insane hunger that can never be satisfied, a wound that can never be healed, an unnatural desire to consume. Our hunger traps us inside a prison as big as the world. There is no escape. Black Iron Mountain comes for us all."

JD stood up. He took off his horned helmet and stepped into the light.

"I bet you wish you hadn't thrown me out of your band now."

He stood before her, a short, hairy potato of a man wearing

a faded "Valhalla . . . I am coming" T-shirt, radiating intensity.

"Jesus, JD," Kris said, clinging to sanity by her fingertips. "I want to believe you, I really do. And if I was totally out of my fucking mind what you said would make all kinds of sense. But imagine delivering that lecture to someone outside this basement. You sound crazy and paranoid and totally insane."

She braced herself for JD's reaction. Instead of flipping out, he fixed her with a calm eye.

"Kris," he said, "it is possible to be crazy and paranoid and totally insane and still be right. Maybe the problem with everyone is that the world has become so insane they're not out of their minds enough to comprehend it."

Kris thought about the things in the basement JD had called the Special Ones. She thought about contract night.

"You said they ate our souls?" she asked.

"That's what Terry offered them in exchange for fame and fortune," JD said. "When Rob offered him a contract, he didn't sell Black Iron Mountain his soul—he sold them all four of your souls instead. It's worked out pretty well for him."

"I tried to fight," Kris said. "I went after him."

"Where'd that get you?" JD asked. "Stuck in Bill's psycho summer camp. That's where they make their slaves. It's standard MKUltra programming. Psychic driving techniques. Massive doses of scopolamine. The erosion of your personality. When you're finally hollow inside, they give you a monarch tattoo, and send you out into the world until they're ready to activate you."

"Where'd you get all this?" Kris asked. "How come you know more about what happened to me than I do?"

JD sat down at the round coffee table in the middle of the

room, picked up an enormous Ziploc bag of pot, and began to roll a huge joint.

"We're out there," he said. "You soulless people call us crackpots and conspiracy theorists, and you make fun of us for believing in chemtrails and UFOs, and you put us on meds, and ban our YouTube channels, and send us to Bill's little concentration camps whenever you can. But we find each other, we collect information, we listen. You've been living inside Black Iron Mountain for so long you've forgotten what it feels like to be free."

He lit the joint, inhaled, and blew out a long plume of resinous smoke.

"Jesus," Kris said, sitting down across from him, waving away his offer of the joint. "It's like the song. You know, 'The Devil Went Down to Georgia'? I can't believe that after a lifetime of playing metal, it turns out the world is a shitty country song."

JD took another long toke.

"I'm sure you figured out by now that *Troglodyte* is a soothsayer," he said in a tight, strangled voice, letting out a plume of smoke. "There's only three tracks left: 'Sailing the Seas of Blood,' where we go to Las Vegas, 'In the Hall of the Blind King,' where we find Terry, and 'One Life, One Bullet,' where we shoot him."

"Whoa, whoa, whoa," Kris said. "We're not killing anyone."

"He tried to brainwash you," JD said. "He murdered Scottie's entire family. He needs to die."

"No," Kris said. "We're not killing anyone."

"Because that will make us as bad as him?" JD asked in a mocking voice.

"No," Kris said. "Because I'm not a murderer. Neither are you. We're musicians."

"What do you suggest?" JD asked. "Because you've done great so far."

"We follow the album," Kris said. "We go to Las Vegas, we find Terry, and then . . . I don't know. But *Troglodyte* will tell us what to do once we're there."

"Like kill him," JD said.

"What is your problem?" Kris asked. "You sit here, in your mom's basement, getting stoned, banging your drums, going on about killing people like a little boy playing video games. Have you ever seen anyone die? It's . . . " Kris saw Angela falling backward, Scottie Rocket's tear-stained face, the woman in the cemetery. She didn't have the words. "No one else dies, JD."

JD balanced the burning joint on the lip of his ashtray and leaned forward, not pissed, but earnest.

"I have waited for so long," he said, emotion choking his voice. "Keeping my head down so Black Iron Mountain wouldn't spot me, wondering who would stop Terry. Did I need to find him and kill him? Was I Troglodyte? I kept trying to get my life together, but the harder I tried, the more I scared everyone away. I used to have my own apartment. I had a job. But every time I tried to explain the world to people, every time I thought I had friends, they fired me. Everyone thinks I'm crazy, Kris. You're the first person who ever came here, who ever came to my house, and asked me for help. You are Troglodyte."

He raised his hairy arm and showed her a thick, twisted silver bracelet around his wrist. It met in two silver wolves' heads, nose to nose, on the back of his wrist. He placed his right hand over the bracelet.

"The most solemn vow a Viking can make is Odin's Oath,

and I make it now," JD said. "I, Jefferson Davis, swear in the name of him that hung on the tree to let no harm come to you, Kris Pulaski, member of my war band and shield companion. I swear this or my life be forfeit. So be it."

Kris wanted to laugh. Here she was in a basement with a Viking metalhead, the two of them going up against Terry and Black Iron Mountain. It was epically stupid. But she knew better than to laugh at JD.

Instead, she asked, "You got anything to eat?"

Kris took a shower while JD cleaned out the minivan. His mom loaned her a red velour track suit with white piping.

"It's mostly clean and it's in your size," she said.

She gave them a bag of sandwiches while JD got on the phone and arranged for his nephew to check in on his mom while they were gone.

"It'll be a week," he said. "At most."

It was already the end of August. Kris realized her family must think she was dead. Little Charles had probably filed a missing person's report by now. JD threw his duffel bag into the back of the minivan and seemed to hear her thoughts.

"You don't have a home anymore," he said. "You can never return to the Wheel. An album only plays in one direction: forward. But I'll be with you. Every step."

When she used to go on tour, Kris loved the feeling of being on the road, because she knew that every tour was a circle and you always wound up back home. Not this time. She didn't belong anywhere. It felt terrifying.

Finally, they stood in the driveway. JD tied a red-and-black Manowar bandana around his head, which made him look more like a pirate than a Viking.

"You take care of each other," Mrs. Davis said, giving Kris a surprisingly wet kiss on the cheek. "And don't worry about me. Gunnar will be over in half an hour. You two go have fun at your concert."

They climbed into the white Ford minivan.

"Seatbelts," JD said.

They strapped in. Then he turned the ignition and paused for a minute.

"Kris," he said. "Let us go into a battle from which we may never return. But I have sworn Odin's Oath to keep you safe, and I believe in our victory. For our hearts are pure, *Troglodyte* is with us, and I just gave the van its annual emissions inspection."

With that, he dropped the minivan into drive.

"Until Valhalla!" he shouted.

And they took off on their final ride.

DR. LONDON: . . . over two thousand respondents, and from that we established a link between belief in conspiracy theories and negative psychological traits.

RENA TATE: In other words, people who believe in conspiracy theories are more likely to have serious mental health issues?

DR. LONDON: If you believe that the government is hiding aliens in Area 51, or the CIA is trying to control your mind through radio waves, you will almost inevitably demonstrate extremely low self-esteem, and, counterintuitively, very high degrees of narcissism.

—88.1 WDIY, "Health Check"
August 28, 2019

With Oden on Our Side

They drove around the corner and pulled into the parking lot of a stand-up MRI.

"We have to keep moving," Kris said.

JD didn't answer. Instead he opened his door, took out a bottle of pills and dumped them onto the asphalt, stomping them into dust with one of his wide, flat feet.

"Paxator," he told Kris. "I'm off that shit starting now. It makes everything feel like it's wrapped in cotton. Fuck that!"

"I don't know if that's a good idea," Kris said.

"We're on Moscow rules," JD said, ignoring her. He tossed his phone to the asphalt and brought his foot down, shattering its screen.

He slammed his door, pulled out, and Kris bit back her worry. She remembered how in tenth grade JD had dumped a fruit cup in a bottle of Gatorade and carried it around in his backpack for three months because he thought it would turn into wine. One morning, in home room, he drank the entire bottle and puked so far up the walls they had to evacuate the building. They'd been on the road for fifteen minutes and he'd already ditched his prescription. Maybe there was a reason he was still living in his mom's basement.

JD pulled back into traffic. "We have to stay unpredictable!" he said.

His fingers fumbled with the boom box on the console until he found the button he wanted and punched PLAY. A scream tore out of the speakers. It was Bathory's "A Fine Day to Die." Of course, Kris thought, he already had it cued up past the minute-long intro.

"So where are we going?" she asked, raising her voice to be heard over the music.

"Hold on," JD said, holding out a hand to shush her. "I love this part."

Quorthon unleashed a gravel-throated scream as the guitars began tremolo-picking up a scale. Then the song settled back into its thrashy groove.

"I am a seiðmaðr," he said. "I reach out my hand and the universe provides. The less we plan, the better. Then our movements cannot be predicted by the Hundred Handed Eye."

"Then how are we getting to Vegas?" Kris asked.

"A seiðmaðr is a wizard," JD said. "I read the signs, follow the omens, I look for gaps in their net, and slip through, my passing but a shadow on the grass."

Kris began to realize that this might have been a bad idea. She felt out of control, pulled forward by forces she could not comprehend, let alone control. She wanted out. As if he read her mind, JD reached across the seat and grabbed her arm.

"I know you think I'm a joke," he said. "No one ever took me seriously—not in the band, not at Vector Print, not at Quiznos. But I've been preparing for this for ten years. You need me to get you to Terry. I'm the only one who can do it. I really can do magic, Kris."

And then she remembered Bobbie Gilroy, the board tech shaped like a washing machine, who always wore suspenders and tiny black bow ties. Bobbie worked all over the northeast, but one month in 1996 Dürt Würk played Robot House in Philly, Swizzles in York, Unisound in Reading, and Bobbie ran the board at every single show. Their next show was at Old Miami in Detroit, over five hundred miles away, and when they walked into the club, Kris stopped cold. Bobbie stood onstage, bent over, her plumber's butt hanging out, adjusting wedges.

"How the hell?" Kris had asked.

"It's a holy coincidence," Bobbie had told her. "The universe puts you where you need to be."

Holy coincidence, Viking magic, *Troglodyte*—maybe these were the forces that worked against Black Iron Mountain, subtly pulling strings, getting them where they needed to go, keeping them out of sight of the Hundred Handed Eye.

"Okay," she said. "I believe you."

"Good," JD smiled. "We ride!"

As they merged onto the highway, "A Fine Day to Die" entered its breakdown in a sheen of shimmering strings and screaming horses, and JD punched STOP and started fiddling with the radio. He jabbed the scan button again and again, finally stopping on K105. Drive-time radio hurt Kris's ears with its fake attitudes and corporate-controlled playlists, but JD batted her hand away when she reached for the dashboard.

"We need to test the air," he said. "See which way the wind is blowing."

Some girly-sounding boy gasped his feelings through the

speaker, voice auto-tuned to an androgynous whine, the electronic beat precision-engineered for optimum BPM. *When did music get so safe?* Kris wondered. Back in Dürt Würk, they wore their hearts on their sleeves. They may not have been the best band in the world, but they left everything on the floor when they played. This crap was all market-researched lyrics, lab-tested signature changes. She could almost understand how Terry's brand of carefully calculated shock rock would feel like a breath of fresh air after this mall music.

The song ended and JD turned up the radio for the Rush Hour Tower of Power with Cowgirl Carol and the Reject Ranch.

"—got in the studio with us this afternoon a real legend," Cowgirl Carol crooned. "In a minute we're going to Jack Hoff in the field for 'Where's My Monkey?', but right now, he's the man who made Koffin the biggest act on the planet—producer, promoter, manager, and musical mastermind Robert Anthony."

A complicated sound effect ensued that began with the Reject Ranch cheering ironically, someone blowing a warble on a slide whistle and a *Wayne's World* riff on an electric guitar, and it ended with a bike horn being honked.

"Hey, Rob," a sultry woman's voice said, "what are you up to after the show?"

"Hanging out with you," Rob said in his California voice.

"OOOooooo," went everyone in the studio.

Everything disappeared except the radio voices. Kris saw Rob, sitting in the studio, grinning like the Cheshire Cat, a shimmering heat mirage of dark blue eyes, blinding white teeth, tousled blond hair. Hearing his voice in the car felt too close, it made her skin feel greasy.

"I don't want to listen to this," she said, reaching for the radio.

JD put his hand over the buttons, angling the wheel with his other hand as they merged onto Route 75.

"I love a man with a tan," the woman said.

"Back, slut," Cowgirl Carol said. "We're here to talk serious business. Rob, we've known each other for a long time."

"Since 2003," he purred.

"I didn't know you were from the Stone Age," a sidekick snickered, followed by a prerecorded clown laugh.

"We met at the Marconi awards, and even back then, I knew you were ahead of your time," Cowgirl Carol said. "You were dedicated one hundred percent to Koffin, and I thought—I still think—single artist representation is the wave of the future."

"I just feel," Rob said, moving closer to the mic and using his sincere voice, "that focusing on one artist gives you a longer career. You take a journey together, you reap the rewards together. It's like watching a caterpillar turn into a butterfly."

Kris put her fingers in her ears.

"Listen!" JD said, raising his voice, startling Kris into dropping her hands. "Every word is information we need."

"And you face dangerous times together," Cowgirl Carol prompted.

"And, yes, these are dangerous times," Rob said. "I wish that wasn't true."

"So I want our listeners to know that you're here for a very serious reason today," Cowgirl Carol said. "Koffin's got Hellstock '19 coming up in Las Vegas, and you've had to hire extra security. Which is crazy."

"What we have," Rob said, "is a very sad story. A lot of

people know that before Koffin was formed, Terry was in a metal band from Pennsylvania called Dürt Würk. They were basically a bar band, and Terry was the real creative talent. And now that he's looking back on all the songs and all the years and celebrating a life in music, one of his old bandmates is very bitter, very jealous, and she's stalking him."

"Oh my God," Cowgirl Carol gasped.

"She's c-c-c-crazy," the sidekick said.

"We live in a country where there's a second amendment, and that's part of our constitution," Rob said. "But it also allows unbalanced people to become a danger to themselves and, as is sadly true in this case, to Terry. This individual, her name is Kris Pulaski, and we know she escaped from a substance abuse treatment facility where her family had placed her for very good reasons. From what we've heard, she is armed, and has threatened to murder Terry."

"That's terrifying," Cowgirl Carol said.

Kris's hands became fists in her lap as she listened to them lie.

"The police are taking it very seriously," Rob said. "Our number one concern is the safety of our fans."

"So what can our listeners do?" Cowgirl Carol said. "Because rock and roll is about having a good time, and when these . . . *fanatics* take it too far, it destroys the scene for everyone."

"I don't want anyone to do anything dangerous," Rob said, and Kris could hear his forehead wrinkle with concern as his voice dropped to an earnest pitch. "But if you see Kris Pulaski, do not approach her, do not speak to her, but alert the police right away. And I would also like to say, that in all my years of working in the music industry, this is the most serious threat to an artist I have ever witnessed. And there's another tragic footnote to this whole story: she may have also killed one of her other bandmates and his entire family. We don't have any hard evidence of that yet, but . . . well, I'll let your listeners draw their own conclusions."

Kris could not move.

"Okay," Cowgirl Carol said. "We've got a picture of this *person* up on the website, and like Rob said, do not do anything dangerous. At the same time, keep your eyes peeled, and if you see this sicko—and there is no other word for her—call the police *immediately*. In times like these we have to protect our artists who give us so much great entertainment."

"Thank you very much, Carol," Rob breathed. "And I know Terry thanks you, too."

Kris's fists were clenched so tight her palms bled. JD punched off the radio.

A brown hatchback passed on the right, and in the back window was a sticker of Calvin peeing on a Nike logo tucked next to a Gothic *K*. The truck in front of them had a Koffin *K* etched into the dirt on its rear doors.

JD's paranoia didn't seem so crazy anymore. The Hundred Handed Eye was looking for them.

MALE ANNOUNCER: . . . three exciting stages, fifty of the hottest bands, at the most extreme musical experience in the history of man.

KENDALL JENNER (prerecord): Avenged Sevenfold, Slipknot, Slayer, Trivium, Kamelot, Cannibal Corpse, Pallbearer . . .

MALE ANNOUNCER: Hellstock 2019, in Strawberry Valley, Nevada, with bungee-jumping platforms, fire sculptures, and X-treme intensity.

KENDALL JENNER (prerecord): . . . Purple Hill Witch, Earthless, Wolves in the Throne Room, Molotov, and me, Kendall Jenner.

MALE ANNOUNCER: Hellstock 2019. Brought to you by Bud Light, the World's Favorite Light Beer.

—Hellstock 2019 Radio Promo Spot
August 20, 2019

Twilight of the Gods

For almost seven days, the Hundred Handed Eye blocked them at every turn. They tried I-70, but before it bent onto I-15, which would take them to Las Vegas, highway construction pushed them onto 191, which turned south toward Mexico, away from Vegas. Every alternate route they tried was clogged with accidents, ICE checkpoints, toll roads covered with cameras, and DUI roadblocks.

JD looked for blind spots in the Hundred Handed Eye where they could slip through the gaps, but there were precious few. Meanwhile, NPR cranked out subliminal tones that induced complacency. Clear Channel encoded messages encouraging despair on low frequencies. Billboards lining the highway featured arrangements of colors that numbed drivers with choice paralysis.

Black Iron Mountain loomed over everything. There were no accidents. Coincidence didn't exist. The world was thick with meaning, and they were both targeted.

JD distracted himself from the hunt closing in around them by investing more and more faith in *Troglodyte*.

"In 'Sailing the Seas of Blood' there are five verses and six repeats of the chorus," he said. "We need to take Highway 56."

Kris found it on the map.

"But that's way north," she said. "And then we have to head back down to McPherson? That doesn't make any sense."

"'Sentinels stride crimson waves,'" JD quoted. "'Their searchlight eyes seeking escaped slaves.'"

He quoted "Sailing the Seas of Blood" at her until she stopped arguing.

"You know, Terry probably has a copy of that album, too," Kris said. "It might not be the best idea to base our route on it."

"*Troglodyte* guides us," JD said.

When he wasn't talking about *Troglodyte* he talked about killing Terry. Eventually Kris gave up reminding him that it wasn't going to happen. For now, she needed him to keep them unpredictable, to keep them moving, to keep them out of sight of the Hundred Handed Eye. And mostly it worked. As JD said, he reached out his hand and the universe provided.

Every few hours, JD stole a car. They pulled into an airport parking lot and drove out twenty minutes later in a rust-red Dodge Caliber. They pulled over in front of an abandoned Ford F-350 with its hazard lights blinking on the shoulder of the highway, took the note off its windshield that read "Gone to get water," and drove it fifty miles before the engine overheated. They swapped it in a mall parking lot for a lime-green Mitsubishi Eclipse. He always found the keys, the cars always started, no one ever spotted them.

"By the time the cops are looking for the car we stole in Provo, we're already in the car from Cherry Creek," he said.

The only thing that stayed constant between cars was JD's boom box, blasting out an endless stream of Viking metal when he wasn't scanning the airwaves for news about the Great Hunt.

A sad banjo played the familiar "All Things Considered" theme, and then one of those professors with a complicated name was speaking.

" . . . a tragic story of greed, and envy," the reporter said. "Onetime bandmate of Terry Hunt, the heavy-metal legend who performs under the name Koffin—that's Koffin with a 'K' . . . "

WABC News Hour Radio.

". . . Kris Pulaski apparently bears a grudge, and police are taking this very seriously . . . "

Clear Channel Wire Service News.

". . . Hunt embarks next week on Hellstock '19, an epic concert in the desert outside Las Vegas with almost half a million tickets sold . . . "

News, traffic, and weather kept them informed of where they'd been spotted at the top of every hour.

" . . . learning that the would-be assassin is traveling with another of Hunt's former bandmates, Jefferson Davis, who goes by the nickname JD. Listeners are advised . . . "

" . . . last spotted near Omaha, Nebraska, driving a white Chevrolet van. Authorities speculate . . . "

" . . . conspiracy? This guy, he plays heavy metal, and we all know they're Satanists, and suddenly after Shillary loses the election his old cult mates want to kill him? This makes Pizzagate look like . . . "

Rob gave interviews and spurred on the Hunt.

"I'm sure the murderer of the Borzek family was Scott Borzek," he said. "But you also have to look at the facts. A member of this band has died while Kris Pulaski was in his house and her therapist at a rehab facility was brutally beaten. She has threatened Terry's life. We're taking this very seriously."

Kris saw how Black Iron Mountain thrust its fist into reality and controlled the world. But that was wrong. Black Iron Mountain convinced the world to control itself.

"'Fifty states of gore,'" JD sang to himself. "'Between Troglodyte and the door / Bound by what we swore / On this sea of horror / It always offers more.'"

Kris watched another billboard go past featuring another celebrity she didn't know hawking another product she didn't want: Hannibal Green for Wine Shooters, Samantha Kay for Diet Now, Karl Charles for Kentucky's Own. More summer blockbusters, more digitally sculpted girls showing pixel-polished flesh. Rappers, athletes, actresses, stock photo celebrities sporting clip art beauty. Dead echoes in an empty room.

And all the time, the Hundred Handed Eye kept searching.

" . . . body count of four people dead and one critically injured. We have to ask ourselves: where does this end?"

" . . . the ugliest stalking incident in the history of rock and roll . . . "

" . . . witnesses and family members are being interviewed and police in eleven states are determined not to let . . . "

JD smoked pot constantly. Whenever he stole a car he rolled a joint. At first, he smoked them while driving, but then Kris insisted he at least park when he smoked.

"You can't drive fucked up," Kris said.

"Without my meds, I need it to level me," he said, eyes streaming. "I'm fine."

"Let me drive," Kris said.

"You don't have a license," JD said. "If I get stopped we have a chance, if you get stopped, it's game over."

Then he imitated Bill Paxton in *Aliens*, saying, "Game over, man," for ten minutes.

Every day he became more erratic and Kris got more and more anxious as the start date for Hellstock '19 approached and they couldn't get any closer to Vegas. They spiraled around the city, unable to approach it directly, kept away by detours, and police checkpoints, and highway closures, no matter which route they tried.

They drove through the night, occasionally napping in mall parking lots. JD shoplifted frozen burritos from supermarkets and let them thaw on the dashboard. He abandoned his boom box in a landscaper's pickup truck outside Garden City, Kansas, and scanned the radio, hopping from station to station, listening to the same wire-service stories about the Great Hunt thirty times a day as the Hundred Handed Eye searched for them. Its gaze was a hundred million spotlights, sweeping the seas of blood for signs of their passing.

Billboards of Terry's blind face, streaked with rivers of black gore, loomed up ahead, over them, and disappeared behind them. All around them cars swirled and swarmed, pushing west to worship their God. Black Honda Accords with Gothic *K*s on their rear windshields, guys driving Ford Tauruses with their windows down, long hair fluttering in the wind, the occasional Chevy Econoline full of girls in black lipstick. Each one heading for the end of the world.

Three days until showtime, they found themselves stuck in New Mexico.

"What if we go south and come at Vegas from the west?"

Kris asked, looking at the road atlas.

"Maybe we should be looping up into South Dakota," JD said, ignoring her. "Wounded Knee might be a blind spot in the Hundred Handed Eye."

"That's hundreds of miles back the way we came," Kris said.

JD sang the chorus from "Sailing the Seas of Blood": "Sailing the seas of blood / Riding a gory flood / From sea to dark red sea / Gettysburg to Wounded Knee."

"It's five hundred miles due north," Kris said, losing her cool. "Do you know how long that'll take?"

"Maybe Gettysburg is the answer," JD mused to himself.

"Jesus Christ!" Kris said. "That's a thousand miles back to Pennsylvania. We have to keep heading towards Vegas."

JD erupted in a fury, pounding on the steering wheel, thrashing his head from side to side, screaming at the top of his lungs, punching the ceiling.

"I don't know what to do anymore!" he yelled.

Kris looked around at the cars approaching them from behind, about to pass them, and panicked.

"Stop," she shouted. "You need to stop!"

He kept screaming, banging his head back and forth so hard his Manowar bandana flew off into the back seat. Instantly, he calmed, breathing hard. The cars passed them smoothly in the other lane. Kris gave it a minute before she leaned over the back seat and picked up his bandana. It was incredibly heavy. Silver metal strips were stapled to the inside. Immediately, she knew what they were.

"You've got a tin foil hat," she said, heart sinking.

He snatched it out of her hands.

"Hold the wheel!" he snapped, tying it around his head. "This is lead foil! Tin foil is for paranoid lunatics. My head is not a baked potato."

His anger melted into a stoned giggling fit.

"Baked potato!" he wheezed.

Kris finally realized this wasn't going to work.

"Pull into this rest stop," she said.

CARSON DALY: I saw the lineup for Hellstock '19 and I think people are going to be amped, they're going to be excited.

ROB ANTHONY: We hope so.

CARSON DALY: Why don't you tell us a little bit about this, because as a huge fan of Koffin, I couldn't be more stoked.

ROB ANTHONY: Terry will play his entire discography starting with the most recent album and ending with the earliest. In a way, it's a journey back through time beginning with *Insect Narthex*, then *Necrosex*, and finally *Witch Slave*, and he may even go earlier than that, back to his Dürt Würk days. As you know, the original bass player and the drummer for Dürt Würk will be at the shows. So who knows?

CARSON DALY: Any chance he'll play *Troglodyte*?

ROB ANTHONY: No, despite the mythology around *Troglodyte*, it's not a very good album. Terry would rather leave fans with memories of his actual good work.

—97.1 KAMP, "Carson Daly Mornings"
September 4, 2019

Master of Puppets

JD didn't say anything, just followed the curve of the right-hand lane off the highway and into the rest area hardscape: a black asphalt parking lot with a grass clearing on the right. In the middle of the clearing was a small brick amenities building with toilets and vending machines. On the southern end were three concrete picnic tables rooted beneath some scrubby pines. There were two parked cars, and all the other spaces were empty. JD parked near the picnic tables, at least thirty empty parking spaces away from the bathrooms. He handed Kris a packet of Kleenex.

"I have to go, too," he said, not mentioning his temper tantrum. He pointed toward a utility shed next to the picnic tables. "You go over there and I'll use the bushes."

A maroon minivan glided in behind them and rolled down to the far end of the lot. Kris put one hand on the door handle and faced forward while she spoke.

"When I get back," Kris said, "we need to reassess."

"What?" JD said. "You're not making any sense."

"I think I'll do better on my own," Kris said.

"But," he said, the car rocking as he turned to face her, "I swore Odin's Oath. I'm not ditching you when we're so close."

Kris opened her door and put one foot on the asphalt.

"That's the thing," she said. "We're not close. I think I have to do this part without you."

Before JD could say anything else, Kris leaned into him. His hair stunk like a wild animal and was stiff with dried sweat. She gave him a one-armed hug.

"You're a good guy, JD," she said. "You got me this far, but I can make it from here. Go home. Take care of your mom."

She got out and slammed the door. JD gaped at her through the passenger side window as she waved goodbye. He scrabbled for his door handle, but Kris knocked on the hood. He looked up. She shook her head. His hairy face got hard and he looked down at his lap, then leaned forward and turned the ignition. Hot air blew on Kris from the front grille as JD slammed the car into reverse and rolled backward. Kris lifted her hand again. JD didn't wave back. He just drove away, burning a little rubber to show he was pissed off.

Kris watched him go, then turned and walked to the bathroom. She felt relieved, and eager to get moving. She didn't know how she'd get to Las Vegas, she didn't know how she'd stay free, but JD had taught her to stay in the blind spots, slip through the cracks, exist in the margins, trust her instincts. She'd keep her ears open for signs. It'd be easier without him around.

Kris pushed into the cool green bathroom and her eyes instantly adjusted from daylight to the artificial fluorescents. She picked the farthest stall, latched the door, and lowered herself to the seat. Her thighs were covered in faded yellow bruises, her knuckles were scraped raw, her right shoulder was stiff. Her body ached like something had been kicking her from the inside. Her ass was sore from sitting.

She took her time, trying to postpone making a decision about what came next. Being in the bathroom felt like a break from the world. From out of nowhere, the urge for a cigarette hit her. She hadn't had one in years, not since her touring days, but right now, on the road again by herself, it sounded exactly right.

She finished up, ran some water over her hands, wiped them on her velour sweatpants, and walked outside. A couple more cars had pulled into the parking lot, and a handful of people roamed the dry grass, stretching their legs. In front of Kris, a girl in a long black skirt and black T-shirt was hunched over her phone, blocking the concrete walkway, thumbing away at a message, a cigarette jammed in the corner of her mouth. Kris could taste the sharp smoke. She followed her instincts.

"Excuse me?" Kris said. The girl looked up. Her black lipstick coated the filter. "Can I bum one of those?"

The girl stared at her, mouth tight, eyes squinted. Kris tried again.

"Just one?" she asked. The girl kept staring, eyes scrunched up like she had a headache. "You know what? Never mind. I shouldn't smoke anyways."

Kris turned to go but the sidewalk was blocked by a young guy, heavyset with a cursive neck tattoo, filming her on his phone, his attention totally focused on its tiny screen. Kris put her head down and walked off the concrete sidewalk, across the crunchy brown grass, headed for the far end of the parking lot, wanting to disappear. She'd get into the woods and strike off alongside the highway toward Vegas, keeping parallel to the road as much as she could. There were too many people here.

Ahead of her, standing between the hoods of two parked Hondas, a man and a woman in matching olive hiking shorts and Patagonia fleeces had their phones out, held landscape, tracking her as she passed. Kris stopped and gave them a hard stare but they didn't waver, and that's when she realized that more cars were pulling into the parking lot: a black SUV with Florida plates, a red Volvo with tinted windows, a white Volkswagen Jetta. The lot was filling up.

Kris started walking faster, and the couple came toward her, phones out. One quick look over her shoulder showed three people in matching UCLA sweatshirts behind the girl in the black skirt, all of them with their phones out, all of them following Kris. She sped up. Behind her, their footsteps got faster.

An electric shock ran through Kris's left shoulder. The girl in the black skirt had shoved her. Kris stopped, turned, and saw a wall of people behind the girl, all of them bearing down on her, all of their phones out, all of them staring at her tiny image on their screens, fitting her into their phones, capturing her in their hands.

In the back of the crowd, stragglers ran to catch up while directly in front of Kris, the girl in the black skirt stood with her phone jammed in Kris's face.

"You dirty slut," the girl spat, hatred in her voice.

The crowd closed in around Kris, making a circle with her at its center. A thicket of arms, each holding a phone, shooting her chest, her crotch, her stomach, her eyes, getting her from every angle. They crowded in, a wall of blank faces staring at her digital image. Kris couldn't breathe. Some were older, middle-aged, and there was even a grandmother with puffy white hair who reminded her of her mom, holding her phone out, standing next to an older gentleman in a black POW/MIA baseball cap. They talked to each other about her, their voices dripping with rage.

" . . . stalking Terry Hunt . . . "

" . . . whore . . . "

" . . . sleazebag . . . "

" . . . fucking lynch her . . . "

The Hundred Handed Eye had found her.

Far back, outside the circle, Kris saw people asking each other what was going on.

"Help me!" she shouted, trying to get their attention.

They heard her, but instead of coming to her rescue they pulled out their phones and shot the crowd, curious to see what would happen next. In the middle of this crowd, Kris stood alone.

Then the music started. A white van by the toilets had its side doors open, and Kris heard the unmistakable industrial howl of the intro, and then Koffin's "Stand Strong" began to play.

The crowd reached for Kris and she stepped back, bumping into hands holding phones. She spun around, but they were everywhere. Fear turned her guts to water. She wanted another chance. A do-over. She didn't want to die here. She felt so stupid. She'd walked right into Black Iron Mountain's arms.

WHOOOOOOOOOONK!

A car horn, loud and sustained, cut through Koffin's anthem, and Kris looked past the reaching arms and saw JD's car screech to a halt on the other side of the line of parked cars. He leaned across the center console and shoved open the passenger side door.

"Odin's Oath!" he shouted.

Kris's heart leapt.

She pushed forward toward him, but they shoved her back,

keeping her trapped. The crowd flowed and reshaped, more of them between her and the cars, blocking JD from view with their black T-shirts, and pink button-ups, and baggy camo shorts, and their beards and their ponytails. Behind Kris, away from the parking lot, the crowd thinned and she took her chance. She elbowed the POW/MIA-capped man in the gut and he lost his footing and stumbled. Kris stepped past him, through the break, and made an end run around the crowd, going deeper into the grassy area, away from the parking lot. The crowd flowed fast, spreading out in a line, pressing her back, putting themselves between her and JD's car.

JD reversed to keep up with Kris as she ran deeper into the field, his passenger-side door open. She heard him shout something but it was lost over their voices:

". . . bitch . . ."

" . . . slut . . . "

" . . . dyke . . . "

Kris broke into a run, triggering the entire herd. They came for her in force, flowing over the field, moving fast. She ran, full out, sprinting for the utility shed. If she could make it past them and then cut between the parked cars and get to the other side, she'd meet JD's reversing car and get in, or jump on the trunk, or cling to the hood.

An inarticulate roar went up as Kris passed the leading edge of the crowd and zagged to the right, stepped onto the sidewalk. The mob was at least eighty people strong now, strung out across the rest area. They were too close, arms reached for her, fingers strained, but then a Chinese girl in jean shorts dropped her phone and bent down and the yoga couple behind her and the heavyset guy with the beard fell over her, creating a human logjam, and Kris gave a final burst of speed and slipped between an electric-blue minivan and a red Volvo station wagon inches ahead of a huge guy with a neck beard. His outstretched fingers brushed her right shoulder, and then Kris was free.

The crowd screamed with rage. Women sustained high notes, while men bellowed lower ones. Their pursuit slowed as they filtered between the parked cars and Kris's heart gave a joyous flex when she saw nothing but empty asphalt between herself and JD's car, gears whining, passenger door open. She closed the gap and caught the doorframe, swinging both feet inside, dropping her butt onto the seat.

"Go!" she shouted.

A fourteen-year-old kid with a gray hoodie and an activity strap on the back of his glasses got between the open door and the car, his legs pumping furiously. Kris let the forward motion of the car help her slam the door and it bounced off his shoulder and the kid went down, eating street in a tumble of arms and legs.

"Until Valhalla!" JD yelled, shooting Kris a victorious grin.

Latecomers who hadn't reached the main body of the crowd poured onto the asphalt in front of them, flying out from between the parked cars, some of them stopping with their phones outstretched while others ran at the car. A young black guy in baggy white basketball shorts and a goatee was the first to get in front of them, and the front bumper clipped his legs out from under him, sending him pinwheeling up the hood, smacking into the windshield, which cracked into a silver star.

JD jammed on the brakes and the kid unwound back down the hood and hit the pavement hard. JD tried to steer around him, but it was too late. The fastest members of the crowd were on them. A middle-aged man in a suit stepped onto the bumper, then the hood, and bounced the car with his feet. Hands slapped Kris's window. People crawled onto the trunk. All Kris could see through the windows were hands, screaming mouths, black rectangles with glass lenses recording it all. The sound of drumming filled the car.

"Go!" Kris screamed, terrified.

JD revved the engine but kept his foot on the brake as more and more people poured in front of them. The car began to rock on its shocks as the screaming crowd pushed it from side to side.

"We have to go!" Kris yelled.

"I can't!" JD yelled back, his voice choked. Kris looked over. JD was on the verge of tears, his eyes wild, nostrils flaring. "They're people!"

His bandana had slipped off his head and lay on the center console, leaving his hair to hang in his eyes. He gripped the steering wheel so hard it bent. They were trapped.

"They're not going to stop," Kris shouted to be heard over the drumming and screaming. "You have to drive through them."

JD whipped the steering wheel to the left, then the right. The pounding got louder. JD eased up on the brake and the car jerked forward, and Kris felt relief run through her body. Then JD's window exploded.

Pebbles of safety glass showered his hair and face and bounced off Kris's neck, unleashing the roar of the furious crowd. Hands slapped into JD's face, grabbing his hair, his shirt, his arms. Kris screamed, and JD thrashed and bellowed, but that exposed his tongue and fingers forced their way inside his mouth, hooked his left cheek, grabbed his tongue by the root. JD clung to the wheel as hundreds of hands pulled him out through the window by his lips. Hands pried his fingers off the steering wheel, breaking them with hollow pops, and JD screamed as his left cheek stretched like bubblegum, and then fissures appeared, filled with red, widened, and his cheek came loose from his face and white gobbets of fat and red blood flowed down his hairy chin and the front of his shirt in a bib.

Kris stretched her left leg over the center console, past JD's thrashing legs. She found the accelerator, stepped on it, and the car jerked forward five feet before it caught on something and the engine revved, threatening to stall. The hands still had JD, and they dragged him backward through the window by his mouth and hair, leaving only his enormous belly and legs in the car. Kris grabbed onto his belt and jammed her foot down on the accelerator.

The air behind Kris's head exploded and pebbles of safety glass blew all over the back of her neck and tumbled inside her tracksuit as hands grabbed her by the hair and hauled her backward. She clung to JD's belt with one hand, held onto the steering wheel with the other, and hands tore at her ears, grabbed her neck, and she thought her elbows were going to shatter, she thought her fingers were going to pop.

Kris threw all her weight onto her left toes as her body slid backward out of the car, and the car lurched forward, hung for a second, then screamed forward again, the front bumper making hollow *thunk*s as it threw people aside. The hands in her hair pulled her head back until she heard the vertebrae at the base of her skull pop, and then there was a searing pain in her scalp and the sound of her hair ripping out by the roots echoed inside her skull, and it was so painful she went blind for a full three seconds. JD slipped from her hand, then she gave a tremendous yank and he was back inside the car most of the way, and Kris was covered up to her shoulder in his hot blood and they were rolling forward.

"Guk!" JD choked, and Kris looked.

The white bone of his throat was totally exposed, and she watched a knob of cartilage work itself up, then down, as he tried to speak. His beard had only a few hairs left now and his left cheek was completely gone, showing a sideways grin. His dislocated jaw jutted out to form a grotesque, one-sided underbite. His left eye was a hole leaking white jelly. His scalp hung in a flap against the side of his face, exposing half a dome of raw bone.

Kris pressed her foot down on the accelerator harder, terrified to stop, people bouncing off the front bumper, spinning to the side. She checked fast over her shoulder as they cleared the last of the crowd and she saw them still running after her car, making calls, sending texts, filming her license plate as she raced toward the highway.

ROB ANTHONY: Not many people know how committed Terry is to helping the people who've helped him, and he views his Saturday night performance at Hellstock 2019 as a tribute to everyone who helped Koffin on its journey. To that end, he's invited Tuck Merryweather, the bass player from Dürt Würk, his very first band, and Bill Thompson, Dürt Würk's original drummer, to join him onstage.

ANN BOX: Unfortunately, there's a sad story there.

ROB ANTHONY: Jefferson Davis, also a member of Dürt Würk, was a troubled individual and Terry has reached out to his family. And Kris Pulaski is . . . well . . . Terry hopes that she'll have the good sense to turn herself in to the authorities. His number one concern is the safety of his fans.

—106.7 KROQ, "The Big Box"
September 6, 2019

Into Glory Ride

Kris stood on the accelerator, all her weight hanging from her wrists, fingers clamped around the steering wheel, trying not to rest on JD. Her butt was on his thigh, right foot trapped on the passenger side, straddling the center console. She roared forward, merging onto the highway.

JD's blood beaded along the top of the doorframe and the wind flicked fat drops away. She yanked the wheel left to merge, trying to put as much distance between herself and the rest stop as possible, and a car laid on its horn, but no one hit her and she mashed the gas pedal all the way to the floor because she wanted to stay ahead of any cars, and their horns faded away behind her.

Wind roared through the shattered windows, making the blood tacky beneath her hands, gluing them to the wheel. Blood drooled down the back of her neck from her torn scalp, and the rest stop was a half mile behind, three-quarters of a mile, one mile, three miles, but she still didn't feel safe.

A big green sign announced the exit for Battery Road and she put her weight on JD's leg and eased up on the accelerator as she curved off the exit, the g-force trying to flip the car. All her weight went into her heel as she switched her foot to the brake, rolled slow through the stop sign at Battery, and took a right leading away from the highway.

JD's body slumped to the left as she made the turn, and didn't sit back up, and she knew he was gone. It took three miles to find what she needed, two miles beyond where she thought she'd go insane if she didn't get away from his corpse. But if there was one thing she was learning it was that she could endure anything, even the unendurable.

She found an abandoned hotel, unbranded, no glass, its exterior walls built and rooms framed before the developers ran out of cash, or maybe discovered toxic waste on the site, or embezzled all their funds and split. It sat at the end of a crumbling road blocked by a single, sagging chain. Kris drove up into the weeds, around the chain, and parked behind the hotel.

She didn't let herself look at JD until she was out of the car. Then she forced herself to take it all in. His exposed teeth and bones were blood-slimed. His broken fingers jutted off in different directions. His face was flayed and hairless. His remaining eye stared at the rearview mirror.

Kris popped the trunk and found three hot Budweiser tallboys in an empty cooler and poured them all over her head, scrubbing her face, knowing it was better to smell like a drunk than be covered in gore. The warm beer burned her scalp where chunks of her hair had been torn out.

She checked herself in the passenger side mirror: bedraggled, wet, skin stained red, eyes insane. Then came the hard part. She rolled JD's uncooperative corpse to one side and pulled out his wallet. It contained $25. She picked up his Manowar bandana from the floor, and tied it gently over her bloody scalp. It pressed down on her raw skull like iron.

"I'm sorry," Kris said to JD's body.

She made herself memorize his swollen tongue, his missing cheek, the wet eye socket. Another person, crushed beneath Black Iron Mountain. She wished she could light the car on fire and give him the Viking funeral he deserved, but she didn't have any matches. Kris turned and walked away.

A three-mile hike got her back to the highway overpass. Only two cars passed her on Battery Road. She was too tired to run, and there was a long list of things that had to be done before she could stop walking. Just thinking about that list exhausted her.

At the Citgo on the other side of the underpass she bought a bottle of water with JD's money.

"Bathrooms are for customers only," the grizzled guy behind the register said. "Five dollar minimum."

Kris added a pair of scissors and a "Just Visiting" Roswell T-shirt and that earned her the key and left her with $9.

In the bathroom, she scrubbed off the remaining gore with the water and then cropped her hair close. She wrapped the pieces in paper towel and buried them at the bottom of the garbage can, not because the gas station seemed like the kind of place that would care if she left a pile of hair in the sink, but because she didn't want Black Iron Mountain to track her here and learn she had cut her hair and changed her appearance.

Then she pressed the lead foil down as flat as she could and tied JD's Manowar bandana back around her head. There was no choice but to think like him now. She had no one to watch her back, no one to keep her safe. She was on her own.

Cleaned up, an ad for New Mexico's UFO industry across her chest, Kris waited in the parking lot and finally intercepted a guy in a Crosby, Stills & Nash reunion hoodie. He had a red goatee and a receding hairline.

"I got in a fight with my husband," Kris said. "He threw me out of the car up the road. Can I get a ride?"

"Your head is bleeding," he said.

Kris wiped the blood away.

"He drinks."

"I can't get involved," the guy said.

Kris saw the clerk giving her the stink eye from inside. It was only a matter of time before he called the cops, and then the Hundred Handed Eye would find her. She needed to get walking.

"Hey," a voice said from behind Kris. "I heard what you said about your husband."

Kris turned around. A young girl on the curvy side with long black hair stood behind her, smacking gum.

"I'm okay," Kris told her.

"Said the woman with the bleeding scalp." The girl blew an enormous bubble and popped it. "Where're you going?"

"I said I'm fine." Kris started to walk away.

The girl stepped in front of her and stuck out her hand.

"Melanie Gutiérrez. I'm heading to Las Vegas." She gestured to a dirty white Subaru with West Virginia plates. "Don't worry. I just got a new transmission."

Kris stopped. You reached out your hand and the world provided. Holy coincidence, Viking magic, *Troglodyte*—whatever you called it, she'd be a fool to refuse.

"I'm Deidre," she said, shaking hands.

"We have to watch out for each other on the road," Melanie said. "The guys aren't going to do it, right?"

"Right," Kris said.

DAVE KING: The crowd was crazy. They looked like they were trying to kill Pulaski and the hairy guy.

CARRIE MOSTE: I understand you were scared, but, Dave, I've got the police report right here, and they saw something different.

DAVE KING: You can see it on my phone.

CARRIE MOSTE: And definitely, in this video you took, there is definitely a crowd around Kris Pulaski, but where you see angry people trying to attack her, I see scared people trying to detain her until the police can arrive.

DAVE KING: No one called the police.

CARRIE MOSTE: They have recordings, Dave.

DAVE KING: I had another video, you could see them surround their car and—

CARRIE MOSTE: —try to stop them from fleeing the scene—

DAVE KING: —they tore the hairy guy apart.

CARRIE MOSTE: On this other video? Can I see it?

DAVE KING: It's deleted off the cloud. I can't find it.

CARRIE MOSTE: I appreciate you coming in to speak with us. Listeners, we'll be bringing you live updates as we get them.

—102.7 KJYO, "The Night Stalker"
September 6, 2019

Little Sparrow

"I like your tracksuit," Melanie said, as they pulled out of the gas station and back onto the highway. "It's very hip-hop."

"Okay," Kris said.

She looked at every car they passed, considered every driver and passenger, trying to see them before they saw her. Had they been at the rest stop? Were they from Well in the Woods? Were they looking for her?

"You want to get on the floor?" Melanie asked.

"What?" Kris asked.

"The way you're looking at all the other cars. I thought maybe you were scared your husband might see you. So if you want to get on the floor, I won't think it's weird or anything."

Kris considered Melanie for the first time. She was just a kid, open-faced, big eyes with lots of eyeliner and mascara, snaggle teeth. Melanie took her eyes off the road and shot Kris a smile that said, "I'm no danger to anyone."

Shit, Kris thought. She'd gotten in the car and with a complete stranger. She would never survive on the road like this. She flashed on the girl with black lipstick back at the rest stop, not much older than this kid.

Shit, Melanie thought. She took a quick look at the painfully skinny, middle-aged woman in the passenger seat. Thrift store clothes, no makeup, banged up from a fight, intense looking, and Melanie knew from Pappy's that intense people always meant trouble, especially women. She'd only picked her up because of the Manowar bandana. She and Sheila Bartell used to sing "Kings of Metal" when they drove home from volleyball.

Both of them thought at the same time: *this is a mistake*.

Kris went back to studying the road, trying to figure out her next move. She heard the wet gurgle JD made as his cheek came off, the sound of ripping meat she'd never be able to get out of her head. She gagged.

"Do you need to throw up?" Melanie asked.

Kris couldn't trust herself to talk, so she shook her head, fast and hard.

Melanie had a bad feeling about this. Like a really, really bad feeling about this. She never should have let a stranger in the car. She needed to keep this woman talking, and ditch her at the next rest stop.

"Why're you going to Vegas?" she asked.

Kris didn't answer.

"I'm going because . . . " Melanie smiled and dropped her voice into a Monster Truck Announcer Voice because humor was the best way to disarm someone dangerous. "Hellstock 2019! The ultimate desert smackdown! Three days! Three stages! Fifty bands! And Saturday night, the final show for Koffin . . . Koffin . . . Koffin."

She risked a look at Kris, who wasn't smiling.

"My sister lives there," Kris said.

"Cool," Melanie said. "Were you guys moving out there with her?"

"No," Kris said. "He was just giving me a ride."

The sound of her hair being torn out at the roots echoed through her head. The white bone in JD's throat moved up and down. His remaining eye stared at Kris, blinked, and the two halves of his torn eyelid crumpled down and wouldn't come back up. Who was going to tell his mother?

"Your husband?" Melanie asked.

Kris realized no one was going to tell JD's mom. The woman was going to hear about it on the news, and they'd have pictures of what happened, and they'd say Kris's name, and this woman, who'd never hurt anyone, would be destroyed. A short, unhappy sound escaped Kris's throat.

"You okay?" Melanie asked. "You need a tissue?"

"What?" Kris asked.

Melanie tried to put things back on track.

"Your husband was giving you a ride out there?" she asked. "I'm just being interested. I've been driving for eighteen hours straight. I'm a little stir crazy."

"Yes," Kris said. "We were heading out there and then we got in a fight."

"Cool," Melanie said, thinking, *This woman is getting out at the next exit.* She made her voice carefree. "I'm going out there to start over. See the show, and then turn over a new page, you know? I've got a guy there, just a friend, but he knows I'm coming. He's waiting for me."

"Yeah," Kris said, slumping down in her seat, drowning in misery as she thought about JD's mom, about JD's agonizing last minutes of life, about how he came back for her. Another death, laid at Terry's feet.

"Stand Strong" by Koffin blasted out the speakers, way too loud. Kris shot upright like she'd been shocked.

"Sorry!" Melanie said, turning it down. "I wasn't used to having people in the car."

"Can we have silence?" Kris asked.

Melanie picked up her phone, where it was plugged into the car, and paused her playlist.

"Sure," she said.

There was silence except for the sound of tires on the highway.

Then Melanie said, "Look, I don't know much about husband and wife stuff, but I got a feeling you're pretty shaken up by what happened between you two, so I'm not going to bother you for a little while. If you want to talk, you can, but I'm not. If you want water, or some snacks, there's a cooler right behind your seat there. There's a first-aid kit under your seat, and if you need to call your sister you can use my phone. I've got it on airplane mode so my ex doesn't bother me because frankly I wasted enough of my life on him and I don't want to hear from him ever again, okay?"

Kris's brain was consumed by images of hands reaching through the shattered window for her and she didn't answer. But her scalp ached, and after a mile she leaned forward and reached under her seat and pulled out the first-aid kit. It was a white box with a red cross on top, and Melanie had clearly stocked it herself because it was insanely organized. Kris grimaced as she pulled the Manowar bandana away from her scabs. Melanie shot a quick look over, and sucked air between her teeth when she saw the raw, seeping patches.

"Use the Medihoney," she said.

Kris unscrewed the cap and applied it to her scalp using the visor mirror. It numbed the burning, throbbing spots on her skull down to a dull ache. They drove on in silence, Kris's head filled with the sounds of ripping skin, JD screaming, "I can't! They're people!" All this blackness crowded inside her skull. She squeezed her eyes shut, but in the darkness she saw his panicked, bearded face, the hands banging on the car windows.

"Can we have some music?" Kris demanded, then softened. "Please."

Melanie reached for her phone.

"Anything but Koffin," Kris said.

"Why not Koffin?" Melanie asked.

"Because they're shit," Kris said, and then she couldn't help herself, and it all came out in a rush. "Terry Hunt's a rip-off Marilyn Manson, someone else writes his music and he never credits them, he uses fake outrage to distract from his weak subject matter, he doesn't even play a goddamn instrument. His lyrics are sentimental bullshit, his sound mixes are sloppy, his bass lines are all ripped off from Trent Reznor, and I've never seen another musician do something great that he doesn't steal a year later."

The temperature lowered in the car.

"Okay," Melanie said, "Because they're my favorite band. I don't know all that musical stuff you're saying, but I like them because I got through some hard fucking times listening to their music, and I've got a lot of good fucking memories listening to their music and if you think you're going to come into my car, when I'm giving you a ride, and tell me my favorite band sucks, then you're an asshole. Don't you listen to anyone but yourself? I'm going to their show! For two whole days! Maybe you shouldn't shit all over something when someone giving you a ride tells you they're their favorite band."

It felt so absurd, so ridiculous to be yelled at over not liking Koffin that Kris didn't know how to react. She was selfish. She'd made JD come with her and he died. She went to see Scottie Rocket and he died. She was cursed.

"I'm sorry," she said.

"No," Melanie said. "Fuck that. I'm sorry, but at the next exit I'm pulling over and you're getting out."

"Okay," Kris said.

A green sign for an exit to Crownpoint flashed past and Melanie started slowing down.

"I never should have picked you up in the first place," Melanie said, half to herself but so angry she didn't care if Kris heard. "Trying to help someone and getting it thrown back in my face."

The exit was one mile ahead on the right. As Melanie got in the lane she needed, Kris said, "Before you let me out, I want to say I'm sorry. Really. You like the music you like. I'm just being a bitter asshole."

Melanie put on her turn signal.

"I'm having a bad day," Kris said. "And I'm sorry. But don't let me make you not want to help someone else next time, okay? You had good instincts. I'm just having a hard time getting out of my own head."

Melanie sighed and turned off the turn signal, pressed the accelerator.

"I'm not going to put you out," she said. "For all I know, your ex'll pick you up and then I'll feel guilty you got murdered.

Come on, we're five hours to Vegas. Just don't work my nerve."

"You don't have to do this," Kris said.

"Thank you would be fine, actually," Melanie said.

"Thank you," Kris said.

"Now find something to play," Melanie said.

Kris went through Melanie's music library on her phone, looking for something they could agree on. It was no to Fugazi ("I was into them when I was vegan for five minutes," Melanie said), no to Bon Jovi ("Those posers had a business manager before they even recorded an album," Kris said), no to Beck ("I can't listen to him after I found out he was a Scientologist," Melanie said), no to Black Sabbath ("I've heard enough Sabbath to last me a lifetime," Kris said), no to Green Day (Melanie: "Maybe if I was twelve"), no to Beyoncé (Kris: "Something without auto-tune, please"), no to Sonic Youth (Melanie: "That's my boyfriend's music. You know what? Delete that"), no to Manowar (Kris: "I need something that's not jock rock"), no to Blink-182 (Melanie: "What's that even doing on there?"), no to Springsteen (Kris & Melanie: "No!"), no to Radiohead, no to Metallica, no to Taylor Swift, no to Linkin Park.

Finally, Kris said, "Okay, what about this?"

There was a brief moment of Ladysmith Black Mambazo crooning from the speakers, then an upbeat guitar picking out a happy riff, and Dolly Parton's voice rolled out of the speakers singing about how she's been happy lately, thinking about all the good things to come.

"Oh my god," Melanie said. "Peace Train!"

"This is without a doubt the best version of this song," Kris said, sitting back in her seat.

"Cat Stevens bites," Melanie agreed.

Melanie juked her head along to the music, caught up in Dolly Parton's voice that sounded like she was singing through a smile. Kris looked out her window at the passing brown desert, and started nodding along. As the song trailed off into its hushed ending there was a brief silence, followed by the urgent cut time strumming of "Jolene," and first Melanie and then Kris were singing along with Dolly, begging Jolene not to take their man.

When it was over, Melanie insisted she put on "I Will Always Love You."

"It's a crime that everyone associates this song with Whitney Houston," Melanie said. "Did you know Dolly wrote this to say goodbye when she left her business manager? God, when she sings this to Burt Reynolds in *Best Little Whorehouse in Texas* . . . "

"Dolly Parton is a genius," Kris said.

They listened while the music stopped in the middle of the song and Dolly talked directly to her business manager, wishing him joy and happiness, but more than anything wishing him love.

"Have you ever heard 'I'll Oil Wells Love You'?" Melanie asked.

"No?" Kris said.

"Yeah," Melanie said. "It's from her second album, and it's not making fun. She wrote it with her uncle years before she wrote 'I Will Always Love You.' It's about a woman who wants to marry a rich oil millionaire from Texas."

"Man," Kris said. "You're like a superfan."

"Growing up, I thought Dolly Parton was Santa Claus," Melanie said.

"What?" Kris asked, and then she surprised herself by doing

something she never thought she'd do again. She laughed.

"Seriously," Melanie said as "Coat of Many Colors" came on. "My parents enrolled me in that Imagination Library program she does, where she mails kids a free book every month until you're five. I used to go crazy when the books came. My mom told me I'd run around and shout my head off about how my friend Dolly had sent me another book. And when I was thinking about Christmas I figured, well Santa probably wasn't real because no one has a job where they only have to work one day a year, but Dolly sent me a book every month, so she must be the one sending me all my gifts at Christmas. So yeah, I thought she was Santa."

"I was Dolly Parton for Halloween, like, three times when I was little," Kris said. "I saw her on *Hee Haw* for the first time when I was five or six and just lost my mind."

After that, the ride was easy. Late in the day, they passed Flagstaff, and the land got flat and covered with green scrub. When Melanie slowed down and took the exit, Kris went on high alert.

"Where're you going?" she asked, as they rolled off the highway, braking hard for the first time in a couple hundred miles.

In her mind she saw the cars flooding into the rest stop, the hands banging on the windows.

"I'm hungry," Melanie said, putting on her turn signal and pulling into an enormous Walmart parking lot. "I like eating here because it's safe."

She parked at the far end of the lot, where the solid mass of car roofs reflecting the dazzling desert sun broke up, scattered, turned into Winnebagos and RVs parked a respectful distance from each other. Some people sat at folding tables and ate, kids running around them. Others sat in lawn chairs.

This is fine, Kris said to herself. *There's no problem*. But she clutched the door handle so hard her hand cramped. Melanie yanked the emergency brake.

"Come on," she said. "Get what you want out of the drink cooler."

She spread a big striped beach towel in the shadow of the Subaru, and opened the cooler. Kris looked in. It had Ziploc freezer bags in it all labeled and dated. Melanie hunted and then pulled one out, then another, and set them up on the asphalt with paper plates, a little plastic bag for garbage, some grapes, some barbecue potato chips, and a Diet Coke for each of them. She tore a weird-looking bun in two and handed half to Kris.

"I hope you're not a vegetarian," she said.

"What is it?" Kris asked.

"Pepperoni roll," Melanie said.

It was delicious. They leaned against the warm car as the sun went down behind Walmart, turning the horizon orange and purple. They left the windows down so they could still hear Dolly.

"See him?" Melanie said, picking up the conversational slack. "That guy over there?"

Kris followed Melanie's gesture to an impossibly skinny husband and wife in their twenties. He followed his wife around, gesturing with his hands, mouth moving nonstop, as she cleaned out the garbage from their car.

"Newlyweds," Melanie said. "See how she keeps stopping to fidget with her wedding ring? And he's actually wearing a "My Favorite Disney Villain is my Wife" T-shirt. I bet her honeymoon consisted of him explaining what music she needs to listen to and how everything she wants to do is lame."

Kris could believe it.

"And him," Melanie said, pointing to a man on a lawn chair. "Sitting alone, staring straight ahead, not even eating. He's going to Vegas for one last binge before he kills himself because he's so lonely. I bet the only time people ever talk to him is when they ask if he's saving that seat next to him at the movies."

"You've got a good eye for details," Kris said.

"I just like to watch people," Melanie said.

"Do me," Kris said.

Melanie gave her a side eye, checking Kris out.

"You bought those clothes at a gas station, I bet," she said. "And that bandana is from a friend. Someone you miss. The guy who you had a fight with isn't your husband."

Kris stopped breathing.

"No wedding ring," Melanie said.

"I threw it away," Kris said.

"Not even an indentation on your finger," Melanie said. "Also, I don't think you had a fight with your husband, or boyfriend, or whoever it is. No wallet, no bag, what kind of man throws a woman out of his car without her bag? Either a real mean one, or one who doesn't exist."

Kris didn't know what to say. Finally, she decided on honesty.

"I'm going to Vegas to settle an old score with someone," she said. "It's a man, but not my husband."

"Always a mistake," Melanie said. "Trust me. I know."

Behind them, Dolly Parton began to sing "Little Sparrow."

"I need to look him in the eyes," Kris said. "Ask him why he caused so much pain. Why he hurt so many people."

A satellite blinked past overhead, a mechanical falling star.

"Any answer you get won't be good enough," Melanie said. "Twisted people do twisted things. That's all. They're more shallow than you think. I'm with Dolly."

"All ye maidens heed my warning," Dolly sang behind them, "Never trust the hearts of men / They will crush you like a sparrow / Leaving you to never mend."

"Dolly always knows," Kris agreed.

Kris couldn't remember the last time she had a conversation with a woman who wasn't her mother or a Best Western guest. The two of them sat for a while, listening as the music changed to "Eagle When She Flies," then "9 to 5." Eventually they got back on the road, talking in the darkness from time to time, listening to Dolly Parton's complete discography.

Identical condos started clinging to both sides of the highway, strung with identical plastic "Now Leasing" banners. Billboards got more aggressive (IN A WRECK? NEED A CHECK? MAKE HIM PAY! SUEMYBOSS.COM!), and suddenly they were in Vegas. A black pyramid glowed on the horizon. The skyline got crowded with massive gold and silver slabs, the Eiffel Tower, the Stratosphere Tower, a cheapjack roller coaster on top of a hotel.

Kris had always thought of Las Vegas as a whore's corpse, covered in glitter and left in the desert to rot, but even that didn't do justice to the Strip. Frat boys carrying plastic yard-long margaritas got in a fist fight with a guy dressed as Batman at an intersection. Drunk parents pushed sleeping kids in strollers across the street, screaming at each other about money, while half-naked women wearing police caps and fishnet stockings posed next to puffy-faced fathers with their hats on backward.

Hookers for Jesus in pink-and-black T-shirts gave a street-corner sermon, while card slappers slapped hooker cards into the hands of ironic bearded hipsters wearing bunny ears and tutus over their cargo shorts. Chinese tourists posed next to a truck stalled in traffic towing a sign that read "Loosest Slots & Sluts in Town." Bored guys with leathery faces handed out bottles of hand sanitizer while wearing green T-shirts that read, "Girls Direct to Your Room in 20 Minutes."

"Where can I drop you?" Melanie asked.

"I'll just get out wherever and call my sister to pick me up," Kris said.

"I'll drive you," Melanie said.

"It's fine," Kris said, letting her know by the firmness of her voice that the subject was closed.

Melanie pulled up in front of a gleaming white castle with red and blue turrets rising into the sky.

"I know it's cheesy," she said, "but they had a deal for really cheap rooms, so why not? How often am I ever going to get to stay in a castle?"

They got out and Melanie waved to the valet parker who was absorbed in his phone.

"Well." Kris paused, on the other side of the car. "Thanks. You sure I can't pay you back?"

"Go," Melanie said. "You did me a favor. It was less boring with you in the car. Good luck."

"With what?" Kris asked, distracted, thinking of where she could find a place to sleep and how she could get out to the Hellstock '19 campground undetected. Maybe she could dress up like a cleaning lady. No one ever noticed maids. Did they have maids out in the middle of the desert?

"Your thing with this guy," Melanie said. "Looking into his eyes. I hope it goes okay, but you're better off without him."

"Thanks," Kris said, and walked away.

She almost didn't hear Melanie running after her.

"Deidre," Melanie said.

Kris turned around.

"How much money do you have in your wallet?" Melanie asked. "Honestly."

The two women looked at each other and Kris made up her mind.

"Nine dollars," she said.

"Come on. You're staying with me."

JACK BLAST: . . . an atmosphere I can only describe as evil. These so-called Koffin Kids, what I call anarcho-radicalists with a globalist agenda, have jammed every room in Las Vegas and Green Valley for their occult ritual this weekend, and I call it occult because that's what Terry Hunt, its organizer, calls it. These aren't children, they have a history of violence, of murder, of wanton destruction of private property. Let's call them what they are: foot soldiers in the One World Government here in Nevada to spread terror.

—WJET, "Radio Free America"
September 7, 2019

Toxicity

Kris woke up from a nightmare of JD's thick, wet screams to Melanie blowing in her ear. She jerked up with a start, skull exploding with fear, eyes rolling wild as she looked around the dark room, not knowing where she was.

"Relax, it's me," Melanie said, squatting next to Kris's bed.

She was fully clothed and the bathroom light was on. Kris had the impression that Melanie had been up for hours. The girl put a plastic shopping bag on the end of Kris's bed.

"I thought you might want some clean clothes," she said.

Kris opened the bag and found a "What Happens in Vegas Stays in Vegas" T-shirt, and a pair of stonewashed jean shorts with "Juicy" appliquéd on the butt in sequins.

Kris closed the bag and handed it back to Melanie.

"I can't pay you," she said.

Melanie pushed the bag back at Kris.

"It's my last good deed before I spend two days partying," she said.

Kris sat up in bed, body stiff, back aching, skull throbbing, and looked at the white plastic shopping bag.

"Why are you being so nice to me?" she asked.

Melanie stood up and began doing yoga poses.

"Buy me breakfast," she said. "They've got a $3.99 special downstairs for guests. You can meet the guy I'm going out to Hellstock with. If your radar goes off, I won't go with him. I just need you to give me a thumbs-up or thumbs-down."

Even at nine in the morning the streets were baking. Through the window of the hotel diner, Kris saw emergency vehicles shimmering in the heat haze rising up from the street. Someone had slammed their red Honda Accord into the fence around New York-New York Casino, killing themself and some pedestrians the night before. Two metalheads in Blind King corpse paint handed out thumb drives with their band's demo on it to the crowd of rubberneckers shooting the crashed car on their phones.

The waitress who led them to their table had blood encrusted around one nostril and a scabbed-over earlobe where someone must have torn out her earring. The local news blasting from the corner-mounted TV told them that police were still looking for a naked clown who tried to set the Little White Wedding Chapel on fire.

"Everything looks worse in the morning," Melanie said.

Something thumped against the plate-glass window hard. They looked up to see a guy in an MMA "Fight Everyone" T-shirt slamming one of the metalheads against the glass. A cop got involved. The MMA guy took a swing and then there were five cops on top of him, pepper-spraying him in the eyes.

"Wow," Melanie said.

"It's a little tense out there," Kris said.

Melanie stirred a spoon idly around her coffee cup.

"This is all a mistake," she said. "I don't know anyone except you, and I don't even actually know you. And now I'm spending an entire weekend with these guys."

Kris was never impressed by women who made plans, then got depressed because they hadn't thought them through. But Melanie had taken her in off the street, and helped her hold her head together in a situation where otherwise she would probably have lost her mind.

"Look," she said, leaning forward, talking confidentially. "You don't have to—"

"Boo-yah!" a male voice shouted.

Kris leapt halfway up the wall. Five guys surrounded their booth, standard issue dude bros in cargo shorts and button-up shirts. A muscle tee and a couple of porkpie hats added variety, otherwise they were all gym-toned, perfectly tanned, exquisitely coiffed examples of thirty-something white guys.

Melanie and Kris stared at them in horror.

"It's me!" One of them with a sparse beard and a deep tan said, spreading his arms out. Melanie looked uncomprehending. "Hunter!"

Kris watched Melanie's age drop five years as she let out a girlish high-pitched squeal, and then she and Hunter were hugging, rocking from side to side like clumsy dancers at an old folks' home. They stepped back, held each other at arm's length, then did it again. Kris could not follow this kind of radical mood swing. Everything hit maximum volume now that the boys were there.

"This is my crew," Hunter said. "Chisolm, we all know what that rhymes with, Spencer"—the two fist bumped—"who just closed a mega-deal with me for some sweet condos over in the District, and last but not least, bringing up the rear, as always,

Owen McSlowen."

Everyone fell silent as they waited for Melanie to introduce her crew.

"Oh!" Melanie said. "This is Deidre. She's a hitchhiker I gave a ride to in New Mexico. She's awesome."

The word hitchhiker immediately gave Kris an exotic air. No one hitchhiked anymore unless they were making a political statement. Hunter's crew filtered into the booth, all eyes on Kris, squeezing Kris and Melanie against the wall, while Hunter squatted at the head of the table.

"How do you know she isn't a serial killer?" he asked Melanie.

"I thought serial killers picked up hitchhikers," Melanie said. "I don't think they *are* hitchhikers."

"She might be trying to confuse you," Hunter said seriously, eyes locked on Kris.

Then he burst out laughing and broke eye contact.

"We're just messing with you," he said, and held out a fist. Kris bumped it with her knuckles. "That's awesome. Roaming the US of A. Nothing tying you down."

Spencer started to eat their toast. Slowen asked if Kris was finished with her bacon.

"So when do we leave?" Melanie asked, eyes shining. "I've been waiting all summer."

"Ask the navigator," Hunter said, and Chisolm pulled out his Android and laid it on the table.

"So the concert is up in Strawberry Valley," he said, showing them on Google Maps. "That's near where they used to do the atomic bomb tests and less than a hundred miles from Area 51."

"It's why he's doing it there," Slowen said. "They said the

radioactive sand attracts UFOs. Koffin's going to do an extraterrestrial summoning on Sunday night."

"So our boy Jones is holding the campsite," Chisolm continued. "Along with about four hundred thousand other people. Last night was madness, so let's haul ass and get up there fast. We'll come back early Sunday because all the bands that day are bullshit doomcore acts, so we're not missing anything. Traffic's going to be a bitch."

Melanie looked like a kid getting ready to go to summer camp, clamping her hands between her thighs and rocking back and forth with excitement.

"Do I follow you up in my car?" she asked.

"Why don't you park it at my place?" Hunter asked.

Kris instantly spotted it. They were going to take this girl up into the wilderness without her own way home. She would be totally at her mercy.

"Mel—" she began.

"Awesome!" Melanie said. "I'll see where you live! I want to meet Lars!"

"Here he is," Hunter said, and showed her a picture of an Irish setter mix on his cell phone.

"Aw . . . he's a cutie," Melanie said, and showed it to Kris. "Are you a dog person?"

"I should get going," Kris said, wondering how the hell she was going to get to Strawberry Valley. She reached into her pocket for her nine dollars. Maybe if she moved slowly enough, Melanie would offer to pay for breakfast instead.

"I know what!" Melanie said.

Kris realized the girl was staring at her.

"Do you still have that ticket, the extra one?" Melanie asked Hunter.

"I was going to sell it at the gate," Hunter said. "It's $150."

"Come with us, Kris," Melanie said. "You can use it."

The boys looked uncomfortable.

"I don't know if we have room, Pixie Sticks," Hunter said, and Kris instantly hated the way he just assigned a nickname to a woman he'd only met twenty minutes ago.

"You've got two trucks," Melanie said in a suddenly serious voice that brooked no bullshit. "Of course you have room."

Hunter cocked his head and considered the tabletop for a minute. "All right," he said. "It's all yours. But you owe me. For the ticket."

"I can't do that," Kris said. This was too much. "I should get going."

"No, wait," Melanie said. "Come here."

She slid out of the booth, and Kris saw her as these boys saw her: a young girl with soft curves, wide eyes, shorts that showed off too much leg, a tight top. She seemed exposed and vulnerable in a way she hadn't when they'd been alone together.

Melanie took Kris by the elbow and guided her to the hostess stand.

"I'm not taking your $150 ticket," Kris said.

"Listen," Melanie whispered, looking over at the boys and flashing them a smile, then ducking out of sight in front of Kris, her face getting serious. "I don't know these guys. I know Hunter, but not these other four. And now I'm getting in their car and going camping with them in the middle of nowhere for two days. I'm not bringing you because we're best friends, I'm bringing you because I get a feeling you can take care of yourself, and I need some insurance. I may be young, Deidre, but I'm not stupid."

Suddenly, all her problems were solved at once. Black Iron Mountain was looking for her traveling alone. Now she'd be traveling in two trucks with a bunch of rowdy boys, like she was their cool aunt. She'd have a ride to Hellstock, and she'd be making Melanie feel safer and repaying her for the ride and the room.

"I'll go," Kris said. "But I can't pay you back for the ticket."

"If you keep me from getting murdered, it's worth the $150," Melanie said. Then her face lit up like a little girl again and she charged back to the table, leading Kris by the arm.

"Woohoo!" she cheered. "Deidre is going!"

They settled back down to general merriment and inane conversation. After putting up with enough of it to seem polite, Kris said, "I'm going upstairs to shower. Then we'll leave?"

"Sure thing," Melanie said, and Kris left the table.

Banter continued until Hunter saw Kris get into the lobby elevator and the doors close. Then he turned to the table.

"Holy shit," he whisper-breathed.

"Jesus Christ," Spencer said.

"What are you guys talking about?" Melanie asked.

"That's her," Hunter said.

"Who?" Melanie asked. "What did she do?"

"The chick you're with," Hunter said. "Oh my god, you're clueless. That's adorable. She's the one trying to kill Terry Hunt. That's Kris Pulaski."

"No," Melanie said. Then thought it over for a second and did a verbal double take. "Nooooo."

"Yes," Hunter said. "Show her."

Chisolm spun his phone around. Melanie looked. A photo from about seven years ago of Kris, plus a police sketch of how she probably looked today. The set of the jaw, the thin mouth, the sharp cheekbones, the intense stare—even in a crappy police sketch it was obvious.

Melanie sat back and put her hand over her mouth.

"Oh, my shit," she said.

The four guys looked at each other and burst out laughing.

"Oh, shit!" Spencer said.

"Whaaaat?" Slowen asked.

"She really didn't know!" Hunter said, laughing. He pulled Melanie's face to him and kissed the top of her head. "You are the most trusting person I ever met," he said.

Everyone razzed her, in good spirits, until Melanie got serious.

"I can't narc on her," she said.

"No one's asking you to narc," Hunter said. "But she's going to try to kill him. I mean, you could probably be arrested as an accessory."

"Not before now," Chisolm, who was a tax lawyer, said. "Now that you know her identity, the burden is on you to do something about it since there is a high likelihood that a crime will be committed."

Melanie sat in the middle of their urging and coaxing and bantering, shaking her head. Refusing to believe it, but actually knowing it was true. It made too much sense.

"You picked her up in New Mexico," Hunter said. "That's right after she killed that guy she was traveling with. I can't believe everyone in America has been looking for this skank and you had her in the front seat of your car the whole time, doing a *Thelma and Louise*."

"I won't turn her in," Melanie said.

"The cool thing is," Hunter said, "that 800 number isn't a cop number, it's a hotline run by Terry Hunt. So it's not like you'd be turning her in to the cops."

"I guess I could call anonymously," Melanie said.

"Anonymously?" Hunter said. "Are you kidding? If it's Terry Hunt, he'll owe you his life. He'll give you VIP tickets. We'll get to go backstage. Dude, this is your chance."

"Give me a minute," Melanie said, grabbing her phone off the table and sliding out of the booth. "Don't call anyone. I need to think."

Outside on the baking sidewalk, she walked in circles, threading her way through the rubberneckers watching the tow truck pull the Honda off the casino fence. She couldn't do this to Deidre—Kris. Who would have her back over the weekend at Hellstock? Although Hunter and these guys would be so grateful to her if she got them backstage that they'd probably treat her like a goddess. But this was wrong. She would call upstairs on the house phone and tell Kris to run, then call the tip line. Would they let her up to get her clothes out of the room or would they put crime scene tape all over it?

Melanie's wanderings took her close to the car crash. Everyone had their phones out, taking pictures of an enormous blood smear on the sidewalk, like someone had swiped it with a gory mop. There was a single white Reebok in the gutter.

"That's where the kid hit his head," one bystander said in

a slight Russian accent. "I heard it all the way up the block. It sounded like a watermelon exploding."

Melanie felt sick and her vision swam in the heat. People shouldn't get hurt like this. These were real people's pain these tourists were taking pictures of. Overcome with nausea, she shoved her way through the crowd, away from the crash. It was disgusting the way people got off on other people getting hurt. Why did people want to hurt each other all the time?

Why did Kris want to kill Terry?

She looked at the empty shoe, forgotten in the gutter. She thought about Greg yelling at his video game, pretending to murder strangers over and over again. She thought about a bullet shattering Terry Hunt's face. She thought about the scabs all over Kris's scalp from her not-husband.

People had to stop hurting each other.

Kris got out of the shower. She opened the door to the room and called, "Melanie?" to see if the girl had come back yet. No answer.

She left the bathroom door open and changed into her new clothes. The shorts were shorter than she'd have liked, and she wished she still had her Bones with her. Not having a suitcase, she shoved her Roswell T-shirt into the plastic shopping bag. She'd have to borrow a jacket from Melanie. It got cold in the desert.

The closer she got to Terry, the more it seemed like *Troglodyte* was opening doors. She tried to think if there was anything in "Sailing the Seas of Blood" or "One Life, One Bullet" about this part of the journey. Did Hunter and those guys come up in any way?

She couldn't place them on the album. She'd just keep moving forward. JD and Scottie Rocket, all those sad souls trapped at Well in the Woods—there were a lot of things Terry needed to answer for.

She felt herself picking up momentum, moving faster as she approached the center. She didn't feel happy, but she was filled with grim satisfaction that she was off Terry's map and the initiative was hers. She was coming at him from his blind spot now.

Melanie knocked on the door.

"Hold on," Kris said, toweling her hair, walking to answer.

The kid had probably misplaced her keys. Kris looked through the peep hole. It was black.

The knock came again.

"Ma'am?" a muffled voice said. "UPS."

DR. CRAIG BORWIN: . . . got black helicopters, white noise generators, cell phone jammers, the city is occupied territory. This morning, a shell company registered the domain name NevadaStrong.com. Something big is coming.

TODD FIXX: Who is the enemy?

DR. CRAIG BROWN: We don't know anymore. It could be Soros-funded antifa terrorists, NWO goons wearing FEMA IDs, ATF, the deep state, no one knows who it will be because they are always one step ahead. They monitor everyone. They listen to everything. I implore all patriots to lock down their property, assume an armed posture, and be ready for anything.

—Genesis Communications Network On Demand Radio,
"Fixxing Freedom"
September 7, 2019

In the Nightside Eclipse

The traffic jam was epic. Hour after hour of slow rolling and sudden stops, people getting out and strolling between cars, sitting in lawn chairs on the side of the highway. But in the late afternoon they finally edged over the rise and saw Strawberry Valley and Melanie forgot to breathe.

A massive comet made of garbage had hit the desert, leaving behind a trash-strewn crater. Drones crisscrossed the sky. Rows of tents stretched to the horizon, flatlands of parked cars sparkled under the blazing sun. Cars crept beneath a three-story-tall spider made of scrap metal straddling the road, and a vivid fiberglass clown's head on top of a merry-go-round spewed fire.

"Aaand there goes the network," Spencer said, as the three dots on his phone turned into "No Service."

Cellular coverage in Strawberry Valley was never good, but the 440,000 people, plus 21,000 support staff, plus 5,000 volunteers broke its back.

"I've never seen so many tents," Melanie said.

"It's pretty in-tents," Hunter said, and everyone busted out laughing.

Melanie wondered where Kris was. She wondered if Kris understood. She knew she'd done the right thing because the boys had spent all morning reassuring her, but she couldn't seem to stop feeling like she'd betrayed her friend. Looking out over all those parked cars, the lines of tents stretched beneath her, she thought they looked like rows and rows of graves.

The four UPS men wore brown shorts, their dark brown socks pulled up tight, their hairy knees sticking out. They had a pass key.

They poured into her room, making it small. They didn't talk. Two of them took her by the arms and laid her on the bed, holding her down, while the other two searched the room. It took them five seconds. Then they put on the chain lock, closed the curtains, and turned on the bedside lamp.

"I'm going to scream," Kris said.

The one holding down her shoulders put his finger to his lips and shook his head once. Kris gathered her breath. When she opened her mouth to scream, he placed his hand on the bottom of her ribcage and stabbed his thumb into her diaphragm, hard and deep. All the air whooshed out of her in one big rush. So did the $3.99 breakfast special. She turned her head so it landed mostly on the pillow.

Another UPS driver examined the bathrobe belt, rejected it, and settled on the iron. He yanked the cord out and tested its strength. Kris watched him take it into the bathroom. In the room mirror, she saw him tie it into a noose and loop it over the shower head.

"I want to talk to Terry," Kris said.

The two UPS drivers with her looked at each other and one of them produced a bottle of Paxator. That's when Kris realized that all four drivers looked identical. Each one was dark-haired and trim, with a neat mustache lying across their upper lip.

The one who'd jabbed her diaphragm gripped her jaw in one big hand, his fingers digging into its hinge. The other took a Paxator out of the plastic bottle and held it up.

"Package," he said.

Kris knew that meant he wanted her to open her mouth. She shook her head. The one holding her jaw squeezed, and the way his fingers pressed into her glands gave her no choice. Her mouth creaked open. The driver popped the pill inside. His fingertips tasted salty. Then he relaxed his grip on her jaw.

"Sign here," he said.

And Kris knew that meant swallow.

The sun slammed down on Strawberry Valley. Their tent was by the Google Challenge Zone, where the noise acts played, and in the scorching heat haze the distant sound of crashing chords and an amplified male voice shouting at the crowd felt like a dream. Girls in bikinis and sunglasses strolled past, shirtless guys walked by wearing gas masks, wearing bong masks, wearing skeleton bandanas that turned the lower halves of their faces into grinning skulls. A makeup crew from LA had opened a zombie workshop, and the living dead shambled through the tent city, red Solo cups in hand. Mountain bikes rolled by, hover boards got jammed in the sand, the few cops Melanie saw were on four-wheelers.

It took them ninety minutes to get from their car to the campsite, where they found Jones sitting in the middle of their three blue dome tents, clearly baked.

"Dudes," he said. "I just joined the army."

Everyone serviced Hellstock '19. You could sign up for the army, you could sign up to consolidate your student loans, you could sign up for an American Express card with 0% APR for the first year, you could sign up to win a free iPhone, you could sign up for Rise Up, for We the People, for Earth First, for Amnesty International, for Change.org. People put their signatures on everything.

Most of the support staff had walked off the job on Friday night and hadn't come back. Garbage curdled and stewed in the cans. Every weak breeze carried the barnyard tang of shit.

"Yeah," Jones said, giggling. "They tipped the porta-potties. They're calling them the Shit Pits now. But some dudes rigged up their own chemical toilets and it's one dollar to piss, five dollars to shit. Chicks are lucky, they can just flash their tits and pee for free."

All this disorganization scared Melanie. The boys took off their shirts to reveal gym-cut abs and chiseled pecs. They shared a vape, they had food in their coolers, and when some Jehovah's Witnesses tried to give Melanie a tract about how this was the end of the world, they closed ranks and drove the Witnesses away. The boys wanted her to feel safe, but she'd glance up sometimes and catch them breaking off a look that seemed to communicate some secret. Something about the way they talked to her felt like they all shared an inside joke and she was its punch line.

As people shot fireworks at the drones zipping back and forth overhead, they decided to head over to the Pepsi Peace and Love Arena to see Gwar. They were shouldering their backpacks when a drone fell out of the sky, turning from a speck, to a dot, to a humming spider dangling in front of their faces.

"Hello?" a tinny voice said from its tiny speaker. "Can you hear me?"

"Uh, yeah," Chisolm said, laughing.

"Which of you is Melanie?" it asked.

"Me?" she said, raising her hand timidly.

The drone rotated to face her.

"Terry Hunt is grateful for what you did," it said. "He's grateful that you're keeping this event safe and fun for your fellow fans. He'd like to invite all of you to a private backstage tour of the Crypt and a brief one-on-one so he can thank you in person. If you make your way to the Bud Light stage and tell security your name they'll take care of you."

Then it rose into the air and turned into a busy, darting speck again.

"No! Way!" Spencer said, and the guys all high-fived each other.

Hunter pulled Melanie aside.

"Look," he said. "I know you don't know us, and you must feel out of place, but I'm watching out for you, okay? If anything feels weird, just tell me."

She wanted to feel relieved.

"Package," the UPS driver said.

His fingers dug into Kris's jaw joint. Her lips cracked open.

"Sign here," the UPS driver said.

She swallowed. He tipped some water into her mouth to help

loosen the bitter clot of pills dissolving in her throat. Kris swallowed the lump. It was better than suffocating.

The UPS driver came out of the bathroom and nodded to the one giving her the pills. Then they turned all their attention on Kris and that's when she knew she was going to die. Another pathetic rock-and-roll suicide in a dingy hotel room with holes in the sheets, cigarette burns in the carpet, and the TV nailed to the wall.

"Please," she said.

"Package," the UPS driver said.

They were giving her an overdose, then they would hang her from the electrical cord in the shower, probably pulling down on her feet to make sure the cord crushed her throat, blood building up in her skull, pounding hot in her temples.

She bet they even had a note. Something in her handwriting about a last-minute wave of remorse, or how she couldn't bring herself to hurt Terry. And no one would ever hear *Troglodyte* again. Dürt Würk would be forgotten. Her entire life led to this dark hotel room in Las Vegas in the middle of the afternoon.

"Sign here."

"Package."

"Sign here."

"Let me talk to Terry," Kris said.

"Package." This time he really dug his fingers in.

"I need to speak to Terry," she said. "Can you call him? Just call him? For two seconds."

"Sign here."

"Please," she said. "I have something to tell him."

"Package."

"You have to tell Terry I brought him something."

The pills were starting to dissolve into her bloodstream, she could feel them slowing her down, making her face numb.

"Sign here."

"I wrote a sequel to *Troglodyte.*" It just popped out. She didn't know what part of her brain decided to try that, but she ran with it. "It's a sequel and it's the same as the first album. Tell him, it does the same thing. And there's a song about tonight, there's a song about this show."

"Package."

"You have to let him know," she said, and began to weep. Tears dripped onto the back of the UPS driver's hand.

"Sign here."

"It's not going to go like he think it will tonight," she said. "I'll play it for him. The riffs, the words, they're all in my head. It's six songs, a full album about what's going to happen."

"Package," the UPS driver said.

"Sign here."

At some silent signal, the UPS drivers stopped feeding her pills and lifted her up, fingers digging into her armpits, and carried her toward the bathroom. Kris lost it.

"No," she screamed. "Nooooo!"

She thrashed her body from side to side, but that only made them press her ankles tighter together and clamp down on her wrists. They took her to the tub. The white electrical cord hung from the showerhead in a perfect noose.

"Please," she said. "Just tell Terry. Tell him I'll play it for him. Tell Terry."

They raised her up, and looped the electrical cord around her neck.

In the other room, the phone rang. A soft electronic trill. The UPS drivers stopped. They looked at each other. It trilled again. Kris's heart leapt, but she knew it was probably only the front desk calling to make sure she knew checkout was at eleven.

One UPS driver went into the other room and picked up the phone mid-ring. Kris saw him in the mirror, pressing it to his ear. He listened for a minute, then hung up. The other three UPS drivers watched him.

"That package is out for delivery," he said.

They put Kris on her feet, wiped the vomit out of her hair with a wet towel and, still controlling her arms, marched her out of the hotel and put her in the back of their truck. Then they pulled out, headed for Hellstock '19.

Behind the Bud Light stage sprawled a tent city of trailers, air-conditioned walkways, chain-link fences, fabric walls to block paparazzi shots, a helipad, honey wagons, makeup trailers, generators, catering services, three full bars, an ice cream fountain carved out of a single massive block of ice, a Starbucks, two gyms, a Pilates studio, a day spa, and an above-ground pool. Everything needed to entertain fifty visiting acts, conjured out of the desert by the power of money. At the far end, close to where sixty-three eighteen-wheelers sat in long rows, waiting for Sunday's strike, was Terry's private compound, open only to invited guests. In the middle of the compound stood the two trailers housing the Crypt.

A mobile museum highlighting major landmarks in Koffin's career, the Crypt was accessible to two hundred "super-fans" who purchased the $1,200 "Koffin Experience" tickets. Inside, industrial-strength air conditioners pumped ice-cold air into the dark rooms where pinpoint spotlights picked out a golden microphone presented by Osama bin Laden's brother after Terry did a show for his son's thirteenth birthday, the hand-drawn designs for the corsets sold by Shroud, his fashion collection, and a twisted leg of metal from the sound tower fans tipped over on the *Insect Narthex* tour. There was absolutely no mention of Dürt Würk except for one photo, next to a picture of a fourteen-year-old Terry standing with his parents at a track meet.

"That's her," Hunter breathed, and Melanie crowded up close to the glass.

Kris stood onstage at Robot House in Philly, feet planted wide, head down over her guitar as Terry stood in front, shirtless and thin, blood crown on, fake blood oozing down his face and dripping onto his shoulders as he screamed into the mic.

"She looks so young," Melanie said.

Melanie longed to be that intense woman onstage in the picture, the one so focused on what she was doing that she shut out the world. She hoped Kris was okay, wherever she was.

"Even psychos started small," Hunter said.

They regarded with appropriate awe Terry's guitar (which he never played), three books from his occult library (which he'd never read), and a pair of his skinny leather jeans from the *Witch Slave* tour (which he'd never worn because they were too small). The last stop was the meet-and-greet room where an assistant named Stephen told them to wait.

A woman with a headset scanned the room and left, then two security guards came in and took up stations on either side of the door and stood there for so long that the group forgot about them, taking pictures of themselves on the American Airlines–branded step-and-repeat, until suddenly, in a whirl of entourage, Terry was there.

The guys crowded around him, all wanting photos and autographs, but Melanie hung back. He was smaller than she thought, a perfectly formed miniature man with skin made out of the same substance as the beautifully moisturized handbags she could never afford. He looked like an elf, barely older than she was, even though she knew he was almost fifty. He was lineless and smooth, his hair fine and golden, illuminated by some inner light like a digital effect in a movie. He looked more real than she did. He didn't smile, just stared at them from behind his enormous mirrored shades.

Finally, he said, "Who made the call?"

The guys parted like the Red Sea to reveal Melanie as she mumbled, "Me," and Terry stepped forward and shook her hand. It was cool and dry and she didn't know how he did that in this weather. Even with the air-conditioning blasting she was wet beneath her arms.

"Never doubt that you did the right thing," Terry said, taking off his sunglasses. His almond eyes and high cheekbones stared into her soul.

Melanie mumbled something and then Terry was pulling away and she tightened her grip at the last minute. He turned back, caught in the act of putting his sunglasses back on.

"Don't," Melanie said, and she wasn't sure why she felt the need to say this, "Don't do anything to her. She was nice to me."

Terry regarded her through two perfect reflections of her

face, then said, "Kris has to learn that her decisions have consequences."

Then a brisk smile whisked across his face and he turned to the boys.

"You guys need to save your energy for tonight," he told them.

Melanie saw them all pause, that lull in a conversation she'd seen all day out of the corner of her eye, and something secret passed between them and Terry. Then Spencer tried to take one more photo and Terry turned his back, and he was a rock star again, his entourage swirled, and he was gone and they were being propelled, gently, toward the exit.

She followed the boys, quietly, slightly shocked that this moment she'd worked for all her life felt so small.

LAURA TOWER: . . . here at Hellstock '19?

DENISE: To see Koffin!

LAURA TOWER: Why?

DENISE: Because they're the greatest band in the history of music.

LAURA TOWER: And why is Hellstock '19 so important to you?

DENISE: This is Woodstock for my generation! How could I respect myself and not go?

—103.5 KIND-FM, "Tower-Trax"
September 7, 2019

Diary of a Madman

It was already dark when security scanned the UPS driver's pass and waved the truck through. They dragged Kris down endless tented walkways. The sound of the crowd rained down from the sky like a massive, crashing ocean in the desert. Finally, they stopped at the bottom of a set of flimsy metal steps bolted to the side of a trailer and protected by two matching bouncers, both bald and goateed.

One knocked and immediately the door opened and Kris came face to face with the devil.

There he stood, peaceful and handsome, totally untouched by all the misery and death done in his name. It seemed unfair that he still looked so young and unlined.

"Terry," Kris said.

His sunglasses came off. His dimples came out. His perfect teeth flashed.

"You just won't quit." Terry Hunt smiled.

Kris's blood throbbed in her neck. The air thickened. She was twenty-eight again, and Terry was thirty-one, and she stood at the base of the stairs and looked up at him as he held out his hand and said, "Come on."

And Kris reached out through the heavy air, across all those years, and put her big, calloused guitar-player's hand in Terry's small, soft, rock-star one, and went up the clanging metal stairs, through the door, and found herself back in Gurner.

She stood, letting her eyes adjust, in the dim, cool cavern of the Sporting House on 191, just east of Hecktown Road. It smelled like old beer and sawdust, and the familiar Natty Boh clock behind the bar proclaimed, "Oh boy, *what* a beer!" The wall-mounted jukebox spun silver CDs in the golden gloom.

Kris touched the white plastic door behind her to make sure they were still backstage in a trailer. It was there, the one out-of-place artifact, the only thing still connecting her to the desert. Terry stood in the middle of the floor before her, arms out, a ring-master presenting his circus.

"Isn't this great?" he said.

"But it burned down," she said.

"Nope," Terry said, walking over to the bar with its sagging strings of Christmas tree lights and backlit liquor bottles. "I took it."

It took her brain a minute to put everything together and then the sheer audacity of what he'd done wiped out her voice. She clung to the door handle, keeping some contact with the real world.

"Do you know how expensive it is to steal a building and make sure no one notices?" Terry asked, pulling two Rolling Rocks out of the reach-in behind the bar, ice sliding down their sides. "Rob thinks how much I spent is a sign that I'm unhealthy, but it's not the money, right? It's what you do with it."

He banged the caps off the Rolling Rocks and carried them around the bar, heading for the farthest of the three booths on the left-hand wall, still talking. "I want to hire some actors, get some customers in here, like the black midget. Remember him? Or the one-armed cowboy? That way anytime I come in there's some folks hanging out, the way it used to be. It wouldn't be hard. People are cheap."

He was in the booth now, arms stretched along the back of the seat, leaning back like he owned the place. He did own the place.

"So lemme hear it," he said, and waved his hand toward the far end of the room. "The new *Troglodyte*. Play whichever one you want."

On the tiny stage stood two guitars on stands: a Gibson Hummingbird acoustic, and a hideous Fender Telecaster customized to look like it was covered in black dragon scale.

This was it. There wasn't going to be any chitchat about the good old days. Kris had made a desperate claim and now she had to back it up. She took as deep a breath as she could without letting Terry notice, approached the booth and sat down across from him. The red vinyl cushion sighed. The light from the bar painted one side of Terry's face gold. He drummed his fingers on the scarred wooden tabletop.

"You don't actually expect me to play that thing?" Kris said, stalling. "That's the ugliest guitar I've ever seen."

"You've always got to be a hardass," Terry said. "Relax."

He slid one of the Rolling Rocks across the table and raised his, dripping ice, holding it out for a toast.

"Cheers," he said.

Kris picked up her cold beer, raised it, then as Terry moved to clink necks, she turned hers upside down and let it glug out over the table. Beer ran off the lip onto Terry's lap and he jumped up and danced out of the booth.

"A lot of people are gone," Kris said. "Scottie, JD, Scottie's family. They didn't die so we could hang out together in your backstage vanity bar."

"Memorial funds were started," Terry said, brushing at his wet crotch. "Flowers were sent. But right now: do you have a second *Troglodyte* or not?"

Kris had been lying about it for so many hours she'd almost convinced herself it existed.

"I got screwed by you on a deal before," she said, thinking fast. "That's not happening this time. I'm not playing until we talk terms."

For one second, written plain across Terry's face was a look of naked hunger. Then he sat down at one of the tables in the middle of the floor. He pushed out the chair opposite with his foot. "I'll make you a deal," he said.

Without any other options, Kris went and sat down across from him.

"You shouldn't even be here," Terry said. "But when I heard you in the hotel room saying you had a new *Troglodyte*, that gave me this brainstorm. See, there's two ways this can go, Kris. The first way, you're a rock-and-roll suicide, a sad, washed-up, bitter old has-been, hanging from her showerhead, another answer to a trivia quiz. But when I realized you're still writing—good job keeping that secret, by the way—when I realized that, I mean, look, the past is the past. We're better together than we are apart. Write for me."

"Are you fucking kidding me?" Kris said, so genuinely taken aback that it just popped out.

"Do you know what it's like not to be able to make anything

new?" Terry asked, in the desperate tone of a junkie hard up for a fix. "Do you know what it's like to have nothing but sand inside your head? To create something you have to dream it first, but Black Iron Mountain ate my dreams. I've parceled my soul out, and I made them pay for it, and I got so much in return, but that's the problem with selling something: eventually it's all gone. Why do you think I released a greatest hits album? Why do you think *9 Circles* bombed so hard? Why do you think I'm retiring? I pay a guy whose only job is to listen to what I lay down these days and tell me who I ripped off.

"I'm dry, Kris, and I still haven't gotten the one thing that matters. I don't even want the money anymore. If the money mattered, we'd all still be going on about Liberace. He had more hits than me, but now he's a punch line. I've got all the money in the world and it doesn't mean a thing because I'm not a legend."

Kris felt the spit in her mouth go dry.

"People are dead," Kris said. "People we know. Just so you can be famous?"

"Legendary," Terry said. "There's a difference, and you know it. Legendary leaves a mark, it creates a myth that lasts forever. Don't you dare make this sound small. It's what you wanted your entire life, too."

He was right, and for the first time since contract night, Kris could see the future. A house. Respect. A cell phone bill that always got paid. Playing in a studio again.

"They lied to me," Terry said. "Back in '98 when I went to LA with Rob and learned what Black Iron Mountain could do, they demanded one soul to make me a star, and I gave them four. I thought you guys would be happy with the deal, I thought we'd keep playing together, but you went and fucked it all up. So, I adapted. But they kept wanting more and more and more.

"When I went dry, I asked them what else I could give them, and they laughed. Or I think they laughed. It's hard to tell. But I kept asking, and finally Black Iron Mountain told me they'd give me my dreams back if I got them more souls. A lot more. All at once. And so I did the farewell concerts, and all those kids who signed up for tickets, when the show was over, when they all went home, they fell asleep, and the Special Ones ate for days."

"How can you do this to us?" Kris asked. "Tuck, Scottie, me, all these people?"

"I'm where I am because I'm willing to do what no one else will," Terry said. "It's not like anyone misses their souls. And it doesn't matter because they lied!"

He smacked the tabletop with the flat of his hand.

"I was supposed to be singing new material tonight," he said. "I did what Black Iron Mountain asked, and they gave me nothing. Nothing! So now I'm doing this, I'm giving them even more—hundreds of thousands of souls, all tonight—and this time they have to give me what I want.

"But when you started talking in that hotel room I realized that you weren't a problem to be solved, you were a sign. You came when I needed you, like you always used to. *Troglodyte* freaks them out. They didn't make it. They can't control it. They don't understand it. And it's about them. Give me the new one and I'll finally have some leverage. We can ask for anything we want. This is what we dreamed about back in your basement when we were kids. It's a win-win."

"Not for JD," Kris said. "Not for Scottie."

"This is the omelette," Terry said. "They were the eggs. Black Iron Mountain keeps getting hungrier and hungrier, they keep pushing me for more, and all they give me in return is money! But you wrote *Troglodyte*. You made it out here despite everything they did. There's something that doesn't fit in about you. And if you're writing for me, I finally have a weapon. If they're lying to me again, I can finally push them back."

He had the same high-pitched whine in his voice he always got when he didn't understand why everyone wasn't giving him his way.

"You're out of your mind," Kris said.

"What is your problem?" Terry asked, eyes wide. "There's no heroic fight here, no war between good and evil. The war is over. They won. We're just hiding in the ruins and trying to survive. Let me protect you."

"I want my soul back," Kris said.

That wiped the smile off his face. He leaned forward.

"Jesus Christ, Kris," he said. "We're friends. When *Troglodyte* is around reality gets crunchy around the edges. Things happen that *they* don't like. You and I, we're on the same team."

"You sold Scottie's soul," she said. "You sold Tuck's soul. I don't give a shit about Bill, he's an asshole, but you sold my soul. And it wasn't yours to sell. I want it back."

Ice shifted and settled in the cooler behind the bar. Terry looked embarrassed. He looked away.

"That's not how it works, Kris," he said. "It's gone."

She'd made her way out here in the unspoken hope that the deal could be reversed. That hole in the center of her world, the one that gobbled up all the joy, all the hope, that sucked in all the light, that kept her poor and crushed her down, she'd dreamed that maybe she could finally fill it, that seeing Terry could finally heal the wound. But now she knew he wasn't lying and in an instant, her world came undone, and all her anger came rushing back.

Kris stood and picked up her chair and raised it over her head to bring down on Terry's face, to wipe that expression of pity off it, but he looked the same as he used to, and they were in the Sporting House and it felt like years ago and suddenly she felt stupid and overdramatic, the one still screaming when the argument was done. So she turned and hurled the chair across the Sporting House, over the bar, sent it crashing into the mirror. The sound of exploding liquor bottles was a small satisfaction, but it was something.

"You sell-out motherfucker!" Kris shouted. "You took what I had and used it to build your kingdom of bullshit. You're the reason everything in this world feels so secondhand and shitty, not me. There's a hole in the center of the world, Terry, and it's you."

Quietly, Terry got up and walked over to the bar and surveyed the damage. Then he reached behind it and pulled out a clear plastic bottle. He cracked the seal and took a long pull. Kris's legs gave out and she dropped into one of the chairs.

"Give me my life back," she said, and her voice cracked.

Terry took another long gulp from his bottle of Pedialyte, and wiped his mouth. Then he put on his salesman's voice, thick and slow with sincerity.

"It went to a good cause," he said. "Look at what I've built: the world's biggest concert, the Koffin brand, Shroud, this whole empire, and in some small way, you helped. And now we're so close. I just need that album so I can make Black Iron Mountain give me what I need to make people remember this forever."

"You took my music," Kris said. "You stole our lives. You killed Scottie and JD. I'll keep fighting you, I'll fight them, I'll—"

Terry talked over her.

"It's over, Kris. There's no one left to fight."

"We'll see about that," Kris said. "I can pick a fight in an empty fucking elevator." Kris paused. "'No one left to fight.' Fuck you."

"I can protect you, Kris," Terry said, full-on wheedling now. "All I need is the album. I need to know if you really have it."

"It doesn't exist," Rob said from behind Kris. "It's just more of her bullshit. That's her whole life, right? One big line of BS."

Terry's shoulders slumped.

"Can I not get any privacy even in my own bar?" he asked.

Rob had slipped in the door at some point while they were arguing and he stood there, hands in his back pockets, grinning, hair perfect, looking exactly the same as he did when Kris signed her contract, way back in 1998.

"There's a face I never thought I'd see again," Rob said to Kris, walking over to their table. "Sorry you wasted so much effort getting here."

"I've been hearing you on the radio," Kris said. "A manipulative fuck, right down to the end."

Rob raised his eyebrows in mock surprise.

"The end?" he asked. "What's ending? I'm not aware of anything ending tonight, except you."

"I'm working with Terry," she said, and that wiped the smug smile off his face. "I wrote a new album for him."

Terry looked up in surprise and Kris felt the power she had. The escape she offered him from Black Iron Mountain was something he wanted more than anything. Rob carefully kept his reaction neutral.

"You need to get ready," he told Terry. "It's almost eight, and you have to head over to yoga, do your warm-ups, I'd love it if you had some meditation time, then you're getting a massage, and you need to be backstage by nine thirty."

Terry reached over and put his hand on Kris's arm.

"Play it now," he said.

"You actually believe her?" Rob asked.

Terry ignored him.

"It's now or never, Kris," he said.

Rob pulled out a chair and dropped down, slapped his palms on his thighs.

"All right," he said. "I raise and I call. If you're really going to do this, let's hear it. Show us what you got, or shut up."

No more excuses. Kris needed to play. She stood, grabbed a heavy bar stool by the seat, and dragged it to the stage where the little Hummingbird glowed golden on its stand. She hated acoustic guitars—they reminded her of Mr. McNutt, her first teacher back in Gurner.

But she picked it up now, amazed at how light it felt in her hand, and sat on the stool. Terry shot Rob a look, and the two men watched her, both of them hiding how scared, how eager, how needy they were. It wasn't just Terry, either. Rob wanted it too. He didn't believe her, but he wanted what she was about to play so bad that his naked hunger overcame his doubts and charged the air with electricity.

Kris strummed an open chord, and Terry practically leapt out of his shoes, then settled down when he realized she was just warming up. After a moment, Kris stopped, took a breath, closed her eyes, and she prayed. She prayed to *Troglodyte*, to holy coincidence, to Viking magic, to anything and everything that was the opposite of Black Iron Mountain. She prayed for inspiration. She emptied her mind and waited to be told what to do.

"We really have to get—" Rob began.

"Sssh!" Terry slapped at him with one hand.

Kris sat there, guitar balanced on her thigh, and did nothing. Terry looked at her, and instead of looking away, she met his gaze, and she realized that this was it. She didn't have to hide anymore. She let him see it all in her eyes: his betrayal, the years of fear she'd lived, watching her best friend kill himself, hiding in the closet while the UPS men murdered Scottie's family, the long mindless months of Well in the Woods, the hunger of those weeks on the road. She let him see it all. And she refused to play. After a minute, he shook his head, looking like he wanted to say something, then he paused, holding his words in his mouth, looked at Rob, then at Kris, then he shrugged.

"I tried," he said, and turned and walked to the door.

"I knew it," Rob said. "Just more sad little lies."

Kris stood up.

"I'm leaving, too," she said.

Terry stopped with one hand on the door handle.

"Sorry, Kris," he said without turning around.

"You're ditching me?" Kris asked. "Again?"

Terry turned to face her.

"I always tried to protect you from yourself," he said, and

put on his sunglasses. She hated him for timing the move so perfectly. "But your decisions have consequences."

Then he pushed out into the bright backstage hall and left Kris alone with Black Iron Mountain.

(LAS VEGAS, NV)—Fires are burning, people are walking off the job, and police are saying the situation is "extremely critical" at Hellstock 2019, the music festival one hour north of Las Vegas. Headlined by Terry Hunt, lead singer for the heavy metal supergroup Koffin, Hellstock has drawn almost half a million people to this quiet desert community. Nevada State Police are on hand, but desperately outnumbered by festivalgoers, a situation that was made even more dangerous when almost two thousand volunteer security workers walked off the job Friday night. Looting, a lack of water, and a disregard for crowd-control barriers have created a situation best described as volatile . . .

—WABC News Radio
September 7, 2019

Devil Is Fine

The moment was undermined a second later when a maid in a green Polo shirt and smock came in, plastic bucket of supplies in one hand. She stopped when she saw Kris and Rob.

"Oh, sorry," she said. "I'll come back later."

"No," Rob said, waving her in. "Go ahead."

The door closed behind her and the Sporting House was cool and dark again. The only sound was the gentle tinkling of broken glass as the maid swept up behind the bar.

"Do you want to know something funny?" Rob said. "We expected it'd be you who came to us first."

Every tendon in Kris's body was stretched to the breaking point, every muscle vibrated, her shoulder ached, her mouth felt dry. She was a bullet, fired from a gun, ready to smash through Rob's perfect face, tired of all this dancing around.

"Who the fuck are you?" she snapped.

The maid stopped sweeping for a moment and looked over. Rob shrugged and gave her a goofy grin. *Women*, his expression said. The maid went back to sweeping. Rob perched on the edge of a bar stool like he was posing for a photo.

"Who do you want me to be, Kris?" he asked. "Should my

name be Louis Siffer? Mr. Beezle Bub? Did you ever see that movie where the vampire is named Dr. Acula? Genius."

"This isn't a joke," Kris said.

"I'm the same guy you've always known," Rob said. "The one who wants what's best for you. The one who paid for *Troglodyte* out of his own pocket because he believed in your sound. The one who drew up a pretty good contract for all of you. One that, and I feel rude pointing this out, but one that you messed up because you operated a motor vehicle under the influence."

"This isn't my fault!" Kris shouted.

The maid paused again, Rob gave her a grin, and she went back to sweeping.

"Volume, dude," Rob said. "Look, I don't mean to be confrontational, but you are where you are because of one person: Kris Pulaski."

"We are where we are because you sold our souls to those things, whatever the fuck they are."

Rob laughed and shook his head.

"I know, right?" he said. "What are they? What is Black Iron Mountain? You'd think that if anyone would know I would, but you've got me. I am literally at a loss. I couldn't even describe them to you. I've caught glimpses, here and there, over the years, but I make sure I'm nowhere near when they come creeping out of their corners." He gave a cartoonish shudder. "I don't even like thinking about it."

"Then help me," Kris said.

"All I've ever done is help you," Rob said. "But right now, there are bigger considerations. Right now, everything is riding on Terry."

"What does he want?" Kris asked.

"What he wants doesn't matter," Rob said. "It's what they want. And you want to know something funny? We don't know what they want. But they *want*. The only language we have in common is commerce, exchange, you trade this for that. We don't even understand their body language. I've always wanted to get a linguist in there, record the noises they make, see if they could be analyzed. I outsourced that to one of my old professors at Reed about nine years ago. I still feel guilty about what happened to his family. But there are no mistakes, only lessons. Onwards and upwards."

"You sold us out to those things," Kris said.

"Except for you, I don't see anyone complaining," Rob said. "I mean, sure, occasionally we ask a bit more of someone like Scottie, and sometimes they just can't handle the responsibility and they go a little off the rails. But in general, everyone watches TV, argues over politics, tweets about their favorite wrestlers, watches football, goes to superhero movies, eats at Chipotle, enjoys the great taste of light beer. From time to time the hole inside of them gets a little too big and you get a dead girlfriend, or someone marches into work one day with a gun, but that's a small price to pay for a neat, orderly world."

"Not anymore," Kris said. "I'm stopping this."

"How?" Rob asked. "The only thing you're going to do is head back to Bill's. You'll receive a small surgical procedure and then none of this will have happened. You'll be on Paxator and back at that Best Western in no time, and all of this will be a hazy dream. It's the least I can do, for old times' sake. Although, if you really want, you can stick with the rock-and-roll suicide in a discount hotel. We held your room."

Kris looked at the maid for help, to see if she heard, but the maid was tying up the black plastic garbage bag full of broken glass and hauling it to the back.

"Just one more dead body on Terry's road to success," Kris said, trying to sound cynical, but only sounding scared.

"You're an ignorant person," Rob said. "Terry is trying to save the world."

The idea was so ridiculous that Kris laughed out loud. She couldn't help it.

"I know, everything's a big joke to you," Rob said. "But Black Iron Mountain is metastasizing. Every year it grows faster. It always wants more souls. Its greed knows no bounds. So Terry made a deal. He offered Black Iron Mountain something new. They've been signing people up all weekend, getting them with unlimited data plans, petitions for gay rights and against fracking, registering them to vote. And tonight, the Special Ones will come creeping out of their corners and feast on almost half a million souls."

Kris saw the desert moon slip behind scraps of cloud, and in the darkness she saw kids falling unconscious, passing out on the sand, going into their tents, lying down on their sleeping bags. And then the cold, white faces came crawling out of the dark, hundreds of them, thousands, hundreds of thousands, creeping up from a hole in the center of the world, picking their way over warm bodies, turning open mouths into slop bowls, lapping up the best part of them.

She wondered if Melanie was out there.

"I tried to warn Terry," Rob said. "When this is over, they're going to be just as hungry as before. But Terry doesn't listen. He really thinks he can appease them this time. He actually believes they're not lying. His hunger clouds his reason, but nothing is ever enough. Not for him, not for Black Iron Mountain. I think tonight will be a tipping point. After this, they'll eat the world."

The only sounds were the refrigerator motors humming, the neon buzzing, the *wisk-wisk* of the maid spraying disinfectant on the bar.

Kris thought about the kid holding out her hand at the gas station, saying, "Melanie Gutiérrez. I'm heading to Las Vegas." She heard her singing along to Dolly. She thought about her out there in the desert, alone with those soulless boys, the Special Ones creeping through the crowd, she thought about Melanie unconscious in the sand, black foam gushing from her mouth.

Kris's heart gave a low, slow flip. Blood drained from her head, her legs were hollow straws, and her voice was weak and far away when she said, "You don't have to do this. You don't have to do what they say."

Rob blinked and for a flash his face looked his actual age. He gave Kris a rueful smile.

"About thirty years ago, I was in a band," he said, his voice genuine and quiet. "I thought we were going to change the world. But my dad woke me up one morning and took me out on the beach and made me take a hard look at my life. He told me the story of the sparrow and the mountain. You ever heard it?"

"Jesus, you people like the sound of your own voices," Kris said.

"I just want you to know I'm not a monster," Rob said. "See, Black Iron Mountain is, well, a mountain. And you're a sparrow.

So you want to destroy it and you fly over and you pick up a pebble in one of your talons and you're all angry and arrrrgh arrrgh arrgh, and you carry it away, and you drop it in the ocean. It takes all day. Then you fly back to the mountain and take another pebble. Arrrrgh arrrgh arrgh. Do you see where I'm going with this?"

"Yeah, the sparrow kicks the mountain's ass," Kris said.

"No." Rob shook his head, taken aback. "The mountain's enormous, the sparrow can only carry one pebble at a time, and it has to fly to the ocean, which is hours away. Hundreds of sparrows will die and the mountain never changes. For all intents and purposes, the mountain is eternal. It's a really depressing story. And that morning, my father asked me: do you want to be the sparrow or the mountain? Do you want to die in a flash, and no one will even notice, or be part of something bigger than yourself that will live forever?"

"I'll get a million sparrows," Kris said, but even to her it sounded empty. "We'll take a million pebbles at a time. Your fucking mountain is toast."

Rob shook his head, and got up off his stool, and if he'd left then, Kris would have been stuck. Rob could have just walked out of the room and left Kris to Black Iron Mountain and then nothing else that happened that night would have needed to happen. But Rob was a man, and men never know when to shut up.

"It must be nice to be you," Rob said. "Everything must seem so simple."

And he gave her one of his patronizing smiles. The same one he gave her when he explained the contract with Black Iron Mountain in the Witch House that night. The same one he gave her when he showed up at the hospital while Tuck and Bill were still in the emergency room. The same one he gave her from the other side of her coffee table as she took his pen to sign the contract, pretending to read clauses she didn't understand in a desperate attempt to delay the inevitable. The same smile men had been giving Kris her entire life.

Every promoter who'd shorted her on the door because she "didn't understand how clubs work." Every house tech who'd explained to her where her monitor really needed to be, how her guitar should be tuned, what songs she actually should play.

Everyone who told her to calm down, who told her no, who told her to wait, who told her to be good, act nice, do what they say, sign a contract, play this kind of music—all of them gave her that same patronizing smile when they explained things to her and here it was again, on the last night of her life, right there on Rob Anthony's face.

Kris couldn't help herself. She punched him. As hard as she could.

Her fist clipped him on the chin, and it hurt like hell, but Kris didn't care because it was so satisfying to see the shock on Rob's face as he stumbled back, as his legs went out from under him, as he went down like a sack of cement, whacking his head on the edge of one of the tables. As he lay motionless on the floor.

The maid stared at her, frozen, cleaning rag in one hand, spray bottle in the other.

"Will you trade clothes with me?" Kris asked, pulling her shirt over her head. "I won't tell anyone."

The maid only hesitated for a second.

"They aren't paying me enough for this," she said. "I'd rather be home with my kids."

Five minutes later, Kris walked past the two bouncers outside the Sporting House, clanged down the metal stairs, and melted into the crowd. They didn't say a thing. After all, who ever notices the maid?

DONALD PUPINO: It would be hard to describe the chaos. Just after 9 p.m., the first fire broke out by the Pepsi Peace and Love Arena during a performance by the band Woods of Ypres. It was extinguished shortly thereafter, but not before thirty festivalgoers were injured in a stampede. Over the next two hours, attendees looted merchandise booths and set multiple fires throughout the campground. Nevada State Police are undermanned, and we are witnessing sheer anarchy. We've been told by authorities to retreat to the highway for our own safety.

—89.9, KNPR, "Nevada Impact News"
September 7, 2019

You Can't Stop Rock 'n' Roll

The crowd was trying to murder Melanie. All day long the enormous mass of people had basked in the heat, slow and torpid, like a snake. But after the sun went down and a full yellow moon came up, the crowd became a grinding, crushing, whirlpool of bodies sucking Melanie down.

Hunter, Jones, Chisolm, Spencer, and Slowen formed a protective pocket around her as they pushed their way into the dense, hot crush of people jammed motionless in front of the Bud Light Stage, 440,000 strong, a big dumb animal whose microsurges caught Melanie in its undertow and crushed her beneath its waves. But the boys repelled intruders, pushed back against freaks having freak-outs, picked her up when she went down.

As Cannibal Corpse took the stage, cans of Budweiser got passed around, bottles of Pacífico, burning joints, the occasional edible. Melanie tried to do all things in moderation until Slowen passed her a blunt and shouted over the guttural sounds of George Fisher destroying his vocal cords, "What're you saving yourself for? Marriage?"

Melanie realized he was right. This was Hellstock '19. When was she going to rock out harder than this? So as Cannibal Corpse and Kamelot gave way to Pig Destroyer and Abbath, things got funky.

By the time Slipknot wrapped up their set, Melanie could feel the beat coming through the earth, up through her feet. She closed her eyes as the crowd surged forward and crushed her into Chisolm's and Spencer's backs, everyone excited for Slayer, Jones reciting trivia about how Terry Hunt got thrown off a Slayer tour because he was too much of a badass. Melanie imagined that the beat through her feet was fists buried deep underground, corpses banging on their coffin lids.

She felt a sharp, invasive scratching, and realized someone had put their fingers up the back of her shorts. It took her a second to register it through the stoner haze, and she whirled to find Slowen grinning at her. He pulled his fingers out and sniffed them. Melanie tried to tell Hunter, but Slowen pushed around her fast, grabbed Hunter by the shoulders and whispered in his ear. Melanie grabbed his other shoulder, staying away from Slowen's hand, but Hunter ignored her, then turned and shouted, "Let's move up!"

The pocket of boys plunged forward into the wall of backs, Melanie caught in the middle, unable to escape their flying wedge. Women in bikinis were passed hand over hand through the crowd. Tossed two feet, five feet, ten feet, high over the crowd, going down into the sea of hands and emerging with their tops off, breasts flapping free. The boys shuffled forward, getting shoulders and elbows in their chests and faces, pushing deeper into the airless mass as Slayer took the stage.

Melanie couldn't breathe. A woman got passed over her head

and she held her hands up to help, saw the strong male hands all around her dipping into the girl's shorts, up her shirt, pulling her hair. Then the girl was gone, sucked away into the crowd, and the boys stopped moving. Melanie was too short to see the stage. She had a few inches of sand to stand on. Next to her loomed the metal struts of the sound tower where the mixing engineer sat twenty feet in the air. She looked over her shoulder and saw a solid wall of faces piled up behind her. Bodies pressed in on every side. There was no way out. Slayer started to play "Altar of Sacrifice."

As Kris melted into the crowd flowing through the backstage hallways, she felt it. A heavy, oppressive weight in the air. The walkway air conditioners had broken down and now they just blew hot desert grit. Techs passed by with filter masks pulled up over their faces. The warm air was thick with the smell of scorched plastic and burning weed.

Slayer boomed from backstage monitors, filling the air over the tents, winding down their set, and the traffic in the walkways thickened as everyone prepared for the main event.

Kris emerged into a courtyard formed by a ring of RV dressing rooms parked around a massive square of bright-green Astroturf. Tables with umbrellas were scattered across it, crowded with wives, and girlfriends, and agents, and visitors from other bands. There were three Koffin pinball machines at one end. Waiters took orders for coffee and cocktails, serving them from an open-air bar. Someone's girlfriend danced topless on one of the tables, and everyone ignored her because nothing was less cool than paying attention to another band's groupies. Kris climbed the stairs attached to the nearest RV, pushed the flimsy door, and stepped into the clean, well-lit interior.

It was a white plastic shell that smelled like disinfectant. A dressing table ran down one side with a long mirror screwed into the wall, and a rolling wardrobe rack jammed with clothes stood against the opposite wall. On top of the rolling rack were a series of foam heads with different wigs: curly, blonde, long brunette. Hanging from the ceiling in the corner was a flat-screen monitor showing a live feed from the stage.

The monitor went dark and a counter started running in the upper right-hand corner, displaying the seconds and minutes until Koffin went onstage. Kris went through the clothes on the rack and found a pair of black jeans about her size, took off the maid's uniform, and slipped them on. She found a white tank top and slipped it over her head. She took a glance at herself in the mirror. She looked like hell. Her hair was patchy and cropped, her face yellow and tight with exhaustion.

She did a quick wipe with some Wet Ones and found a lipstick and some eyeliner in the countertop debris. She used a little of the lipstick to make blush. She considered the results. Not very good, but it'd do for stage work.

On the monitor, Terry came onstage and the trailer shook with thunder from half a million throats. She grabbed a yellow windbreaker and pulled it on over her shirt.

Behind her, the door opened. She turned and stood breast to belly with Tuck.

"What the hell—?" he started.

"Close the door," Kris said, ducking under his arm, pulling it shut behind him.

He took an automatic step into the room to avoid getting hit by the door.

"What the hell, Kris?" he asked again.

She stepped out of his reach, just in case.

"What are you doing here?" she asked.

"I was invited," he said. "And I know you weren't."

"You're in stage makeup," she said. His skin was even. He had on foundation and eyeliner. It wasn't conspicuous, just enough to make him camera ready.

"Terry invited the old band to join him onstage," he said. "Well, me, anyways."

"For *Troglodyte*?" Kris asked.

"Hell, no," Tuck said. "For 'Chinagirl.' You're not supposed to be anywhere near this place."

"'Chinagirl' sucks," Kris said. "I can't believe that's what he's going to play."

"That's really not the immediate issue," Tuck said.

"I need your help," Kris said.

"No," he replied.

Kris reached out and tapped a fingernail against the all-access ID on a lanyard around his neck. Tuck didn't pull away.

"You owe me," she said.

"No," he repeated. "You're not going to make a mess of Terry's big moment. I'm not a huge fan of the guy, either, but we put you in Well in the Woods because you have a problem."

"I'm not even mad at you about Well in the Woods anymore," Kris said. "I just want your pass."

"To do what?" Tuck asked.

"You know what I want," Kris said. "Just once. I need to

bring him home."

"I cannot believe you're asking me this," Tuck said.

"You know something's wrong," Kris said. "Honestly, tell me anything feels right out here."

"We can agree on that," Tuck said. "This whole concert is dangerous, and kids are going to get hurt. The air smells evil, bad vibrations are everywhere, people are snarling at each other like they've got a hangover, and no one's doing anything about it."

"That's the way Terry wants it," Kris said. "This'll help. I promise."

"And now Terry again," Tuck said. "You're obsessed."

"He seems normal to you?"

"Of course not," Tuck said. "He's on some kind of Satan trip. To be honest, I'm embarrassed about going out onstage with a man who's bought into his own hype this hard."

"Then help me," Kris said. "Whatever you think of him, whatever you think of me, he shouldn't have buried that album. It was my life. I just want to end it."

Tuck really looked at her for the first time in years. Kris met his gaze.

"And then it'll be over?" Tuck asked. "You'll stop all this? You'll go back?"

"Behind the bars, there's a superstar, who never had a chance," Kris said, reaching deep.

Tuck's face was a confused blank as he tried to place the lyrics, then the first smile Kris had seen him make flickered across his lips as he recognized "Dead End Justice." The atmosphere in the trailer changed, and the two of them were in Dürt Würk again.

"The problem is," Tuck said, sitting in one of the folding

chairs, shaking his head, "this pass has a photo of a large and handsome black man on it. And you are not him."

"OK," Kris said. "What's the plan?"

"You grab the guard, in the prison yard," Tuck quoted. "Get his keys and gun. We'll run."

Terry put on a hell of a show, counting down his discography, starting with *9 Circles*, then *Insect Narthex*, then *Necrosex*, and finally *Witch Slave*. Everyone roared as his trademarked IP appeared onstage at the appointed times: the thirty-foot-high locust, the forty-foot inflatable maggot with its twelve puppeteers, the twenty-foot Witch Slave operated by pallbearers in black.

The crowd surged and shoved and Melanie held on to the sound tower so she wouldn't get sucked away. At one point she heard high-pitched female screams piercing the air over the crowd, electrifying because they were in the register of pure terror, then they were cut off. She tugged on Hunter's arm, but he was chanting along with "Hellmouth."

Koffin's lighting was better than the other acts—the video screen got more use, the sound came through clearer. But Melanie was depressed by how empty the music felt. "Stand Strong" sounded commercial and clichéd, "Burn You Down" sounded like Greg yelling at her.

Hunter tried to get her to sing along to "InFANticide," and she mumbled her way through it, but the song didn't resonate with her the way it did in the hospital, waiting to get word on her dad. Everything that had sounded deep, and private, and meaningful back then now sounded ugly, and flashy, and cheap.

When *Witch Slave* started she cheered along with everyone else, but she felt alone, cut off in the crowd. The boys surged and crushed in around her, but this time they didn't withdraw. The pressure compressed her lungs.

"I can't breathe," she squeaked.

She felt hands on her body, on her butt, worming their way down her shorts, on her breasts, her stomach, her sides. She tried to push them away, but her arms were trapped. Hands squeezed her breasts until they bruised.

"Hunter," she tried, her voice lost in the crowd. "Hunter!"

She realized that the hands on her breasts were his.

The boys' true faces surrounded her, baring their teeth, grinning, eyes wide and excited. Their hot breath stole all the oxygen from the air as Terry's voice drowned everything out. She started to cry as they pushed in, pushed down, pressed her back into the metal strut of the sound tower, harder and harder until her ribs bent, then started to fracture, bruising her lungs.

"Help," she said, but her voice sounded weak and pathetic in her ears, lost in the sound of "Die for Me."

Spencer grabbed her hair and banged the back of her skull on the sound tower, and Melanie saw blackness and flickering pinpricks of white light. She clung to the tower as hard as she could, but hands prised her fingers up, pulled them away. The boys crowded in eagerly, standing on her toes, crushing her, pushing her down, and she knew she wouldn't come up again. Hands found her neck and squeezed. And Hunter leaned into her ear and hissed the last thing she'd ever hear him say:

"Die, bitch."

There was a brisk knock on the RV door.

"Half hour," a woman's voice called, and Kris and Tuck looked at each other.

"Are you giving me the badge, or do I have to fight you for it?" Kris asked.

"Don't be stupid," Tuck said, standing. "Get under my arm."

What security saw when they came out of the holding area was Tuck, the enormous guy they'd been told was going to play, with a giggling, drunk, blonde groupie clinging to his side.

"I'm sorry, sir," the security kid said. "If she doesn't have a pass she can't go backstage."

The kid was one of the few remaining volunteers brought in to fill out the ranks. No one expected any trouble backstage. The guys with experience were out front fighting the crowd.

"You got a problem with a black man dating a white woman?" Tuck asked, and the kid waved them in fast, not wanting to get fired for being racist.

Kris and Tuck followed the cables, up the stairs onto the back of the stage, and the noise of the crowd hit them like a punch to the face. Kris actually rocked back a half step. The two of them walked past hard cases and rolling cases, dodged roadies carrying coils of cable on the fly, past security guards, past lighting techs looking for a missing gobo. Koffin sounded terrible because all the speakers were in front, facing out. Back here the music echoed like a cheap radio turned up too loud, heard from three blocks away.

They finally found a place to watch in the darkness behind the guitar station. Three rows of guitars stood on angled racks while two beefy guitar techs with long hair moved between them, bending and pecking at the instruments by the light of their tiny flashlights, fishing out guitars and handing them to runners.

Kris watched Terry on the monitor, feeling she was exactly where *Troglodyte* wanted her to be. She was in the right place; now she waited for the right time. Her life was a bullet, headed for the target.

Terry ended "Die for Me" and the crowd roared.

Over the PA, Terry said, "I'm going to play a song now called 'Chinagirl.' I haven't played this song in a while, but it tells you everything you need to know about a band I used to be in called Dürt Würk. A band we've been hearing a lot about recently."

That was her cue.

She'd always hated "Chinagirl." A song isn't a commercial for an album. It isn't a tool to build name awareness or reinforce your brand. A song is a bullet that can shatter your chains. "Chinagirl" would never be that song.

A bullet took Scottie Rocket away. A bullet killed his family. A bullet was what she had become.

One life, one bullet.

Kris stepped away from Tuck and reached for his big hand, lifted it up, held it to her face and kissed his palm, closing her eyes and inhaling the scent of his skin. She'd known this hand all the way back to the beginning. He was the last person she was going to see before she finished what they'd started all the way back in 1987.

Kris dropped her windbreaker and came up over the shoulder of the guitar tech whose beard was way too big for his face.

"Hey," she said, indicating a Strat, as Terry's hoarse voice rambled on. "What's that tuned in?"

"What?" the tech whispered, giving her a quick look. He decided she was probably the big guy's girlfriend, and turned back to the stage. "Standard."

"Sounds good," Kris said.

Without giving herself time to think, Kris Pulaski picked up the instrument and stepped out of the shadows and walked into the stage lights in front of 440,000 people, strapping on the Strat as she went. With the guitar bouncing off her hip she walked over the cables, past all the gear, to the front of the stage, into Terry's space, into the limelight, into the focused force and intensity of 880,000 eyeballs and their unblinking camera phones.

She didn't worry, she didn't smile, she didn't feel out of place.

A girl with a guitar never has to apologize for anything.

JASMIN AHMED: . . . over forty million dollars of damage and that estimate is still climbing. There are 1,566 persons who have received emergency medical care, as well as reports of countless sexual assaults, our colleagues from local station KNPR are still missing, and police have been making arrests into the early morning hours . . .

—BBC World Service, "Newshour"
September 8, 2019

Troglodyte

The audience noise was a blasting physical force, a black ocean smashing into her chest. Their sound never stopped. And when the crowd saw Kris before Terry did, noticed her standing right behind him, their noise shifted, modulated, leapt impossibly higher. Terry turned, and he had three seconds before the camera jibs craned in close, and he used them to say, "You can't be here."

Then she stepped around him and reached for his mic stand. He tried to block her, then realized what that would look like to the cameras, so he dropped his arms, and Kris took the mic and said, into the pounding black ocean, into the biggest audience she'd ever seen in her life:

"I'm Kris Pulaski, the guitarist for Dürt Würk." She heard her voice bounce around the desert on a system of 30,000 speakers. "The Blind King asked me to join him onstage to play an album I don't think many of you have heard. It's gotten a bit of a reputation over the years. We wrote it back in 1998 when we were still in Dürt Würk together. It's called *Troglodyte*."

Terry held two expressions on his face at once, displaying a cool thin smile for the cameras projecting his image a hundred feet tall on the screen, sending his face around the world, recording this moment for all time. The other expression was just for Kris: hatred mixed with disbelief. But Terry was nothing if not a professional, and he easily pried the mic out of Kris's hand.

"Are you sure you're up for this?" he asked. "I didn't think you'd have the lady balls to join me up here on stage."

Kris didn't answer. She didn't have the words Terry did. She only had one thing and she prayed that she wouldn't fuck it up. Not when it finally counted.

She bent her head over her guitar and without tuning or running through any warm-ups, trusting that the techs had done their job, without giving Terry a chance to make another comment that would diminish this moment, without hesitation, without a count-off, she crunched into the opening chords of "Beneath the Wheel."

Terry had taken that riff and bastardized it on *Insect Narthex* so at first the audience thought she was recycling something they'd already heard. Then the ones who'd heard *Troglodyte* on bootleg realized what was happening and started to cheer. It swept backward to the next pocket of people, and the next, and the people who didn't know why they were cheering further back, and the people behind them, racing through the crowd like a fire. A storm of air blew through vocal chords, a hurricane, an ocean, a vast black sea of sound. And across its surface, lightning flickered as cameras went off, flashes over a vast and sunless sea.

The sudden disruption brought the boys up short, and they turned from Melanie, looking up at the stage. Through her bruised and swollen face, Melanie saw Hunter's lips move in the shape of, "What the fuck?"

Melanie hauled herself to her feet and a hand smacked her face. She flinched, then realized it didn't belong to any of the boys. She looked up. Above her, clinging to the struts of the steel sound tower, a fat woman in suspenders with a tiny bow tie leaned down, one hand stretched out to Melanie, the other held by an enormous dude with long hair lying on his stomach above her on the tower floor.

"Sweetheart," the woman said, "gimme your hand."

Terrified, Melanie froze, but the woman snapped her fingers in front of her face, and Melanie took her hand, and the woman hauled her up out of the crowd, into the sound tower, and the boys didn't notice until her sneakers were scrambling up the struts, on the same level as their faces, and they reached for her, but it was too late—she was flying. The woman hauled them both up until, panting and sweaty, she stood Melanie on her feet on the swaying tower, next to the sound board.

"Whew," the woman said. "I won't do that again. Now what the fuck is going on?"

The long-haired guy at the board scrambled to mix what was coming off the stage as Kris Pulaski played the intro to "Beneath the Wheel" again and again, and Terry stood onstage, paralyzed.

Melanie looked down at the surging, whirling crowd and it seemed impossible that they wouldn't topple this little spindly tower and suck it down into the bottomless sea of bodies. The hairy guy did something violent behind her, and she heard him say, "No access!" before he was back up, brushing his hair over one of his ears, and the fat woman with the bow tie was taking over the board, running her fingers across its sliders and knobs.

"Holy shit," the woman said, taking in what was happening onstage. "That's Kris Pulaski."

As the crowd began to boo, Terry realized he had no choice, because Kris wasn't going to stop playing that goddamn opening riff, and if he didn't do something, the crowd would turn. And so he grabbed the mic, and shouted:

History
Is a boot
Smashing your face
Forever

The crowd roared back, giving him the juice he needed to sing the next verse.

Eternity
In the mud
Crushed like a bug
Whatever

Born with a squeal
Die where you kneel
All that is real
Crushed!

Then he reached deep and pulled out his Cookie Monster growl, an effect he never unleashed anymore because it was so identified with death metal, black metal, with doomcore, and because it shredded his vocal chords. But it electrified the crowd, crackling out of massive speaker towers, lashing the sea of bodies like a whip.

```
Beneath the wheel
```

The roar from the crowd blasted into Kris, almost blew her off her feet. Even all these years later, even with just Kris and Terry, it still worked. And when they got to the end of the song, the screaming roaring chaos got inhumanly louder, and bodies charged the stage, barely held back by security. Their screams slammed into Kris like a tidal wave, and before Terry had a chance to shut it down, Kris tore into the bluesy love song solo from "My Master's Eye."

She saw Terry's shoulder's hunch when he realized what she was doing, and then the crowd realized what she was doing, and even the ones who had never heard *Troglodyte* before knew that this was a once-in-a-lifetime moment, and the roar was like pushing your face into a jet engine.

Kris grinned and took her solo higher, making it sarcastic and jeering, punching Terry's back with it. Terry was nothing if not a creature of the crowd, and when she stopped playing for the three beats of silence before the first verse, he cut loose with a pure, sweet, 1950s doo-wop falsetto:

```
Everything I do he studies
Everything I do he knows
He watches me wherever I am
He follows me where I go
```

Kris looked back at whatever mercenary drummer Terry had playing rhythm and miraculously, the guy was watching her, and even more of a miracle, he seemed to know the album because he came in with a nice four-by-four beat on the cymbals and snares, a lover's shuffle, for the next verse.

He has one hundred hands
He has all-seeing eyes
He is all I am
Without him I die
And die
And die
And die
And die

Kris brought in the monster riff that gobbled up the last of those words and the song took on its pounding, crashing speed, and the drummer and Kris drove it to its conclusion, not perfectly, and with two terrible tempo changes because the drummer still had the click track in his ear, but somehow they both went silent on the exact same beat, letting Terry deliver the last verse a cappella, into the seething crowd with its forest of pale arms throwing horns, its flashing phones, its cameras, its laser pointers, its glow sticks.

And all that I am
And all that I was
And all that I am
And all that I see
And all that is me
And everything
Everything
Everything
Is he

Kris leaned into Terry's mic and said, "Hey, Mr. Sound Board. Kill the click track. We're way off book here."

There was another roar of approval from the crowd who were thrilled to be in uncharted territory. The fat woman in the bow tie chuckled and made an adjustment, and now the only thing Kris and Terry and the drummer were getting fed was the monitor mix, so they could actually listen to each other.

"And one more thing," Kris said, doubling down. "Can we get Mr. Tuck Merryweather out here? Dürt Würk's original bass player."

She stepped back from the mic, and Terry turned to stop her, but Kris was already playing the riff from "Eating Yourself to Live" over and over again, each time with more confidence. Amped up it sounded way more like they'd stolen it from Black Sabbath, so she bent it, drew it out, chopped it up, tossed it back, killing time until Tuck appeared. Just when Kris was about to give up, she heard the crowd roar and turned to see a follow spot pick up Tuck, shambling onstage, bass already strapped over his shoulders.

He was too far away and the crowd was too loud to say anything, so Kris played the riff from "Eating Yourself to Live" at him, then again, then again, and he looked at her, and she nodded, and the dark ocean roared when he fired the bass riff back at her.

They did that for a minute, just swatting it back and forth between them, and then Kris gave him her back and took the song forward. Onstage, Terry realized that they were all chained to this whale and the only way out was through, so he kept going.

As they rolled through "Eating Yourself to Live" Kris forgot the audience. She focused on remembering her chord progressions and time changes, thrilled to realize she'd never forgotten them. Even when she couldn't see them ahead of her in the song, the second she needed them, they were there, like Tarzan swinging through the jungle, reaching out into the air and always finding another vine.

Melanie watched from the vibrating, swaying sound tower, the feel of the boys' hands on her body fading as she stared at this woman onstage, the one she'd listened to Dolly Parton with, the one she'd decided was crazy, the one she'd betrayed. Under the stage lights, this woman glowed.

The arrangements were skeletal and shaky, and the drummer just barely kept time and didn't play any fills. To Kris, the lack of Scottie Rocket felt like a phantom limb, but she did her best. Scottie loved "Eating Yourself to Live" so she used it to pay him tribute, soaring off into rocket runs, flashing across the sky in blink-and-you'll-miss-it note drops. Even Terry seemed to feel it as he brought it to an end, cranking things up higher, and higher, and faster, and louder.

Everything's a game
And everything's been tamed
And everything's the same
And everyone's to blame
And no one sees the pain
And everyone's insane
The Blind! King! Reigns!

The song cut off, unplugged, hit a wall, and there was a second of silence and then the roar returned and Kris was shocked, because for two minutes, she'd forgotten the crowd existed. It had just been the three of them, older, but together, a band again, surrounded by darkness.

She put her pick in her mouth and started the fingerpicking for "Poincaré's Butterfly," praying that Terry remembered the words. There was only a small stutter when Kris missed a chord change on the intro, but then Terry was there, actually singing like a choirboy in his high sweet voice.

Down
Through the dirt
Through the floor
Through the Blue Door

Tunnels
Made of darkness
Made of whispers
Made of screams
Like a choir

On wings
Made of red
Made of yellow
Made of dust
Made of fire

It lands
On my hand
I see
This strange thing
With its wings

Kris stumbled over the notes, her left and right hands getting out of sync, and the song screeched to a halt. She took a breath and started again, feeling Scottie Rocket's invisible hands on hers, guiding her fingers, and the roar came back. Up here everything felt epic, felt mythic, felt like magic, and lyrics that had been written in the basement of the Witch House came out of Terry's throat like an incantation.

Makes me know
That it's so
Beyond the pain
And the shame
And the blood
And the screams
Past the flood
Of the fire
And the King
And his choir
Beyond the torture
And the wire
And the guts
And the gore

There's a door.

Listening to the roar of the dark ocean, Kris knew why this album was a threat. This was the crack in Black Iron Mountain. She turned to get ready to launch into "Down Where the Worms Squirm" and got a glimpse of Rob in the gloomy wings, his eyes bright and blazing. She didn't acknowledge him, but as they tore into the next song she saw black-shirted security filing into the wings on either side of him, like crows.

Everything you said you wanted
Rots and falls apart
In the kingdom of the Blind King
He'll eat your bleeding heart

Kris knew that there was no way off this stage. Not for her. She was a bullet, fired from a gun. She'd burned all her bridges, and at last she was alone, standing on an island, surrounded by this raging sea. What was it JD said? An album only plays in one direction: forward.

Next came "Sailing the Seas of Blood" and then "In the Hall of the Blind King" and then Kris delivered the buzzsaw riff that ended the song, the riff that took them into the final fight, that tore apart the night like an explosion and dropped them all into the chute that started "One Life, One Bullet."

Military snares snapped off behind her, all harsh angry rattles that became blast beats as Tuck joined in, and Kris waited, listening to the intro batter the crowd. Her brain felt bruised. Then she slammed into the groove with them, her right shoulder aching so bad she thought it would fall off. A numbness radiated down that entire arm, and she knew if she slowed down her arm would freeze up. Terry high-stepped along the lip of the stage, lashing the crowd with the chorus, screaming:

One life
One bullet
Troglodyte
One life
One bullet
Troglodyte

The tempo built, and it grew in power and intensity until it became primal, a summoning, an exorcism, the words taking on a sound beyond their sound, notes appearing that they didn't play. It sounded primitive, tribal, and Kris didn't think about the end approaching, until they were there and she slammed her guitar to a halt.

While her ears still screamed with echoes, Terry launched into the chant:

```
There is a hole
In the center of the world
```

The dark ocean picked it up and 440,000 people chanted, "There is a hole / In the center of the world / There is a hole / In the center of the world / There is a hole / In the center of the world." Kris looked back at Tuck to make a face that said, "How weird is this?" but he was already staring out at this sea and not in awe. Sweat sheeted down his face as he shouted along with them, and Kris didn't miss a beat, she turned forward and raised her right fist and screamed along with them, because it had been there all her life, all their lives, and it was waiting to swallow them up at the end, everything that was good, everything that was free, it took everything. In the end they all fell into darkness.

And Kris realized, as she shouted her throat raw, the crowd shouting along with them, that they were guided by something larger than themselves, some greater force, some kind of holy coincidence, something huge and unseen. And at its peak, miraculously, Kris and Tuck and Terry and all 440,000 people in that crowd, they all stopped at the same time, like they'd been practicing this all their lives.

Then Terry—fucking Terry, the Blind King, the pain in the ass, the boy who tapped on her basement window, the kid who asked her the question that started everything, that caused all this pain, that sparked a thousand shows, the boy who said, "You wanna start a band?"—he grabbed his mic and right on time, right on cue, he said the words that were coming but that Kris thought he would never sing:

"And inside that hole!" Terry shouted, and the black ocean fell silent, its colossal sound held back for three seconds, its power coiling, building up, about to overflow. "And inside that hole!" Terry shouted again, "is Black Iron Mountain!"

Terry raised both fists and let the black ocean rush over him, and Kris looked back and the drummer was standing, saluting the black ocean's roar with two raised drumsticks, and she caught Tuck's face and he gave her a grin, and she saw all the forces of Black Iron Mountain moving into place to block her exit in the wings: Bill in his chair, with Miranda and her dreads next to him, her neck still in a brace, and Rob, and all his black-shirted crows, the Nevada Highway Patrol in their flak jackets and black latex gloves.

And in the crowd, fists pumped, bottles flew, and far in the back, someone set a merch booth on fire. And up in the sound tower Melanie shouted along with the crowd and she felt something running down her face, and the fat woman in the bow tie stood up and gave the stage a brisk little salute. And onstage, Kris stepped up to Terry's mic one final time.

"There's," she started, but the black ocean broke over her and sucked her down and she was silent for a minute as she drowned. "There's . . . there's . . . " she repeated, trying to be heard, as the dark ocean slowly stilled and subsided, and finally, she was able to say into the darkness, "There's one last song," and everyone went silent. "On this album that we, um," and here she gave Terry a look.

His makeup was running down his face, and he looked so vulnerable. He was just a little boy in love with himself, making deals without ever asking the price, thinking he'd never have to pay. She saw him, not evil, not good, just another boy who thought he was the only person in the world who mattered. So she did him a final kindness, and in her hour of truth she didn't say that he'd cut the track, she didn't mention the betrayal that still hurt after all these years, the way he'd just taken her baby away from her and mutilated it, and instead she said:

"We, um, lost the tracks, they got damaged so it never made it onto the album."

And like a little boy, Terry gave her a grateful grin.

"But I want to sing it for you now. Because it's the song that means everything on this album. Without it, Troglodyte wanders forever. Tonight, I want to bring him home. Tonight, I want to set him free."

There was a roar from the black ocean, and Bobbie sitting at the board, shaking her head, reached over and held Melanie's hand and said, "Sweetheart, I don't even know what the fuck."

Kris hesitated at the microphone, feeling the spotlight on her face. She had so much to say, and she thought about it for a few seconds which is an eternity in stage time, and finally said:

"They want to tell you what to do, what you should want. They want to control your life. And there's so many of them. There's too many of them," she paused, about to say something else, but it was disappearing over the horizon of her brain and she couldn't catch the tail of her idea, and she saw the bottom of the hole coming up fast as she fell and Black Iron Mountain was in the wings waiting, and so she let it go. "Fight," she finally said. "Just fight. Don't ever stop."

The ocean crashed and thundered as Kris raised her lips to the mic and sang "The Door with Cerulean Hue."

Up the tunnels
Out the maze
Towards the daylight
Through the caves

Every step closer
He hasn't been here before
Every step closer
The Blue Door

She came in with a minor chord on "Blue Door" and there was no drummer, no bass player, just Kris, the ghost of Scottie Rocket standing behind her, and instead of the crows waiting in the wings she felt JD, watching the woman he'd died for play the final song of Dürt Würk's final show.

He's past the barricades
No longer a slave
Beyond their reach
Beyond the caves

Step by step
Out and through
These things you want
He will not do

Troglodyte seeks
The door with cerulean hue

And everyone you saved
Everyone who died
Everyone who slaved
Everyone who thrived
Everyone forgotten
Those written in stone
Everyone together
Everyone alone

They build up behind him
An unstoppable flood
A furious storm
A song made of blood

The words were a pillar of sound growing up through her feet, through her stomach, out the top of her skull, rising to the sky, suspending her on a crystal column of music between the dirt and the stars.

Step by step
Out and through
These things you want
He will not do

Troglodyte seeks
The door with cerulean hue

It wasn't the same song, it never is, each time you play it the song changes, but the feeling remains the same. It was a song for the Dürt Würk that could have been, a song for the band that finished the last track on *Troglodyte* and stood in the cold basement of the Witch House looking at each other in absolute silence for a moment. Back when they weren't a bunch of fuck-ups looking for a place to belong. Back in that moment when they knew they could be legends.

Back before they threw it all away.

Kris drew the song to a close. She'd had her forty minutes. There wasn't anything left for her here, and so she wrapped up her song, and set Troglodyte free.

Up the tunnels
Out the maze
Towards the daylight
Past the caves

Each step closer
He's never been here before
Each step closer
The Blue Door

A key change and she slowed her rhythm down to almost nothing, finger picking a simple riff over and over again, getting slower each time. The dark ocean was silent, listening, the burning merch booths flickering far away.

One more step
One step higher
One more body
Thrown on the fire

There is no more
It's time to fly
It's not a door—
It's the sky.

One final note. A moment of silence. She looked at Terry, and Terry looked at her, and she turned to Tuck, and for a minute Dürt Würk was all that it ever could have been. For a second, Kris stood in that other world, parallel to ours, where nothing was ever broken, and all her friends were still alive, and it was never too late.

Then, the dark ocean crashed into the stage with a roar, broke over the barricades, smashed through the thin line of security, and the lightning blazed and burned and the noise deafened them all. And Kris Pulaski stood alone in the chaos, guitar on her hip, and turned to face Black Iron Mountain, a dark wave rising at her back.

KIM HUNT: What's it like to be a woman in a metal band? Do you face any problems when you're touring? Is it harder to get fans to respect you? And what about the image of women metal portrays? Do you think heavy metal creates positive role models for women?

KRIS PULASKI: I don't know about all that. I just want to play.

—101.7 WFNX, "FNX Weekends"
March 23, 1994

3 YEARS LATER

For Those About to Rock We Salute You

Hellstock '19 ended in disaster. The merch booth fires were only the start of it. That night the crowd, almost half a million strong, rampaged through Strawberry Valley. They stormed the stage, trashed the equipment, tipped cell phone towers, lit bonfires. Kids ran through the flames. Two of them got burns so severe one lost an arm and one lost a foot at the ankle.

Merch booths burned to ashes, ATMs were cracked wide open, sixteen eighteen-wheelers were tipped and looted. In the morning, a vast tide of humanity surged back to their cars and drove back to Las Vegas, leaving behind a crater filled with trash, and mud, and human shit. Not a single record was salvaged. All the sign-ups, all the scanned tickets, all the names of the people who came, were lost in smashed hard drives and burned paperwork.

By the time the swirling carnival of chaos ended the next morning, there were 2,016 people awaiting medical attention, 431 arrests, Kris was missing, Terry was gone, and Tuck couldn't get a straight answer out of anyone.

He called a few people his sister knew in law enforcement,

filed a missing person's report wherever he could, and put the word out on gig boards to keep an eye open for Kris, but Kris had disappeared, leaving nothing behind but her wig. They found it on the ground behind the drum kit. Where she went was a mystery and theories proliferated online, cross-bred and intermingled, spawned mutant sub-theories which birthed even more baroque conspiracies.

One theory said Kris had powerful enemies. Terry was connected to power brokers who controlled Hollywood. According to this theory, she was smuggled out of the venue in the trunk of Terry's limo, and taken to a soundproof room in the basement of his house in Vegas. They'd kept her there for a few days, probably tortured her, then killed her, and buried her remains in the desert. Everyone was paid to look the other way. No one ever found her body, but evidence showed up from time to time in the sand: scraps of her leather jacket, the charred remains of her guitar, a Manowar head wrap lined with lead foil.

The other theory said Kris had escaped in the chaos. That someone saw a cleaning woman help her slip off the side of the stage. That a sound tech smuggled her out of the venue in a rolling case. This theory said that a network of metalheads got her out of the country, to someplace where heavy metal was still treated with respect.

Someone said she'd been spotted in Brazil. Other people said she was in Chile. A few claimed they'd seen her in the Philippines. Wherever they came from, they all said the same thing: this woman showed up at open mics and random shows. She'd ask to borrow a guitar and they'd let her plug in and play. Sometimes she'd tear through the classics: Sabbath, Slayer, Megadeth. She loved

"Reign in Blood." Sometimes, if the night was right, she'd play *Troglodyte*. More and more often, people said, she played new material. Most of it was pretty good.

She never gave her name, no one knew where she came from, and after the shows she always slipped out the back or disappeared into the crowd before anyone could get her picture. The new songs got recorded on phones and uploaded online where they were traded and obsessed over by the most passionate Troglodytes.

Some days Tuck believed one theory, some days he believed the other. But he listened to the new songs that got uploaded and he thought, yeah, they sounded like his girl. And now, today, on the third anniversary of Hellstock '19, Tuck came out of Funkytown where he taught kids bass after school, and realized that he missed her. He didn't want to go back to those times, and that night at Hellstock had been the most terrifying night of his life, but life always felt a little more real when Kris was around.

As he walked to his car, something familiar tickled his ears and he realized it was "Poincaré's Butterfly." Across the street, a girl sat against the wall of a closed check-cashing joint, the velvet lining of her open guitar case pocked with quarters and pennies and a couple of bills. A pit bull puppy lay beside her, muzzle on his front paws, a thick rope tied around his collar. The girl had scabs all over her face and played a battered guitar. Her voice wasn't half bad. Wasn't half good, either.

Tuck looked in his wallet but all he had was a five-dollar bill. Then he figured, why not? He'd consider it royalties for Kris. He dropped it in the girl's case, walked to his car, and drove home to his family, "Poincaré's Butterfly" playing over and over again inside his head.

In LA, Bobbie Gilroy, the board tech, uploaded her pristine bootleg of *Troglodyte* for the nine-hundredth time while she rolled a joint and listened to her girl in the shower. She loved doing this. What had happened in the desert that night had turned into a pop culture moment, like Ozzy accidentally biting the head off that bat, or Michael Jackson catching his hair on fire shooting the Pepsi commercial. It was the kind of cultural landmark that everybody knew.

Bobbie figured she'd been put there to capture it and get that sound out into the world. Something she was proud to do because she thought it was one of the greatest performances she'd ever heard, and that wasn't just nostalgia talking. Sure, there were plenty of technical problems, but emotionally it hit like a freight train. And her bootleg caught every second of it in perfect digital clarity. Avoiding the takedown notices had turned into a game. She was going to keep uploading this until she was old and gray. Which, come to think of it, wasn't too far away. Then her girl was out of the shower, wet and wriggly, and she hit upload and turned her attention to more immediate matters.

In his home recording studio in Los Angeles, Terry Hunt sat alone, trying to avoid his reflection. He didn't like seeing what Black Iron Mountain had done to punish him. Instead, he hunched over in his studio chair and listened to what he'd laid down that day. He was going to release this album. He was not going to let Hellstock '19 be his epitaph.

He listened, and realized that the guitar attack he'd woken up dreaming about in the middle of the night wasn't his, it was from Iron Maiden's "The Trooper." And that riff he'd polished for hours was actually from Mastodon's "Blood and Thunder" and that bass line he was so proud of was from Tool's "Schism" and everything he'd written for the past three days was stolen from somebody else. He dragged every single one of the sound files into the garbage and emptied it with a terminal *click*.

He needed to keep going. It was only a matter of time. He just had to get these influences out of his brain, he just had to keep trying. A simple three-chord progression popped into his head and for a minute he got excited, and then he realized it was from Wolves in the Throne Room's second album. He balled his hands into fists and pressed them to his forehead and he wanted to scream, but he couldn't open his mouth that wide anymore.

In West Hollywood, Rob Anthony walked through Largo before an Aimee Mann surprise acoustic show and shook hands and bought rounds and worried that people's smiles didn't seem as wide as they used to, that their handshakes seemed shorter, their banter didn't sound as sincere. He felt like people wanted to get away from him. He caught a whiff of something rank, like a wet, rotten wound and he was sure it wasn't him, and then he reassured himself that even if it was him—which it definitely was not—no one else could smell it. Then, when the room got dark and the show began, he slipped out the door and drove home alone, keeping all his windows down.

In Valley Center, Kansas, Ethel Davis lay in bed, trying to fall asleep but mostly missing her son. She'd managed to doze off earlier, but now she'd woken up because someone was in the house. From downstairs in the dark basement, floating up the stairs, came the sound of drumming, some heavy metal ruckus, pouring out of the open basement door.

She smiled and settled back against her pillows. This happened at least once a week and she actually found it reassuring. JD wanted her to know he was okay. Her son didn't want her to worry, and so he came back to let her know that he was someplace better, playing his music as loud as he wanted. He always was a thoughtful boy. She imagined him flailing away behind his drums in the basement, wearing his horned helmet, lost in his music, having a wonderful time. She couldn't help it. She smiled. No parent should outlive her child, but who would she be without her Viking?

And in a basement in Los Angeles, California, down behind the laundry room, away from the neighbors, Melanie Gutiérrez sat hunched over her guitar, trying to play the beginning of the song that saved her life. Her wrists were bony and weak. The thin metal E, B, and G strings sliced her fingertips. The knock-off Chinese guitar she'd gotten on Amazon bruised her ribs where she leaned over it. Her left wrist throbbed.

She wrapped a claw around the guitar's neck and pressed her first sore finger to A, her third finger on D, her fourth finger on G, raked her pick down the strings, and the magic happened: the same sound came out of her amp that had come out of Kris Pulaski's amp. The same sound 440,000 people heard in Nevada that night was right here in the basement with her.

But this was too hard. Her hands hurt too much. She was too tired from working a double. Her wrists were too weak. She couldn't do this, she couldn't hold all these notes in her head, she couldn't make these songs sound right. Then she played that chord again and it smashed out of her amp, and she moved to the next chord, and the next one, and the one after that, and she fell forward from chord to chord, making her basement shake, "Beneath the Wheel" blotting out everything in her life, blotting out the world, blotting out Black Iron Mountain, and she knew . . .

She could do this.

How does a sparrow destroy a mountain?

One pebble at a time.

Troglodyte would not be possible if not for the hard work of all these subterranean creatures:

First and foremost, thanks to Rob Anthony whose vision and dedication have changed our lives forever. The future looks dangerous!

Thanks to producer and engineer, Jason Rekulak, for his studio magic and flawless musical judgment.

Those are Rick Chillot's synths you hear on "One Life, One Bullet" and they don't let anyone tell you that synths aren't metal.

Word up to Nicole De Jackmo and Ivy Weir for their angelic backing vocals on "Down Where the Worms Squirm" and "Sailing the Seas of Blood."

The look of Troggie and that bad-to-the-bone logo are the responsibility of one Mr. Doogie Horner.

For the killer mixes, Mary Ellen Wilson and Jane Morley are owed a debt of blood.

The whole team at Roundhouz Studios in LA made this album possible: Katherine McGuire, Moneka Hewlett, Brett Cohen, David Borgenicht, John McGurk, Mandy Dunn Sampson, Andie Reid, Blair Thornburgh, Megan DiPasquale, Elissa Flanigan, Rebecca Gyllenhaal, Kelsey Hoffman, Christina Schillaci, Kate Brown, and Molly Murphy.

No one does it better than the PRHPS Sales Team and we know you guys are going to make this album release completely shred.

For inspiration on the road and for lending us $20 in Denver when we needed it most, thanks to Thom Youngblood and Mary Schreck.

As always, this one is for the fans, Sarah Nivala, Evan Vellela, Michelle Souliere, Patrick Wray, Chris Ryall, Carson Evans, Jo-Jo Gervasi, Miles Foster, Mariah Cherem, Chris Dortch, Lisa Morton, Mitch Davis, Jonathan Lees, Eric Bresler, and all the rest of you Troglodytes. Keep on Trogging.

IN MEMORIAM

AMANDA COHEN

We'll always remember your dedication to Dürt Würk and letting us crash at your place whenever we came through Toronto.

We're sorry we forgot you were standing behind the van the last time we left.